£3

Haydn Middleton was ~~...~~ ~~...~~ y at Oxford, where he now ~~...~~ ~~...~~ has worked in advertising and publishing, lectured in British myth and legend, and written a dozen works of fiction and non-fiction.

'Haydn Middleton is doing something unique in this cycle of novels. He is bringing to light a dark and violent dream of birth, death, blood and the Matter of Britain. He has revealed something in the Arthur/Mordred/Morgan story that was always there, but never so boldly painted, namely the power of the erotic charge between the principal characters in the myth . . . No Idylls here: this is the real blood soaked thing'
Philip Pullman

'The story of Mordred feels as if Haydn Middleton has hacked it with the strong blows of a primitive axe, instead of written it. He has hewn out of the violence of British history a terrible and disturbing legend'
Sara Banerji

'Middleton combines a poet's feel for language with a startlingly original insight into what myths actually mean: above all, he understands that the best use for a tradition is as a beach-head for innovation'
Tom Holt

'Haydn Middleton has tunnelled deep into the myth of Arthur . . . to explore its sexual and psychological underworld. He has emerged with a dark, brooding, visceral vision (that looks back to Oedipus and Electra and forward to Freud) and adds strange, powerful layers of new meaning and mystery to the legend'
Tim Pears

THE KNIGHT'S VENGEANCE

A
Mordred Cycle
Novel

HAYDN MIDDLETON

WARNER BOOKS

A *Warner* Book

First published in Great Britain by Little, Brown and Company 1997
First published by Warner Books 1998

Copyright © Haydn Middleton 1997

The moral right of the author has been asserted.

*All characters in this publication are fictitious
and any resemblance to real persons, living or dead,
is purely coincidental.*

A CIP catalogue record for this book
is available from the British Library.

ISBN 0 7515 2370 4

Typeset in Bembo by
Palimpsest Book Production Limited,
Polmont, Stirlingshire
Printed and bound in Great Britain by
Clays Ltd, St Ives plc

Warner Books
A Division of
Little, Brown and Company (UK)
Brettenham House
Lancaster Place
London WC2E 7EN

And Arthur disclosed the head of Bran the Blessed from the White Hill, because it did not seem right to him that this Island should be defended by the strength of anyone, but by his own.

The Triads of the Island of Britain

Part One

DAWN

ONE

The sky was huge. Dyfric had never seen a sky so huge. The longer he gazed at it, the more he felt drawn upwards, as if a bunch of invisible fingers were plucking them all into safety.

He felt no fear. No one on the ship felt fear. The talk about the prodigy stayed calm and measured. Some thought that Arthur's island realm of Albion had been flooded from within; others that the land had independently contracted to the strip of rocky shore still lining the horizon.

No one knew for sure, and no one was troubled by not knowing. More than enough ships had been on hand to save all those who had wanted saving. In the first momentous hours, nothing else had mattered.

Dyfric himself, a priest of almost forty, had been trained to take the miraculous in his stride. Besides, he had little affection for the land they now had left behind. Wherever they fetched up next, it could hardly fail to be more congenial than ramshackle Albion.

Several times he felt obliged to rise, to lead the rest in prayers of thanks for their safe deliverance. But something held him back. Prayer at this moment seemed inappropriate: either too soon or too late to be effective. And although he hardly dared admit this, he felt little of God in what was happening. It was as if in the general suspension of the laws which governed the universe, God too had been bypassed.

Word was already going around that when they made landfall, it would be somewhere quite wonderful. A kind of Eden. 'Logres' was the name that Dyfric kept catching. Albion elevated into Logres. Again and again since being hauled aboard, Dyfric had also overhead the phrase 'great remaking'. It was even possible that he knew it from before.

Minute by minute his memories of his own life in Albion were thinning. Now he could barely picture the northern hilltop camp where until the previous night he had served as chaplain; and every time he looked around himself, the faces seemed to have grown a little less familiar.

The heavily-bearded figure standing with his back against a mast was almost certainly Lot, King Arthur's Warden of the North, although in this throng he appeared to be exerting no authority whatever.

Seated close to his feet was an older, dome-headed man whom Dyfric knew to be a joiner, Nabur. Any more about him, he was unable now to say. It was possible that the large-eared, dreamy-eyed fellow squatting next to him was his son. Dyfric eyed the pair of them sidelong. If this were a family, then he fancied that there had been a second son: a difficult, gifted boy. But however often he scanned the rest of the crowd, he felt no flush of recognition.

He drew his vestments tighter about him, undisturbed by the forgetting. Albion deserved oblivion. Even if Dyfric could be sure of nothing from more recent times, the miseries from further back were vivid still.

Albion: a land braced in constant anticipation of a return

to the wars of before. Like a man thrashed too often in childhood, it had grown up sullen and graceless. A kingdom so disturbed by the violence of Arthur's final victory that it had never learned how to live without conflict.

Two decades earlier, great Arthur had emerged to halt the Sea Wolf invasions and seize a throne which no one had then disputed with him. Nobody else would have wanted it. The king himself must soon have regretted his success. His kingdom never slipped out of the shadows cast by its own benighted past. For twenty years of peace its people continued to wade through undried blood. Suspicious, watchful, circumspect; brother mistrusting brother, stranger hating stranger.

In that sorry world of endless fences and ditches, fear corroded all. Grown men went on tiptoe, as if in dread of angering the very earth beneath their feet: a farming folk with no sense of their own surroundings, no confidence even in the weather on which they depended so heavily . . .

In relief Dyfric raised his eyes skywards again.

It was as if he and the millions with him were being held in abeyance – removed from their own dimension while another was prepared into which they might return. He felt like a tightly-swaddled child pegged to a wall while its mother cleaned the house. And while he was lodged there, he drowsed, teetering on the edge of sleep, a sleep which seemed enormous.

Everything here was vast. For a moment small-boned Dyfric felt himself filling the ship, the sea, the sky; merging with all that was around him, animate and inanimate alike. The sky's expanse was seducing him anew. It turned his sedated thoughts to the island's older gods: the so-called Mighty – colossal guardians who had lived first on the land, then in the seas and at last, it was said, they had made the air their own.

The air that Dyfric breathed here felt safer than any he had ever tasted. The waters, too, posed no threat. The sea beneath the forest of masts was graveyard-still. Although no sun had risen yet, its surface sparkled as if with reflected light, and all the ships shimmered with it. Dyfric narrowed his eyes and the sea was like a great glass wall, the ships on it rising as battlements. It was beautiful. All of it was huge and beautiful.

He twisted around and tried to peer into the depths, expecting to find the remains of drowned Albion: trees as underwater tendrils, entire submerged shanties, gore-smeared fortifications threaded with seaweed.

But all he could see was his own sleepy, smiling face.

The bearded man by the mast had folded his arms and crossed his ankles, studiously cultivating a sceptical air. Too studiously, Dyfric thought. His jaw was tense, his eyes a little too defiantly averted from the land they now appeared to be heading towards.

Dyfric hunted in vain for the man's name. Already he could not remember how his voice would sound, if and when he deigned to speak. He wondered if he had even known him before.

The next time Dyfric glanced his way, it was as if for the first time ever.

And he knew from the quietness around him that he was not alone in his forgetting. He saw from the way his fellow survivors looked at one another that they too were being unburdened. Released from the past, to move forward the faster; Albion's grisly baggage sliding overboard like ballast.

Dyfric felt physically lighter by the moment. Perhaps, he

thought, that was why earlier he had sensed a drift towards the sky. But now the pull was definitely landward. There was still no suggestion of waves around them, but the tension in the waters' surface had slackened. It was as if the whole glass sheet with all its human cargo was moving closer to the shore. And although this shore was in the same place as Albion's, it had changed. Its entire sweep was less oppressive; it seemed to be spreading out to welcome them.

Dyfric's heart was hurting with hope; his heart, as one of many. It was not just the land that had been reduced, distilled, remade. Its people too had been stripped down and interlaced. Some memories might have gone, but so much more had streamed in to fill the space.

Everyone in this ship, in all the ships, had come together. Names had been lost but names had ceased to signify. It was impossible now to tell where one person ended and the next began, and that was perfect. Dyfric felt like a pearl on an endless necklace; a single pearl forever linked on an unbreakable thread to all who lived and died around him.

Then, briefly, he felt the necklace being enclosed in a gentle, gigantic fist. A new phrase bloomed in his head: *One name, one head, one hand . . .*

As it did so, a shape gathered above, cloudy but substantial, with a golden light gleaming behind it. Dyfric saw it as the hand that held them all: the shape of their own new aspiration, and it rose like smoke from the land.

As Dyfric blinked in awe, the hand became a face. Benign, full of vigour, swirled about by words: strings of sound that spoke only to the inner ear. And then the great face mutated, its cloud-beard and flailing hair dissolving into softer contours: a woman's face replacing the man's – proud, stately, regal, presiding over the rocks and sand and all that lay beyond.

But she, too, transformed as the land curved up around

the ship on either side, taking them on like cushioned pincers.

The sea had narrowed into a delta of serpentine rivers. The great, still indeterminate shape in the sky was holding the threads of water, drawing the ships ever closer to the heart of Logres. The shape became the figure of a man: lower than the faces but solider too. Dyfric's sigh of recognition fused with the rush of sound around him.

Arthur, it was Arthur, poised on a hilltop, arms outspread, the great warrior king at the head of his people. Dyfric could see him conducting down into himself all the strength of the sky. And through him it swarmed across the land at his feet. Seams of splendour ran through his kingdom like streaks of precious ore.

This was a fresh beginning that Dyfric never could have dreamed of. Moved to his soul, he fixed his eyes on his king, briefly blinded to the marvels of thatch and masonry to either side as they passed. Words surged like winds in his face, words making wonders, fashioning the new land's fabric. The king was both far and near, guiding them in with his eyes. From on high he saw them all as they approached from every direction.

Dyfric glanced away. The crowds around him had dwindled. Even as he watched, people of all ages and stations were disembarking – not from a ship now but from a convoy of wagons.

There was no more water around them, only a lush, steep-sided valley. The wagons did not stop as colonies were set down at village after stone-built village. Each magnificent dwelling and church and barn and winding street looked as if it had stood there for ever, so deftly had they all been harmonized with the land.

And as the king grew less distant, Dyfric could clearly see

his city taking shape around him on its hill. The sandstone walls and turrets forcing their way up first from the waters and then from the land. The king with his court had been hatched from the wholeness. A king like a black-maned angel: swordless, all-seeing, the lynchpin of Logres. Arthur: the king for whom this kingdom had been made.

Dyfric's spirit soared as the wagon tilted back to climb the slope to where his lord was waiting. Here, in rapture, he was coming into Canaan.

The spell stretched and broke: the spell that had held the king's sister in thrall for so long.

Standing up high in the hill-figure's fist, looking back hard across late-summer Logres, Morgan knew that she was freer now than she had ever been. Barely able to contain herself, she touched her stomach.

In spite of Arthur's savage efforts to erase all trace of her, she had escaped with not one life, but two. And in time there would be more, countless more.

She closed her eyes and humbly prayed her thanks for that. Not to God the Father, nor even to God the Son. Her gratitude went deeper, to the heart that still beat at the core of this island.

One island, two kingdoms: first Albion, now Logres — this kingdom which they said had been remade for the king. Great Arthur the king. Arthur: Morgan's brother, and in older times her lover; the sire of an innocent child whom twice he had failed to slaughter, and now had set out to expunge from his people's collective memory.

But in her humility Morgan was safe; here she could keep the boy even safer. She had no fear. Here, instead, brute Arthur would learn to fear her. So too would the twin architects of his glistering new regime.

Guenever and Merlin would be no match for the powers that Morgan had already started to harness. Through that unholy pair,

Arthur had worked against nature to achieve his Great Remaking, but Morgan now would tap that nature to its root. By going back to go forward, hers would be more than a mere reconquest, it would be a reversion.

She let her hand fall from her belly to the bone-handled knife that she wore at her waist. It was reassuringly warm; hotter than the sun of Logres could have made it.

There in the hill-figure's fist she sank to the ground. Taking the knife from her girdle, she scratched with its tip near the outline of chalk.

Soon red streaks appeared. Morgan carved harder. She felt the pull and loosened her grip. As the blade was sucked gratefully down, she let go of the hilt.

Blood bubbled up – heavy, old, black-red blood that needed to be purged. The knife was swallowed whole. Morgan's offering, her pledge, her own part of the bargain.

She smiled at the slit in the ground. It ran back through the generations to the time behind time, bypassing Arthur, Merlin, Guenever and anyone else rash enough to believe that a kingdom could ever be made for a king. She knelt forward and put her ear close to hear its oracle-promise: The stone shall be healed, the head will be replaced.

Effortlessly Morgan rose to her feet, closed her eyes and started to walk. Upward, northward, still inside the great chalk giant. And after this giant there would be another, then another – forming so much more than a mere colossal race. Morgan would be the agent of their making: new scions of the Mighty, new shining moons within which each of Arthur's men, women and children would be but the thinnest slivers.

She felt as if she were ascending a stairway of air. The reversion had begun. In the name of Morgan's own reborn son this island would be restored to the Mighty.

The head, truly, would be replaced.

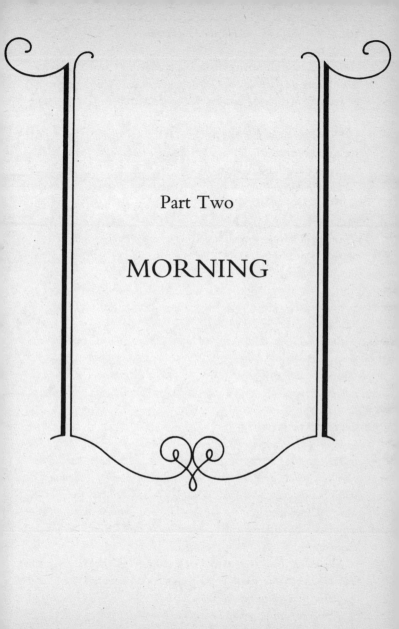

Part Two

MORNING

TWO

Lanslod came late to the great stone-vaulted hall. Over sixty armed men were already inside, none of them seated. Most milled dreamily around the central granite slab, some trailing their fingers across its surface as if it were liquid.

With his head still full of hissing, Lanslod tried to smile.

This was all so new. The light was natural: firm September sunshafts emblazoned with dustmotes. But the alcoves were so dark that a whole army could have been lurking hidden in the shadows.

Lanslod felt dwarfed as he entered, and was glad to find a handful of faces that he knew: older warriors than himself who had fought for Arthur against the Sea Wolves. Urien, Carados, Lot, Ryens, Clarivans, Auguselus. Like Lanslod they had all come safely through the deluge; they too had left Albion behind, to find this new land of Logres waiting.

The echoing rush hissed on in Lanslod's ears, a little more faintly now. Ever since the landfall, his head had been full of it – as if he had jumped from a great height on this stillest of days and a whole world was now tearing past. The old drowned world of before, perhaps, out of which this new one had evolved.

He fell into step around the stone slab. Although perfectly circular, its grain looked rough. He found it was good to keep moving. As reassuring as it had been to climb the steps from the courtyard. No one had summoned him – had anyone summoned the others?—but now that he had come, he felt less troubled. This was right. The more he walked, the more would become clear.

He met the eyes of several unfamiliar men in mail who were wandering in the opposite direction. At twenty-five, Lanslod was far from the youngest here. Some were little more than boys, their beardless faces tight with fright or wonder. None of the others acknowledged him, none spoke. They circled like newborns awaiting their first slap. The kingdom too seemed to be waiting: safely delivered, but waiting.

And Lanslod was sure that Arthur now was close; here in this court that was being called Camelot. Soon the king would come again. Soon he would speak. Not to explain. Simply to instruct. For Lanslod, at least, that would be enough. He had always known enough if he had known that he was the king's subject.

There were benches, he saw, drawn up hard against the slab – seating enough for all sixty and more, a second circle enclosing the first. Directly opposite the entrance arch stood a simple throne of slate: a curved seat, straight backrest, crossed struts between its legs. Lanslod fixed his eyes on it as he passed, imagining the king upon it.

But it felt like decades since Lanslod had seen Arthur. And as he walked on, his memory of Albion darkened farther. Only scraps and shards remained of its end; those final blighted days when the king had seemed to be decaying on his feet –

or rather on his side, in the hole he had made for himself in the hill beneath his court.

Whoever had then ruled in Arthur's name – his queen, his wardens like Lot in the north, and during the climactic floods the apparently self-appointed Regent – a pall had hung across Albion. The kingdom had seemed to be preparing for some massive blow, not by bracing itself but, like the king in his abyss, by making itself softer, more listless. No one then could have imagined so great a remaking of the land. But Lanslod for one was far keener to know how its lord had been restored.

A figure appeared in the archway.

The walkers paused but when they saw that it was not the king, they all moved on. Lanslod caught the newcomer's eye and smiled. He was tall, shock-haired, clean-shaven but swarthy, dressed in a black soutane: the Regent.

Lanslod's smile faltered. The Regent was staring through him to the throne. Then he entered, skirted the slab and stood, slightly stooped, behind the king's unoccupied seat.

'Please, be seated,' he invited them in a rich panoramic voice, limply holding out both hands to indicate the benches, 'and our king will come.'

There was a moment's hesitation. The eye of the veteran, Lot, glinted before he showed the rest the way by dragging out the nearest upholstered bench and sitting. Brumart, ever-combative, may have stayed on his feet just long enough to be noticed, but in the end he too did as the Regent had asked.

The splendid hall seemed to grow disproportionately taller with their sitting: so many men around a stone, their knees turned sideways to give them extra leg-room. Lanslod found himself almost opposite the throne, with Brumart to his left just in front of the archway and a stranger to his right.

'Your king will be with you soon,' the Regent said more

softly. 'Your' king – moments earlier it had been 'our'. He was still standing, his hairless hands now clutching the throne's backrest.

Lanslod knew him hardly at all, nor where he had come from to pilot them through the hiatus between Albion and Logres. 'Merlin' he had heard the lesser people in the wagons calling him. But this was not so much a name as a title.

Albion's influential breed of itinerant messenger-story-tellers had been known as merlins. 'Strays' too; and even 'Arthur's men'. With his unkempt hair and strong, unsurprisable face, this Regent indeed resembled them. But very briefly he loomed larger than that for Lanslod, like a kind of Trojan Horse in which the others were all still contained – although why there should be a need for subterfuge here, now, he could not say.

The noise in his ears grew loud again. It sounded as if someone had clamped great seashells over both his ears. He was sorry to be stationary. Everything in Logres made more sense while he was moving.

Dizzied, he gazed around the stone's circumference. Lot's son Walwen, Osla, Manannan, Pwyll . . . There were others whose names escaped him; and some whose faces he had recognized only minutes before but now were quite alien. There seemed to be vast distances between each of them; and they looked so queasily bewildered, as if they were all still out at sea.

The moment lengthened. The Regent stared dead ahead. One or two of the seated at last started to murmur to their neighbours. Lanslod turned to his left to see the restless Brumart frown and scratch his head. His beard and hair had been close-cropped, which somehow accentuated the size of his attractively crooked nose.

Lanslod swung around to his right. The man on that side,

roughly Lanslod's own age, was spidering his fingers across the stone surface. He inclined his head close to Lanslod's ear. His breath stank of garlic and ill-digested nuts. A meal he must have taken in the last moments of Albion.

'They say that once this stone was water,' he whispered like an overgrown child, the words cutting straight through the hiss in Lanslod's head. 'That it formed itself from water at the coming of the king.'

Lanslod could only smile, and wonder who 'they' were. A long period then seemed to drift by. During it, Lanslod several times came close to falling asleep where he sat. The tumult in his head appeared to be flowing directly in and out of the low drone of conversation around him.

He could not explain his sudden torpor. The journey up from the coast with the convoy of wagons had been long but hardly over-taxing. Already that ride felt very distant; as if he had made it not just hours but months before. And when he tried now, behind fast-blinking eyes, to recall details of the earlier jubilant landing, almost nothing came to mind.

Farther back than that, it was as if he were trying to salvage images from some other person's life altogether. Nor, later, was he able to remember quite how the king finally came into the hall with its great stone dais. All he knew for sure was that Arthur did not enter under the arch like the rest of them. It was almost as if the assembly's intense anticipation had willed him into its presence. In one long, slow moment the slate throne was empty; in the next the king was poised upon it, filling out the shape of all their expectations.

For a while Lanslod continued to believe that he was looking at a mirage: the king's haphazard outline made all the hazier by the fact that Lanslod's eyes had – to his astonishment – brimmed over with tears.

Plainly Arthur moved to a rhythm all his own. Even in

Albion Lanslod had seen him less as a person to be known than as a force to be channelled. Not elemental exactly. He was a thing of flesh, blood and bone like anyone else. Yet his parts had always added up to a different sum than other men's. His big, opaque eyes seemed to be on Lanslod but Arthur's eyes could appear to be on everyone at once. Before his withdrawal in Albion, he had been ubiquitous, seeming to fill any given space with himself. Any gathering of men had been over-arched, even absorbed by the king's majestic presence.

The noise in Lanslod's ears changed again. Rousing himself, he saw that at least half the assembly were clapping their hands in a new kind of salute. Lanslod could not help but join in. The Regent too, still on his feet and slightly to one side of the throne, clapped in an expansive way which suggested that he was orchestrating the acclaim.

On and on it went. The king sat straight-backed, staring into the eyes of each and all. Lanslod's tears snaked down into his beard. His throat felt hoarse and stretched. He was unbearably glad to see Arthur like this: a figure of some forty years of age, dressed in simple royal purple; unarmed, uncrowned – he needed no baubles of that sort. His kingship glittered in his cascade of black hair, it was chiselled into his orientally-high cheekbones, and shone from the line between his pursed, implacable lips.

But the prospect of hearing as well as seeing his monarch touched Lanslod with real fear. Perhaps it had touched the others too, and they were making this uproar to postpone the moment when his voice would ring out again.

Then it was among them. Insinuating itself around the handclaps rather than silencing them. Lanslod stilled his own hands and watched the king's mouth move. Despite the clamour the words came through clearly, but at first they seemed not to be linked. Then Lanslod realized that he was hearing a single sentence over and over. The Lord of War was making no speech, just sharing one secret. A secret that they might already have guessed, but which still had the force of revelation, if only because it was coming from him.

'This,' the king was saying without intonation, 'is the land of promise.'

This is the land of promise. As the six words kept washing over Lanslod, it seemed to him that he was being lifted and cleansed. Purged of the last remaining taint of Albion. Islands of memory stood in an ocean of welcome forgetting, but even they were just shapes without sense to him now.

Transported, he closed his eyes and suddenly he saw a sword contracting into a short, bone-handled knife; a pale child growing smaller, smaller – shrinking in blood like Lanslod's own picture of the past . . .

Then, as abruptly as he had begun to speak, the king fell silent. The applause thundered louder than ever, reaching new crescendoes driven on by the stamping of boots.

Lanslod, choked with tears, felt lost inside his own din. He hardly noticed the king rise and take a curved path around the throng to the archway. Unlike his coming, there was nothing ambiguous about Arthur's going. Lanslod even caught his distinctive hot-metal stink as he passed behind them all into the late-afternoon sunlight. It was as much as he could do not to bound out like a hound after him.

Slowly the uproar ceased, then the silence seemed to scintillate. Lanslod, ecstatic, was on the point of rising when he saw the Regent resume his former position behind the throne.

'This is the kingdom that was made for the king,' he announced – sound etched on pure silence, his clarity almost shocking after what had gone before. 'Think only now of Logres, let Albion wither away . . .'

Lanslod found this hard to follow. His head still pounded from the frenzy that had surrounded the king's appearance, although now at least the cavernous rushing noise had almost completely faded.

'Think of Logres,' the Regent repeated, and this time Lanslod understood it to be an order. An order he saw no reason to disobey. Wherever this Merlin drew his authority from, he had surely brought them all to safety. He had been the Noah whose Ark had ferried them through the deluge.

Dutifully Lanslod tried to picture the country he had ridden across from the coast – so familiar yet so new, not so much following old Albion's contours as leading them into a perfectly finalized form. He recalled it as if through a golden gauze: flat, harvestable fields; neatly-coppiced trees; a sprinkle of stone-built, confidently undefended settlements. A good, sound, sun-drenched landscape; a place that seemed to be totally at ease with itself.

But then, unbidden and far more starkly, the earlier images of the crude domestic knife and of a child growing smaller returned. A child in the arms of a woman who undeniably shared the king's cool, dark glamour. And the woman and child were going down in blood, down into the foundations of this kingdom made for the king . . .

'Once this was Albion, but now there is only Logres. Albion is over, its darkness has been dispersed.'

The new words came like a release. Lanslod's little vision of the bloodied couple blurred then disappeared, as if a sea had been parted to reveal it, only for the waters to come flooding back in again.

Yet only when he refixed his gaze on the Regent – eagerly bent forward, gripping the back of Arthur's throne with a hank of hair obscuring one eye – did he realize that somebody else had spoken the last few words, someone with a lighter voice, from close behind his own head.

He blinked and breathed deeply but did not turn. The speaker had been Guenever, Arthur's queen and the island's first lady. Lanslod had caught sight of her on first arriving at Camelot. An elegant, rather sombre woman only a few years older than himself, standing rapt above the gatehouse as if she were counting the convoys in.

Diagrams of her in Albion flitted through Lanslod's tired mind. As a retainer of no great status, he had known her no better than he had known the king. Once or twice he had been detailed to escort her train across that grimmer terrain. There had never been a reason for them to say more than a few words to each other. But although he barely knew the woman, Guenever's voice was unmistakable. He wondered now if she had been standing behind him all the time.

This is the land of promise . . . Again Lanslod looked from side to side. He could remember so few of the others' names now. His need to be on the move almost overwhelmed him. He felt as if this whole assembly were sitting inside the joint embrace of the Regent and the queen: her arms snaking out from behind to clasp his hands halfway around the dais.

But even as they tried to bring the armed men closer, to press them together into some larger body, Lanslod had never felt more isolated, more asphyxiatingly apart.

'The new land awaits you,' the Regent resumed, flinging up his hands awkwardly, as if in imitation of a conjuror. 'Go out now into it and take what is yours.'

Lanslod needed no second telling. He rose, vaulted the bench, and paused for only a moment when he found no Guenever behind him.

Without looking back he descended the steep flight of

steps to the courtyard across which spidery evening shadows were beginning to creep.

He made for the stables and directed the ostlers to bring him the horse that looked fittest. Move, move . . . the logic of his body was screaming at him. Logres was awaiting him, but nothing else, no one else. He could ride in any direction; all that mattered now was to leave.

Before that night finally swallowed him up, he had put twenty-five miles between himself and Camelot — and a further incalculable distance between himself and Albion.

THREE

Peredur would remember for a long time the sight of Lanslod breaking from the shadow of the city on its hill, then striking out across Camelot's flatlands as if all the demons of dead Albion were at his back.

Standing on the platform outside the citadel's hall, the roaring in his ears at last began to subside. It was the most extraordinary sound. Not exactly like the noise made by the beat of your own blood when you held a shell to your ear – more like the endless gush of somebody else's blood altogether.

In Lanslod's wake, others were dreamily descending the majestic stairway to the courtyard. Peredur took just one step down, to a small dark smear he had seen on the sandstone. As he stooped to touch it with the tips of his fingers, he heard a raucous shout from inside the hall.

'What happened to the boy?'

Peredur inspected his fingers to find sticky blood on them. Without looking up, he was aware that the men still behind him had parted so that the voice shot between them like an angry arrow.

'Can anyone tell me that?' the speaker went on more loudly. 'The boy? Any of you? You know there was a boy? Here.'

Peredur straightened and looked back into the shadowy hall. The man nearest the entrance arch had not yet left the bench. Straddling it, he levelled his finger at Peredur. '*His* age, to begin with. I know he was here.' His voice quivered, with fear more than fury. 'I won't forget that. I won't! So where is he now? The boy? The bastard . . .'

'No,' barked the most senior-looking man still standing on the platform – probably Lot if his age and irritability and streaky, mud-coloured beard were anything to go by. 'No, Brumart. Enough . . .'

Peredur felt the air clot around them all. For a giddy moment he thought that this Brumart might be hauled out and hurled down the steps just for having spoken. Instead he simply rose from the bench and shambled out.

Peredur had noticed him in the hall: young, outsized, huge-boned, oddly-proportioned. He gave the impression that he had agreed to be human only after failing to succeed in becoming some other order of creature. His arm was slung across his body, hand on his undrawn sword's hilt. Glancing down, Peredur saw that the stain had gone; so too had the mark on his fingers. It was as if the stone had wept a tear for him to dry away.

Brumart's eyes blazed over the handful of men who remained. Then they narrowed, and Peredur could see him fighting with his own mind, clearly battling against the inexorable obliteration of his memories. 'The boy . . .' he faltered one more time, and it sounded like a plea.

At that, the Regent stepped forward. He had been standing to the side of the arch, his arms folded tight across his chest, his hands inside the sleeves of his soutane. His eyes seemed to swivel before he said: 'The child is back with its mother.' The statement was so brisk and slick that briefly Peredur thought he had said 'in', not 'with'. 'The child is no more. It has no place in Logres.' The Regent was not looking at Brumart and had aimed his words over Peredur's head, as if at the distant dust-cloud kicked up by Lanslod's horse.

'You're saying he's dead?' Brumart challenged the back of his head.

'He will be forgotten.' It sounded like an instruction. 'He will be forgotten as Albion will be forgotten. Or, if that land is remembered at all, it will seem only like the Egypt from which we were all mercifully delivered into this land of promise.'

'He is dead?' Brumart growled, refusing to be deflected. '*She* is dead?'

Peredur had no idea what he meant. Unnerved by it nonetheless, he raised his eyes and noticed, carved on the hall's arch, a procession of mounted men led by a king on the back of a goat. It was then that a black tide seeped behind his eyes and an old strays' saw from Albion curdled up out of it: *A seed sown in darkness will surely blossom in an evil way . . .*

'They have no place in Logres,' the Regent finally replied – so softly that he could just have been assuring Peredur.

Brumart snorted, but the Regent then began to pick his way down to the courtyard. Peredur, feeling his stomach contract, looked back up to where Brumart stood, all alone now on the platform. At once he too launched himself down the steps, yelled for a horse to be brought, and minutes later became the second man out of Camelot after Lanslod.

Peredur had known only by chance that the first man to leave was Lanslod. Two women on the passage up from the coast had identified him. He was the kind of man, Peredur thought, whom women would be likely to remember. Rangy, tousle-haired, his features soft but confident. Peredur himself did not remember the name. Lanslod had looked too young to have fought against the Sea Wolves; thus he would not have figured in the stray-tales – Peredur's main source of information for all that he now found around him.

For him, the forgetting had begun even before he came ashore in Logres. At eighteen years of age, he had little to remember anyway. But by the time the Regent had dismissed them from the hall, his amnesia about his own history in Albion, as opposed to story-fragments he had heard there, was almost total. All he could recall was setting out months earlier on a journey from the old kingdom's western backwoods. He had left behind his mother and headed in hope towards the king's court, which in Albion was called Camlann. He had never arrived. The Great Remaking had intervened, and a personal quest that had begun on horseback was continued by ship and completed in a wagon.

Peredur believed that his dream had been to serve with his sword a king he had never seen. Now, miraculously, it seemed to have come true. More miraculous still, he seemed to have been expected. On walking into the hall, no one had challenged him. He had assumed his new position as of right, which thrilled and scared him in roughly equal measure.

Now he let his gaze wander away from the horizon to the nearer shimmering gables of Camelot's roofs, to the armourers' workshops, the neat streets teeming with livestock and vendors, the cavernous amphitheatre just inside the lower wall, ringed around with gaming houses and taverns. This, inside the cloud of forgetting, was the heart of the new kingdom.

Logres, Logres . . . It seemed to Peredur like Albion's own dream of itself. The triumvirate of king, queen and Regent had seemed as bemused by it as everyone else in the hall. Clearly they were still feeling their way, running their hands in awe over this fabulous new construct, wondering what in the fullness of time they could make of it.

But he could not yet guess why the assembly in the hall had been held. Surely not to hear those peculiarly terse speeches. At one point he had sensed an attempt at some other kind of inauguration, an almost physical amalgamation of everyone who sat. But by the end of the session the distances between each of them had seemed even larger than at the start.

His eyes roved over a series of tall hedges away to his right, arranged in a kind of maze close to the royal quarters. Looking harder, he saw uncrowned Arthur strolling there, apparently lost in thought. Several steps ahead of him walked the stately, blue-gowned queen. From the high citadel it looked as if Guenever were leading him around on an invisible thread.

The sun was setting immediately behind them. Peredur squinted to keep them in view. Round and round they meandered, too far apart to speak, too close to break out of each other's orbits. And over them both loomed the new court, the new kingdom, and the massive new burden of their maintenance.

After leaving the citadel, Peredur found temporary quarters high above the main gatehouse. From there, before nightfall, he watched rider after rider depart, each presumably with his own idea of what he was riding out for.

It had been the strangest day, and in its way exhausting, mind-tiring. Peredur lay on his bed in the dark and drowsed for several hours.

Intermittently the roaring in his ears returned. It sounded to him now like a kind of song. He imagined a whole choir of strays filling Logres with their words just as once they had saturated Albion. '. . . the seed came to fruit and then withered . . .' he heard more than once. And '. . . its blood has bound the new foundations . . .' When he fell into a deeper sleep, the choir rearranged itself into a huge human face, the Regent's, which solemnly but silently went on singing.

On waking, he went out into the well-lit, leafy streets, turning over the earlier words and phrases but failing to make any great sense of them. Wafts of jasmine and juniper soothed him as he walked. So too did the unexpected quietness, broken only by the distant screams of peacocks. But still he felt tired, impossibly heavy on his feet for so slight a man. Maybe like this former hill-fort, he thought, he too was being remade.

He tried to imagine how Camelot had looked as Camlann, but he had so little to go on. From chance remarks overheard on arrival, he had gathered that these stylish villas had once been filthy shacks, that the jousting-lists had been mass latrines. He was intrigued by the way different people seemed to remember different things from before. For one person it was buildings; for another, a bastard boy; for him, it was words from old fireside tales. Maybe only by fitting all the fragments together would they be able to recreate Albion. It did not occur to him, then, to wonder why they should ever want to do so.

Almost without noticing, he had strolled beyond the main drag into a darker, treeless area that ran quite steeply down to the city's west-facing wall. A single lamp burned above the porch of a small chapel. Surprisingly it was the first place of worship that Peredur had seen here. White-limed and squat, protruding at an angle from the slope, it looked like the only tooth left standing in an otherwise clean-swept gum. Turning aside to approach it, Peredur pulled up short when a wide, circular opening appeared in the unkempt grass between him and the building.

He could think only that it was a grain silo, but when he peered in, he knew it was more than that. The silence inside seemed uneasy. He had the oddest impression that a face should have been staring back up at him.

Raising his eyes, he saw that the chapel door was ajar. By a dim light inside he made out a waxy-skinned, flop-haired chaplain – a man whom Peredur was fairly sure he had seen before, maybe near the citadel steps during Brumart's peculiar outburst. His arms were now extended in the act of blessing bread and wine at the altar. But from where Peredur was standing, it looked as if he were addressing the hole in the hillside – trying to exorcise whatever lurked inside, or what had already come out.

Peredur found it hard to tear himself away. When he did, he climbed back on heavier legs than ever to the brighter streets and turned in to a tavern for some chops and a flagon of ale.

The simple meal was as good as any he had ever tasted. Around him a rash of enthusiastic conversations drifted in and out of his grasp like underwater seaweed. For some reason the word 'night' kept coming through. He had an idea that sometimes the drinkers were talking about him, behind their hands, but respectfully enough. They laughed a lot too. Camelot's rank and file appeared to be responding with more gusto to the Great Remaking than the peers at the dais. Slowly, however, the low-ceilinged room began to empty.

Although it was late, and Peredur was by now the only customer left, he ordered more drink which the girl brought at once. She was younger than himself and skinnily pretty. When he looked at her a little too long in thanking her, she held his gaze. He felt a charge, but not one that he trusted. Smiling, he drank on in silence as she swept the floor.

'More?' she asked afterwards, straightening and putting one hand on her hip as if to impersonate an older, tireder woman. He picked up his mug, swirled its dregs, then set it away from him with a shake of the head.

'You leave tomorrow, sir?' she asked, leaning on her broom and blowing a wisp of tawny hair off her cheek.

'Is that what you've heard?' He met her eye again.

She shrugged. 'I know that the whole Company is riding out.'

'The Company?'

'All those who sat at the Round Table.'

Peredur nodded. Company. Round Table. The new names seemed suitable enough, and she used them with such confidence. 'What else do you know?'

She blushed, imagining that he was teasing her more cruelly than he really was. 'Tell me,' he said. 'Why do you think we're all riding out?'

'To beat the bounds of the new kingdom,' she answered, furrow-browed, as if he were crazy to think that she did not know. Peredur watched smoke from a guttering lamp drift across the floor between them.

He took some coins from his pouch and slapped them down on the table. The girl started at the sound, but did not move away. Peredur wondered if he needed to dismiss her formally. But the liquor had made him even more torpid than before. He was brought back to himself by a male voice calling something gruff from the kitchens.

The girl smiled, stood a little straighter, let the broom fall, and Peredur thought that she was about to offer him some entirely unnecessary apology. 'Do you,' she asked instead, 'want me?'

This is the land of promise . . . Peredur stared up into her eyes. She was lovely, he could see that. And he longed not to be alone. But he needed more than a woman to slake his craving. It would have been no more natural for Peredur to spend the night with her than to join up the freckles on her face until they made a shape. A whole kingdom, it seemed, could alter its essential nature more easily than he.

Unsteadily he stood, edged past her and breathlessly re-entered the scented night. Long before dawn he was out on the road, but only to circle Camelot.

Land of promise, land of promise . . . As Peredur rode, Arthur's words swirled in his head, sounding now like a hopeful protest, or even a protective charm. Who exactly, he wondered, had done the promising, and to whom?

As day broke he had no intention of heading back west, nor of beating any far-flung bounds. The transition here from Albion to Logres had plainly not been perfect. Peredur wanted to know why. And when the nettle stings, as he recalled from yet another old story, the salve tends to lie close by.

FOUR

Lot of Lodonesia – King Arthur's Warden of the North in Albion, and for many years his senior subject – was the last of the Company to ride away from court.

As he guided his horse down the steep slope from the walled city, he did not know whether he felt more bitter or confused. Half an hour across the plain he reined in his horse, wheeled it around and took a long look back at Camelot. So much had moved on in the past week, and in so baffling a fashion, that he wanted to make sure it really was there.

It was. The conical mound stood up like a gigantic shield boss in the oceanic flatlands. The city's beige stone looked soft in the afternoon sunshine, as if its turrets and buttresses were waiting to be shaped more finely still by some perfectionist hand reaching down from the heavens.

But there was nothing provisional about its appearance. Compared to what Lot could remember of the dilapidated camp that had sat on this hill in hand-to-mouth Albion, it looked most exquisitely finished. Too finished perhaps, like so much else that he had seen while riding in from the coast after the sea rescue. Just as once a goddess was said to have leapt fully-formed from her giant father's head, so Logres seemed to have jumped complete from the drowning mind of Albion.

Lot had stayed on in the city for five full days after the assembly. Having ensconced himself in some splendid apartments near the tiltyards, he had waited in vain for a summons from the king. Nor was he sought out for his counsel by the queen, nor even by that cryptic civilian Regent whom he had heard the city's menials calling Merlin.

The new land awaits you. Go out now into it and take what is yours. That, then, was to be his only brief – just as it had been for the bevy of bumfluffed boys with whom he had been made to sit in parity at the assembly. Four of them had been his own ingrate sons, not one of whom had so much as acknowledged him. It made him wonder whether, along with all the other profound changes, blood-bonds too had been dissolved.

Lot's pride was horribly hurt. If he had no major part to play in this so-called kingdom made for the king, he would at least have appreciated an explanation why. The rest he was ready to take on trust: the deluge, the Great Remaking, the remorseless slipping away of whole stretches of his memory. He was a simple man, brought up to believe in miracles – and the storm of glory around him now was nothing if not a miracle. But he thought he deserved better personal treatment than this under the new dispensation.

He had whiled away his five days of waiting with too much wine and a stream of well-heeled courtesans. Straight after Brumart's tediously incoherent outburst at the citadel he had taken in as many of the city's sights as he had needed to. Already feeling slighted, he had found Camelot aggressively smug in its splendour, as if it had woken up inside this dream of itself and planned never to be fooled again into falling asleep.

He had walked only as far as the chapel just over the crest: an odd little temple stationed above a kind of gaping hell-mouth. Its priest, who with six acolytes was tending to the precinct, had a remotely familiar face. Briefly his eyes had met Lot's but it was Lot who had then looked away first, turned and stamped back up the hill.

If he had known the man before, it must have been in the north. In Lot's lucid moments, the things that he still remembered were almost exclusively geographical. His thoughts kept curving back to the great northern Wall – the ruined giants' Wall which had stretched across the neck of Albion as a sorry kind of collar for that ailing kingdom's head to sit on. He knew that this was the region where he had spent most of his forty-eight years, both before and after helping the king to deal with the Sea Wolves.

The new land awaits you . . . Lot could recall little of how he had held down the old north for Arthur, or picture any of the series of wives who had shared his remit. But now on the sixth morning, having swallowed his pride and cut his losses with the court, he wheeled his horse around and headed north again. He had no intention of coming back. He wanted to be as far away as possible from the heart of this new-flowering kingdom of Logres. Sometimes, he told himself as his horse gathered speed, if you pushed your nose too close to the heart of a rose, you missed all its subtler scents.

Lot had guessed it would take him a matter of days to reach the Wall. In the event it took him weeks. When at last it loomed into sight – a towering peacetime feat or even folly now rather than a fortification – the season had turned, and as many leaves were rustling on the ground as in the breeze-blown trees. By that time too, he was no longer riding alone.

He was not quite sure why his progress was so slow. He could have indulged himself less lavishly at the inns and bawdy houses where he stopped over, festering in beds for up to four days at a time. But even when out on the road he felt dreadfully sluggish. It was as much as he could do at times to mount and dismount his horse unaided. Yet as he clawed his way up the kingdom, he could not avoid taking note of his surroundings.

Once this was Albion, but now there is only Logres . . . Albion will be forgotten . . . The queen and Regent had sounded so emphatic about that. But beyond the plain of Camelot, Lot's more distant memories of Albion began to seep back. Slowly at first, and always in fragments. It was as if the waters of forgetting that had roiled in so dark and deep around the court were spread more thinly over parts of the wider kingdom. For days on end he passed through a sequence of shallows where the riverbed was still quite visible – especially when he rode close to the eastern seaboard.

Over twenty years earlier, after stemming the tide of Sea Wolf invasions, Arthur had allowed large numbers of the disarmed invaders to settle along these coasts. Long before the Remaking, they had rewarded the king handsomely, proving as industrious as they were loyal, dredging great swathes of unpromising fenland, bringing thousands more acres into cultivation, and setting down the bones of rudimentary trading-centres that were now fleshed out into thriving, brick-built ports and cities.

The roads here too, once simple tracks, were fine and straight – just as they had been in the long-gone giants' time. Attractive stone churches stood where rickety wooden chapels had used to burn down regularly. Soaring cathedrals

– vast masonry cobwebs – sprawled high on the air like a warning to God that even His great works would one day be eclipsed. But curiously, although it occurred to Lot only later, during all his time in the saddle he hardly ever heard the ringing of a bell.

If this extensive region was anything to go by – and Lot did not doubt that it was – then Logres was breathtakingly beautiful. A genuine land of promise. It was as if Albion had been a mere sketch for this now completed picture. Nothing had been unenhanced. The blades of grass looked fuller-fleshed, the birds sang sweeter songs, even the workers in the fields seemed to glow in the heat of the early-autumn sun, not wilt. The self-assurance of these firm-featured people made a strong impression on Lot. They were always respectful to him but not overly so. In Albion the king's own subjects and Sea Wolf settlers alike had been submissive to the point of slavishness. Back then, fear had ruled: the age-old dread of the sudden, unannounced attack which two long decades of peace had not been able to dispel. In brand-new Logres, fear appeared to have been deposed.

Once on his route he crossed estates which, the smiling harvesters told him, belonged to the lordship of Sir Gornemant. Astolat, a pretty town in which he stayed thirty miles north-west of there, was apparently a part of the domain of Sir Constantine. Gornemant and Constantine: both, according to local reports, were members of the 'Company' – royal servants with specifically-attributed seats at the 'Round Table'.

It dawned only slowly on the drink-addled Lot that they were referring to that pack of pups perched around Camelot's great stone slab. Neither name meant anything to him. Nor had he heard this particular honorific, 'Sir', before. But these two at least had lost no time in going out into Logres and taking what they regarded, rightly or wrongly, as theirs to take.

Soon afterwards, while putting up at a large inn below a coastal castle called Gard, Lot began to feel seriously out on a limb, and closer to a hundred years of age than fifty.

He had eaten well, and drunk as heavily as ever. The Wall, he knew, was very close now. This stirred but also unsettled him. On the far side of it he intended to take, or rather reclaim, what had always been *his*. But he had to concede that he was ill-equipped for a fight, if it should come to that. He wished he had made one of his sons accompany him from Camelot, or even rounded up a squadron of lesser men to back his cause.

As that evening wore on, the task ahead of him began to seem very large. Amid the inn's flock of young guests – raucously clapping and cheering a troupe of tumblers out in the covered yard – he felt more isolated than ever. And when the acrobatics ended, and a stray stepped up with a string of tales to tell, Lot sank close to blank despair.

He had come across strays earlier on this journey. The long-maned, leather-dressed storytellers looked out of place in Logres. Even in Albion, Lot had never got used to them as pure entertainers. Their original missions were as messengers, speeding with news from one part of the war-scarred kingdom to another. To Lot they still bore the stink and stigma of battlegrounds. It was hard at the best of times to listen to their newer fables of Arthur's peacetime feats, however skillfully they turned the words.

But this bard was different again. Possibly because Lot was drunk, he found it almost impossible to follow what he said. In the traditional low tones, he talked not about the king but of magical quests and duels of men he called 'paladins' or, more obscurely, 'knights'. With a heavy heart Lot finally gathered that these were none other than members of the 'Company'. The yarns, though short, made as little sense to him as Brumart's rant. He was sure this stray was talking too fast, as if he had to fight against time to deliver all his lines. Some of the stories were barely more than lists. One featured an item called a 'Grail'. It seemed at one moment to be a stone, a cup the next, then a kind of salver. Most of the listeners sat spellbound, but Lot saw that a few shared his puzzlement. Their murmured comments to one another did not help his own attempts to concentrate.

Finally he gave up, left unobtrusively and edged his way through to a quieter atrium where he could drink himself into a more complete oblivion, feeling ever more ancient and alone by the moment. Already he had begun to wish that, like some whom he had watched with incredulity at the time, he had refused to come through into Logres. He seemed to lack the necessary zest – or even the belief – to make the most of this promised land. There had to be, he thought, something larger than what he was finding here. But the idea of that cowed him as much as it made him yearn, and drove him into deeper scepticism of the new dream realm.

'The stories didn't please you?'

He had not seen the woman come up. He might already have slipped into a shallow stupor. He shuffled himself on his bench, set down his empty cup on the flagstones and tried to bring her delicate features into focus. She was around thirty, slim with a loosely-bound swathe of raspberry-coloured hair. From her confident bearing she seemed unlikely to be on the inn's staff. Like the chaplain at Camelot, she made Lot think 'north'.

He cleared his throat before slurring, 'They didn't please you either?'

'Some stories need to be told over and over.'

'Yes? Until the tellers get them right?'

'Or until there's nobody left to know that they're wrong.'

He smiled thinly without knowing why and gestured for her to sit. She declined, but continued to stand a very short way in front of him, and her pale eyes searched his, as if for a glimmer of recognition. Lot had no way of knowing how she might respond if she found it.

'Do you know me?' he asked softly.

She appeared not to hear. 'I'm travelling north,' she told him. 'Tomorrow.'

'Alone?'

She nodded then said, 'I have attendants.' She looked as if she needed them. She was beautiful but seriously thin, possibly consumptive. To his surprise Lot felt more concerned for her than fretful for himself. He grew uneasy to be sitting while she stayed on her feet – like a king receiving an envoy – but she was simply too close for him to be able to stand.

'Tomorrow,' he suggested, 'you could ride with me?'

Again she did not answer. Her head was turned from him distractedly, as if she still had half an ear on the stray's gibberish. In profile she was quite exquisite, and more familiar too. The crazy thought flitted through Lot's mind that she might perhaps be his wife.

She drifted away without another word. Lot did not give chase. The next morning, well-wrapped for travel, she was waiting at the stables with seven younger women. Her hair had been scraped back tightly, making her look even more gaunt than before. It also exposed a small snaky scar just below her hairline – years old now, but almost certainly a knife-wound.

She smiled at Lot and introduced her attendants with an array of such bizarre names that he forgot them all at once.

'And this is Sir Lot,' she added with a gracious waft of her hand, 'whose seat is at Din Eydin.'

Lot did not ask her own name until they were saddled up and ready to go. She told him, almost dismissively: Anna. Already he had guessed that they were not going to separate.

FIVE

Christmas came and went, and Lanslod pressed on doggedly around Logres.

Week by week, month by month, he drew out his own minute reconnaissance of the new kingdom. Often he went back on himself, largely avoiding human contact, putting up at small but comfortable taverns only when rain, snow or frost stopped him from sleeping out under the stars. For hours on end he would slip into a pleasant trance in the saddle, riding to the rhythm of the faintest music which seemed to come churning directly out of the air – a welcome change from the hissing in his head before.

At first, although alone, he felt that he was a part of something larger. Often he daydreamed of the sixty men around the dais fanning out from Camelot, each holding a thread like the one Ariadne had given to Theseus to take into the labyrinth. They could all go as far as they chose yet stay for ever linked to the kingdom's heart. The merest twitch on the line would be a sufficient signal for each man to return. But the longer he rode, the less he expected a recall. Still less did he feel like putting down roots.

The new land awaits you. Go out now into it and take what is yours . . . Others might have heard that as an invitation to seize estates. He had already ridden over domains which were said to belong to Gaheris and Pelles. But Lanslod saw his own mission as this unusual reconnaissance – not of enemy land but his own home ground; not to make a reckoning of any damage done, but to marvel at all the grandeur.

Wherever he went, he saw nothing remotely like a fortification. The contrast in atmosphere with what he remembered of distant Albion could not have been starker. When Arthur had employed him to help to keep the old kingdom's hard-won peace, Lanslod had carried out his duties with body and soul. Yet if the peace here in Logres was so effectively keeping itself, he could not help wondering to what use he might be put after his travels.

Meanwhile no one ever seemed surprised by his apparently aimless wandering. He knew that people marked his passing. They referred to him with knowing smiles as a 'knight', which sounded heroic enough; 'knight errant' too. At one December stopover he heard the innkeeper call him a 'freelance'. It transpired that this meant a man who sought out his own battles to fight. There were apparently several such in the 'Company', Brumart being one.

Freelances. Lanslod kept chewing on the word. Armed men of spirit roaming the kingdom for purposes that maybe became explicit only through their movement; purposes that might at times prove to be more personal than national; men whose threads back to Camelot might slacken to the point where they no longer seemed to exist. And slowly his unease increased.

Albion's principle of unquestioning obedience had frankly suited him better. There, until its dismal last days, the only vison had been the king's; the only story, Arthur's. If Logres was to be the sum of many men's visions, including his own, then Lanslod would have to ask more of himself than before. He would have to start seeing himself as someone who mattered. This did not come easily. Nowhere near as easily as it seemed to come to the people of northerly Caer Luel – a town behind the western end of the great Wall, where Lanslod took a room for the night early in the new year.

'We have seen other knights of the Company,' he was told by a lean, heavily-furred man who had sought out Lanslod at his inn-dinner and introduced himself as the burgomaster. 'Several have ridden through, and we have served them in whatever ways we could. What we have is yours, to take as you see fit.'

Lanslod nodded, swilling his mouthful of ale from cheek to cheek. The folk at the other tables had not quite fallen silent, but he knew that they would not miss any reply he gave; and the burgomaster plainly expected something from him. He was standing with one thumb hooked into his belt, a flagon in the other hand – held in such a way as to suggest that he would not shrink from dashing its contents in Lanslod's face if he had to.

'Who have you seen?' Lanslod asked guardedly, hacking off a lump of pork.

'Sir Lucan. Sir Caius.' He smiled. 'Separately, not together.' The room seemed to have quietened further. It was a good, warm place to be; its high timber ceiling vaulted in the exquisite Logretian way. Lanslod chewed his food, studying the animal interlace carved into the lower beams. Lucan and Caius. The 'Sirs' still sounded odd to him, but it seemed to be a general designation of status in Logres. 'Both of them were travelling *back* to court. Both had been back more than once since they first rode out . . .'

Lanslod nodded, chewed, said nothing.

Undeterred, the other went on: 'We were able to recognize each by his blazon. You yourself – you ride without heraldic devices . . . ?' Lanslod glared at him, beginning to tire of this. The words meant as little to him as the new kind of stories being told by the strays. '. . . But you will appreciate that without devices we cannot identify you, and do you the honour which you, specifically, deserve.'

'Lanslod, I am Lanslod,' he spat at the table.

The quiet in the room grew grittier. The burgomaster inclined his head. Someone dropped a knife that rang against the floor. Lanslod felt larger simply for having spoken his own name. 'Lanslod,' he said again, drawing out the first flat syllable, moving his head to take in his listeners. The word could have been a net in which he had just caught them all.

'We welcome you, Sir Lanslod,' the burgomaster told him. 'And when you return to Camelot, we would ask that – like Sirs Lucan and Caius before you – you will present our salutations to the king . . .' A shadow fluttered over his features, as if he were in two minds about the etiquette of going on, '. . . and also of course, to the queen.' He said this almost collusively, eyeing Lanslod as if to encourage an immediate assurance. 'In the meanwhile it is our privilege to meet all your requirements here.'

Lanslod shrugged, eating again. 'A bed and some peace will be enough.'

'Our privilege,' he repeated, backing away as the suspended chat all round began to bubble up again. And although no one else spoke to Lanslod in the half-hour before he turned in, he knew he had hardly taken a breath in all that time without the whole host noticing.

In the night he was woken by a commotion outside in the square. He went to his window and looked down to find a large bonfire burning beside the public fountain. A string of revellers, some familiar from the evening before, were prancing around a tarred stake which rose up from the midst of the flames, festooned with severed ropes.

Lanslod watched for a long while before summoning a young inn servitor to ask what was going on.

'It is in your honour, sir,' the bleary boy replied.

'Lucan and Caius were honoured in the same way?'

The boy looked nonplussed for a moment. 'No.'

'Then what are they doing? Tell me. And why the empty stake?'

'To celebrate the escape.' He hesitated, and then he added as if to cover himself, 'Of the spring from the clutches of winter.'

Lanslod dismissed him and got back into bed but did not sleep. If it was some kind of pagan ritual outside, he was not surprised. Christmas had been an extremely muted celebration. For all the roadside chapels and churches that he passed, few showed any sign of recent public use, while out on the hills the big figures loomed larger than ever: old giants in the chalk scoured back into life; newer shapes limed across the dark winter grass.

Lanslod slipped away unnoticed before dawn. The square was lit by glowing, windblown embers, like a great disassembled mosaic. By the time the sun came up through cold blustery showers, he was heading fast due north.

In the weeks that followed he hugged the ragged coastline, studiously avoiding any more settlements, finding the sight of the water somehow restorative. There were times when he wondered what would have happened if he had never come ashore at all from the wide western ocean.

He had such mixed emotions about the Great Remaking. Still he dwelled more often on what he had lost than on what he might gain. Without his own memories of Albion, however trivial, he found it increasingly hard to orientate himself in Logres. Others might have had no trouble in starting their lives effectively in the middle. Not he.

There was, Lanslod felt certain, something – or someone – specific which this general forgetting had been meant to suppress. He could see no other reason why so much of the past had been blanked out. But surely no true promised land should have been founded on concealment? And surely, somewhere in the new kingdom, his misgivings were shared by others?

He was lucky that the weather quickly grew milder. Night after night he lay motionless in his bivouac, making his mind as empty as he could, hoping in vain to feel a twitch on the invisible thread that ran back to Camelot where Arthur lay in wait. Camelot, where Guenever waited too . . .

He could not forget how suggestively Caer Luel's burgo-master had spoken to him of the queen. But whenever he tried to recall her from the last days of Albion, he saw no woman, only light. She and her handmaidens had always seemed to be reflecting one another's radiance in a dazzle so bright that it was hard to know where each of them ended and the next began.

Then for several nights in a row he dreamed of the fire in Caer Luel's square. And now he was among the flames himself – not tied to the stake but severing the ropes which, this time, held a very palpable Guenever.

Afterwards more memories returned: her insistence on always riding ahead with her girls, although he had nominally been her escort. If their eyes ever met she gave an impression of surrounding him with herself. He had been honoured to be assigned to her at the end, even if he had felt that he could no more have protected her than a tick could protect a cow whose flank it infested. Yet now in all his thoughts she was smaller than this, depleted. The woman he was unbinding in the fire was a bag of bones . . .

As he rode ever northward around Logres' fraying ends, going for weeks without meeting a soul, he came to see that Guenever, for all her beauty, transcended every usual consideration. She existed in a world of her own making – a world which increasingly Lanslod sensed to be under threat.

Albion is over. Its darkness has been dispersed . . .

Weaving his way around the inlets and promontories, Lanslod felt that the queen's words were following him, but slowly changing in tone from a proud declaration into a plea to be believed. Albion's darkness might well have been dealt with. But Logres seemed already to be stippled with shadows of its own.

SIX

Chaplain Dyfric stepped cautiously across the moonlit holy precinct. As Camelot's sole practising clergyman he knew that some people, including the strays, referred to him wryly as the Archbishop. At times it surprised him that even a single priest was still needed. The residual Christian element in this region had risen like fat to the surface of a stew and now lay in danger of being skimmed off altogether.

On entering the chapel, he allowed his face to look startled.

Nobody was watching him – unless the night visitor up ahead had eyes in the back of his head – but Dyfric had long since learned to cover himself. And besides, he was still prepared to believe that any feat was possible for the bulky figure now standing in a darkened recess away to his right.

Only a handful of lamps had been left burning. Dyfric edged his way across to the nave and bowed before the main altar. He made the sign of the cross after a lengthy pause, smiling to himself as if he had deliberately been stretching his heavenly Lord's patience before acknowledging Him.

But God was not uppermost in the chaplain's mind. Dyfric

had not come in to pray. That night was still three hours short of the dawn, and he had crept along from his nearby lodgings purely out of curiosity.

Two nights before, he had noticed from his bedchamber a figure heading past quickly: bowed over as if he were battling through rain, his cloak wrapped tightly round him. On the next night Dyfric had again heard footsteps on the chippings below. This time he had watched the figure stand for an inordinately long time at the lip of the so-called 'abyss' in the precinct. Tonight, on hearing him pass yet again, he had left his rooms, gone out into the night and tracked him finally to the chapel.

Dyfric turned where he stood, just within range of one of the lamps and hidden by no pillar. He was a careful man. He wanted to lay himself open to no charge of spying. He stood with his hands linked inside his pair of voluminous sleeves: alert, receptive, available if he should be needed.

The man in the cloak stood hunched in front of a side altar of no special significance. Even with his head lowered he was huge. But the longer Dyfric looked, the farther away he felt *himself* to be standing. That taut, muscled back seemed somehow to be propelling him deeper into the building.

The chaplain smiled again. So little about the man in front of him was ordinary. So little, that Dyfric sometimes wondered how much of a man he really was. He was a king in every inch of his being. His very skin seemed to be coloured royal purple. He was Arthur. Only, ever, Arthur.

Dyfric shivered. It still stirred him to be alone inside any building with his once and future king. He was glad that they were in a sanctuary, although Arthur's own commitment to his kingdom's official religion seemed no stronger than anyone else's – which made this nocturnal visit all the more intriguing.

In Albion – like countless clergymen who had failed to come through into Logres – Dyfric had often asked his parishioners, 'How do you see your king?' He remembered that much perfectly. And he knew that few had ever been able to answer him. The king was just a faraway cloud to most of them, a whirlwind of violence and appetites, a phenomenon that in their hearts they were relieved not to have to see. But one reply had stuck: 'I see a man from behind. He's walking away. Hurrying. Maybe he's heading towards something as well. But it's definitely away from me. Away from where I'm watching . . .'

Dyfric nodded to himself now in belated recognition.

The king shifted his weight from foot to foot. The balance of his body tilted massively from right to left, briefly revealing a single short candle that was burning on the altar between himself and the wall.

Dyfric did not try to guess why he was here. For most of his thirty-eight years the chaplain had lived in or near places of worship. People came to them for all sorts of reasons, most of which they found hard to explain even to themselves. Had this been one of the Company, or a simple civilian, Dyfric would now have approached and asked if he could help. Outside the festival seasons, it was rare enough to be in here with anyone at all except his acolytes. But in this case, he still hung back.

The king was standing straighter. The cloak that he had taken to wearing in all weathers spilled down from his shoulders in generous folds. Dyfric knew the cloak and he knew the stories about it. Always so many stories. Some said that when worn in battle, it made the king invisible to his enemies. Others claimed that it was a trophy, seized years before, after combat with one of the giants who had once held Albion. Its former owner was said to have sewn into it the beards of all the men he had previously outfought.

At the Christmas feast Arthur had pulled off the cloak and dumped it on a bench near where Dyfric was sitting. The chaplain had stared hard at the material – not daring to finger it, for much the same reason that he did not now dare to approach the king himself. Close to, it stank. Not necessarily badly. Sweaty, nutty, oily-sweet. Its lining was crimson silk, but on its outer side there was indeed nothing but hair. Sleek, dark hair of many different lengths, all carefully combed in the same direction. Some men wore hair inside their shirts to atone for guilt. Did the king's reversal imply that his conscience was clear?

Dyfric had noted the colour's consistency then. If it really was made up of defeated men's beards, they must have come from a single unlucky family. It was possible that some great animal's pelt – a bear perhaps – had been used. But few of the stories, Dyfric knew, had no truth to them at all.

That Christmas night Dyfric had kept glancing back and forth between the heaped garment and the king, who had climbed up into the musicians' gallery to be alone. There was no doubt about it. The cloak's hair completely matched the hair on Arthur's head. It was the same. And whereas wearing the cut hair of others was barbaric enough, somehow it seemed far darker to Dyfric to be wearing one's own. But this was a person who lived by defying convention. A ruler who in the six months since the founding of Logres had only ever issued writs that devolved his own authority. A husband who in the same period had spent hardly a night beside his glassy-eyed wife, while never going out on progress to be seen by his lesser subjects. An able-bodied, reigning monarch whose cryptic factotum still went under the name of Regent. According to this same Regent, Logres was a kingdom made for the king. If so, it fitted the perpetually grim-faced king like an iron maiden.

Dyfric blinked as Arthur flexed his shoulders before the altar and took two steps backwards. The jet cloak shimmered with silver as it caught the shaft of lamplight. If his mood could be read from his posture, the king seemed impatient but helplessly so. He looked as if he wanted to leave, but something was holding him. His head was tilted, almost as if he were trying to pick up a voice. He had looked much the same way the night before, above that abyss which, unsettlingly over the previous months, had defied all attempts to cover it over.

Then Dyfric saw, beside the altar-candle, a small triptych. It was like a set of three writing tablets, hinged together and folded to stand unsupported to give the king a clear view of its images. The chaplain had not seen the icon before, but someone could easily have brought it in without telling him. The king could have come with it himself.

Fascinated, Dyfric took one silent step closer but the three images came no clearer. They looked very dark, inside a paler, richly-decorated frame.

The king hunkered down again where he stood. Frustrated, Dyfric was tempted to steal away now and leave him to it. But the moment passed for him to go. And the moment that fell into place behind it felt as heavily weighted around him as the cloak of the king's own hair.

There was a game played by the children of the local flatlands. They dared one another to sit on certain low knolls at a particular hour of the night. According to lore, the sitter was then sure either 'to see a wonder' or 'to suffer blows and wounds'. Dyfric felt something very similar here. Whether or not the king was aware of his presence, something surely was about to happen.

Arthur seemed to grow larger again inside his circumference of silence. He eased back his cloak on the left and Dyfric saw that he had belted on his scabbard. Only ever the scabbard, never any sword. Just as the cloak was meant to make him invisible, so this leather sheath with its animal-head decoration, a wartime gift from his late sister Morgan, was supposed to make him invulnerable. The strays had used to say that when Arthur marched at the head of his armies, it grew to make a bridge over the widest waters.

The king and his wars. Dyfric had a shrewd idea that Arthur was lost without them, that they were behind so many of his sullen looks and gestures, his stupors and withdrawals. He prowled around his court like a beast in quarantine. He belonged where the blood was; where it ran in rivers to carry him on. A part of this king had remained in the past, a part of him was still at large there. On that account if no other, the cleric felt some pity for him.

The king adjusted himself again. This was the moment. A wonder or some blows and wounds. Dyfric stiffened. He thought he was ready for anything.

It began quickly and then went on – it seemed – for ever.

Arthur arched his back, thrust his hands in front of him, and at first only the sound told Dyfric that he was urinating. A feeble splattering against the flagstones, momentarily muffled as his aim rose to the velvet altarcloth, then – as the now powerful, glittering arc came into Dyfric's view – a loud hiss as it hit the icon, knocked it over, drowned the candle's flame and beat on the chapel wall behind.

By then the smell was coming through to Dyfric too. A ferocious stallion stink that made him gag and throw a hand up over his lower face. But he kept on watching. He might have known that the king would piss as prodigiously as he did everything else. Already the frothing fluid was rushing back in rivulets into the body of the chapel. Arthur's boots and the hem of his cloak were drenched yet he stepped up obliviously to the fallen icon and drummed on it from closer range until at last he was done. He shook himself over the altar, shuddered, then turned on his heel and strode outside, his scabbard flapping at his thigh.

His expression was utterly unreadable. Not for the first time Dyfric was reminded of Job's words: 'Who can open the doors of his face?' But if the king had known that Dyfric was there, or if he saw him only now, he gave no indication. His wide, haunted eyes seemed to be fixed on a point beyond these walls, perhaps even outside Logres.

I see a man from behind. He's walking away. Hurrying. Maybe he's heading towards something as well . . . Dyfric, still cupping his mouth and nose, picked his way forward at once.

Disgusted though he was, he also felt cheated. He had glimpsed a wonder of sorts, but it seemed to lack meaning on its own. It was as if a distant hand had tossed a stone into still water, and here tonight Dyfric had seen only the briefest outer ripple. There would be more wonders, he felt sure. More blows and wounds. And soon.

He splashed on through the pools, too keen to wait until morning to find out what images had so aroused the king.

He came to the altar, stooped, shuffled his sleeve down over his hand and picked up the dripping icon through the fabric. He stared at it for a long time before carefully setting it back down precisely where it had fallen.

Then he left the chapel, more perplexed than he had been on entering.

Dyfric's perplexity deepened early the next morning. Rumours were snaking through Camelot that Arthur was about to summon the Company to an emergency council of war.

At noon the chaplain duly watched messengers fanning out from the gatehouse across the plain. Soon afterwards the rumours were confirmed. In a curt statement, which seemed to surprise none of the assembled citizens, the grey-faced Regent announced from the citadel steps that Logres was at war.

Within weeks an overseas campaign was to be launched. There was, Merlin concluded, no immediate danger of hostilities taking place on Logretian soil. The crowd dispersed without clamouring for further details. These people knew enough, Dyfric presumed, if they knew that they were the king's subjects. The conversations of those closest to him as he made his way back down to his lodgings sounded stoical to the point of indifference.

During the following nights Arthur made no more visits to the chapel precinct. The icon stayed untouched in its slowly-drying pool by the wall. Each time Dyfric entered the chapel to look at it, the surer he grew that Arthur's desecration had been directly connected to his declaration of war. In some sense, his abuse of the triptych was the start of his offensive.

I see a man walking away . . . definitely away . . .

Dyfric had the strongest feeling that Arthur's return to warfare had been spurred by the figures so cryptically pictured on that little icon.

SEVEN

Lot received the king's messengers in his rose garden at Din Eydin.

There were no full blooms around him yet. Many of the buds' colours still seemed undecided, and neither Lot nor any of his people could say how this bower would look in its final summer glory. They had all lived through summers before; and most of them had never lived anywhere but here in the head of the island. But the island itself was no longer the same. Logres was not Albion and a rose in one was not, necessarily, a rose in the other.

Lot dismissed the riders with no return message to take back to Camelot. There surely was none to give. None that the king would not have taken for granted: the king, the queen, their precious Regent or whoever was truly behind this extraordinary new line of policy.

He sat on in the rose garden until the sun set. Littered at his feet lay the remains of maybe thirty unpicked rosebuds. By the time he had pulled them apart with his blunt, quivering fingers, it was too dark to tell exactly what colours they might one day have become. There was blood on both his thumbs where he had split the skin on thorns – at first by accident but then at least partly on purpose out of sheer frustration.

Lot had lost a good deal of ground since returning to the north. He seemed to have been awaited in this palace on its rock above the river port – but as a kind of invalid and not as an active provincial Warden. He could only presume that this creeping debility of his had begun in Albion.

Outwardly, apart from his hair turning waxy-white, he looked much the same as he had seven months before. Internally too, according to his doctors, he was as fit as a man of his age could expect to be. Yet he had so little strength. He felt as if, almost literally, he were being eaten away. Increasingly it surprised him to find that parts of his body were still there. Often he poked a finger in his eye, or cracked his shoulder against a door jamb simply because he had lost track of his own dimensions. All of which was mortifying to a man so given to the physical.

Anna came out to him when he failed to show for dinner.

Dressed for the well-heated hall, she shivered as she came to a halt across the lush square of turf from him. He saw her taking in the ravaged roses, the blood on his thumbs.

By the time he had reached Din Eydin with this beautiful wraith of a woman they had already spent a night together. She too had seemed to be expected by the household officials. They were recognized as man and wife as if by default, and Lot had seen no reason to challenge that. *Go out and take what is yours* . . . Maybe, in dreamy Logres, this was how things happened. But whether he had taken Anna or she had taken him, he still was unable to say.

'Come and eat,' she cajoled, pulling the gauze wrap tighter round her narrow shoulders. 'Everyone is waiting.'

Lot stroked his beard, smiling up at her, at the limited range of responsibilities that he continued to have to bear. She must have known that there had been messengers from Camelot. He appreciated the way she did not press him, even if at times she seemed to know things long before he told her.

'There is to be a war,' he said simply.

For a moment she stared at him as if he were some cheap crystal-gazer taking a wild stab at the future. Then she nodded, a little stiffly, like someone who has swallowed a large nut before chewing it to a pulp.

'A rebellion?' she asked.

Lot snorted. She had to know that this was ludicrous.

'Then what?' She tilted her head to one side so that her sleek sheet of auburn hair shifted bodily. It seemed to be the only part of her that still had any significant weight. 'Is the kingdom under attack?'

'Under threat, it would seem.'

He put his hands beneath his thighs and, like a weary little boy, swung his crossed ankles back and forth under the bench.

'From where? From whom?' Anna's head was still cocked. There was a tremor in her voice but the questions sounded rote-like, remote.

Lot shrugged, and even the effort of that briefly dizzied him. 'From "Outremer" was what the messengers said. A great stretch of land to the south-east of Logres, across the narrow strait. "*Oo-trah-mare*."'

The word was new to him but he liked the way it sounded. He had said it again and again under his breath as a rhythm for dismantling the roses.

'Outremer,' Anna repeated to herself. 'It's a whole continent. What kind of exception can a whole continent have taken to a little island like this?'

It was so dark now, Lot could hardly see her expression.

He wished he had been given some kind of a writ to wave at her, then pass across for verification. Even if he himself was illiterate, there were plenty of others at Din Eydin who could read. He resented the fact that in Logres it was only ever word of mouth that counted. From the crazy tales of the new strays (whom he had in pique finally forbidden to enter his gates) to the notification of his own – maybe equally crazy – raised status after the Christmas court.

'The Company has been summoned to Camelot, bringing retinues,' he went on, planting his boots on the grass again, then pushing himself up on to his feet. 'The fleet, as I understand, is being refitted.'

'And you'll go? You'll take part in this . . . excursion?'

Helplessly, Lot turned his empty palms and bloodied thumbs towards her. He felt so feeble on his feet. He had been sitting for too long with an excessively straight back. His right groin seared with pain. His head seemed too full of blood for his neck to support. The idea of his going to war again was as absurd as that of Arthur facing a domestic rising. Even these baby roses had held out against Lot and succeeded in keeping their colours to themselves.

'I'll send a levy,' he replied, shaking his head. 'But there's no fighting left in me. Not with any man.'

Anna looked away from him to the bush which he had previously depleted. There was a stirring farther down the trellised path from the hall.

Lot strained his eyes and saw the pale shapes of Anna's shy girls. Not just a couple of them; always all seven. Moronoe, Mazoe, Gliten, Glitonea . . . Still he found it hard to master their names. But it barely seemed to matter. They were like seven women in one, almost redundant as individuals. And Anna herself could look incomplete apart from them – not that she was out of their company very often. Soon enough now they would all be together again, doubtless debating the news of this war.

'You say so little to me,' Lot complained with a smile. 'Tell me what you think. About the war, about Outremer – what do you think?'

'I know enough,' she answered slowly, 'if I know that I am the king's subject.' Then she took two steps back towards her waiting women.

'Wait!' Lot cried. She stopped abruptly. Lot, wincing at the pull in his groin, limped across the grass and drew her around by her sharp-boned wrist.

'Are you forgetting that I too am a king?'

'How could I forget?' She met his eyes, refusing to flinch in his grip.

She raised her free hand to his face and stroked the cloud of hair at his temple – but only, he knew, to emphasize the absence of a crown.

This region, in common with several others, had been elevated within Logres. Since the end of the previous year, Arthur's realm and its adjacent isles had become a patchwork of principalities, duchies, marches and two sub-kingdoms – one being Cador's south-westerly Cornovia, while Lot had been designated King of Orcadie, a title which apparently was ancient and resided by right in his bloodline.

When the news was brought north – since Lot had been too weak to leave Din Eydin for the Christmas court – he had not at first been inclined to believe it. His people duly started calling him king, but there was no coronation, no obvious alteration in any other aspect of his life and minimal duties. He still suspected at times that it had all been a bleak, pointless joke.

'Do you think it's not real, this war?' Lot whispered to his uncrowned queen, his ringless wife, releasing her wrist for fear of snapping it. 'Do you think something else is at stake here, that the war is some kind of bluff?'

He was surprised to see her eyes blaze back at him. 'How can a land of promise go to war? What could ever come of it? An empire of Eden?'

'You think there is no threat to Logres?'

'From where? The stars? The weather?'

'Then what does this mean? Why the need to fight?'

'Ask these rose-trees why they need to flower. The ones you haven't yet stripped. You're speaking of Arthur, remember, your Lord of War. Did you really think he would be able to curb his taste for death indefinitely? When he is thrown back on himself, all he can ever do is spill blood!'

She had muttered the words but Lot heard a catch of real passion. She spoke of Arthur seldom but always with such knowing. There was just a chance – and Lot was chastened to find this notion thrilling – that, years before, she had shared the king's bed. If the older stories were true, hardly a woman in Albion had stayed out of it. And Anna, he was well aware, needed to sleep with a man only once to feel sure that she knew all there was to know about him. 'I'm not what you want, my sweetheart,' she had told him when he came to her rooms the first time at Din Eydin. 'Not in that way.'

Strangely, Lot had felt neither outraged nor crushed. In a way she had been right. As a lover, she was barely there for him. Already he had taken as many new mistresses as his lassitude would let him. But still he wanted Anna for something; not perhaps for talk, maybe just to feast his eyes on.

Gently he brushed her cheek with the back of his hand. 'I've had enough of war,' he said. 'I'd thought all that was over.'

'It should be.' She looked away to where her pack of silent

sirens waited. Lot watched her frown. The small white scar at her hairline seemed briefly to glow with the intensity of her thinking. 'It was meant to be.'

'You know that? You remember . . . ?'

She arched her eyebrows. Again the serpentine nick in her forehead seemed to shine. Lot had spoken with her like this only a few times; he talked to her rarely enough about anything. But there always came a point when she would switch from apparent omniscience to mere irritated observation.

'Maybe the king is listening to other voices now,' she said.

'Voices?' Other than whose? Lot wondered. And *When he is thrown back on himself* . . . But by what now, or by whom?

'Voices,' she repeated, stressing the word's unphysicality by fluttering her fingers in an arc through the darkened ether around her. Clearly she intended it to be humorous but her expression stayed severe.

Again Lot stroked her cheek. Voices. The second time she said the word, he had pictured Arthur in grim isolation at Camelot, poised on the edge of that peculiar pit in the hillside. He was seeing the king from behind: his shoulders hunched, his head lowered, almost as if he were trying to pick up a sound from deep inside.

Over the months, Lot's thoughts had frequently returned to the gash in the ground below Camelot's chapel. Its emptiness would fill his head like all the echoing caverns of his own memory. Nothing for him could be certain now, but he fancied that there had been a similar hole in the hill at Camlann. One made – according to the stories of the old-time strays – when the king had dug out some ancient kind of totem, possibly a head.

'Come inside now,' Anna urged, sweeping away to be swallowed by her attendants, who then withdrew *en masse* to the hall.

EIGHT

Lanslod dismounted and let the late sun's warmth slant through him. His horse wandered down towards the fast-vanishing causeway. Although it was not thirsty, it allowed the evening tide to lap up over its hooves. The shore air was fresh and calm. Standing tall, Lanslod felt the muscles and bones of his body slowly composing themselves in a way that he had seldom before been still enough to enjoy.

He stared out into the magical western sea as Logres darkened around him. In Albion, no one had ever known for sure what lay across these sunset waters. The horse roamed in and out of his vision; a smooth grey smear on the shadows. Lanslod rocked on the balls of his feet but could not yet turn from the sea. If he moved now, it might well be to travel all the way back to Camelot. This felt like a turning point. Maybe, he thought, he had just felt the first twitch on his connecting thread.

'Soldier,' called a soft voice behind him.

He closed his eyes. Weeks had passed since he had heard a voice. Behind his eyelids he saw an ocean of his own spreading and within it he was almost sacredly alone. He opened his eyes but did not turn to look at the woman. She sounded confident and he could not believe that she too would be alone. He imagined a child beside her. A son or a father. Some other man.

'This is a good place,' he said, buying time.

'You can stay,' she replied: light, laughing. Anyone can stay, she meant. Any knight from the king's court.

Lanslod breathed in and swung himself around on the shingle. She was squatting in a muslin dress close to the bole of a tilted, leafless tree. Her posture made her look tiny, smaller even than the child he had pictured – but there was no one with her.

'Lanslod,' he said. 'I am Lanslod.'

She smiled, locking her fingers around her ankles under the dress.

'I'd like to stay,' he went on. He thrust a hand back towards the water and snapped his fingers. The horse immediately stepped across to him.

The woman pushed herself to her feet. She was taller than Lanslod had thought. The dress ended unevenly just below her knees and she was barefooted. Her straw-yellow hair, loosely knotted to one side of her head, spilled halfway down her arm. She flicked it behind her with her hand. She could have been older than him, but her gestures were so girlish.

The horse came up for Lanslod to take its bridle. He expected the woman to turn and lead them on. When she did not, he asked her name. She smiled again, seeming to fish around for a suitable answer, as if she had not yet decided who, for him, she would be. 'Elayne,' she said.

She smiled wider. The name had sounded oddly unconvincing, and just for the blinking of an eye Lanslod fancied that he saw another woman through her, rising as if up a stairway, a woman as dark as Arthur, holding a tiny child.

'Come,' she said, backing, skipping around and pointing inland. 'It's hardly any distance.' As Lanslod followed, he again felt sure that wherever they were going, somebody else would be waiting.

The starry April sky gave plenty of light, but before she turned in the clearing, he had noticed no building behind her. He stared up at it now, thinking it might be an abandoned chapel, the kind of place he had often on his travels seen occupied by hermits and charcoal-burners. But if so, only its little tower still stood: squat, flesh-coloured, crenellated, with a low, darkened arch for a doorway.

'This is where you live?' Lanslod asked.

She placed the backs of her hands proprietorially on her hips and nodded, smiling her dazzling smile. *Alone?* he almost pleaded.

'Is there a place for my horse?'

'He'll be safe out here. No one will come. You needn't tether him.'

Lanslod tilted his head, wanting to share her confidence. As she disappeared inside the tower, he let the reins slip from his hand.

A new glow picked out his pathway to the arch. Elayne must have lit lamps inside and somehow they were burning through the wall's fabric. Lanslod could see no windows or other openings. Narrowing his eyes, he felt sure he was seeing Elayne herself. The pale blue dress, her sallow arms and ankles: glimpsed as if through a series of slats while she swept from lamp to lamp. But there were no slats. The tower's facade was sheer and made of stone.

Lanslod approached with one hand in front of him. When his fingertips made contact, he thought the surface was warm. But when he pressed, it cooled, and became a green-shot blue, like grittily primitive glass. Then, again, it was monolithic and streaked with sketchy patterns of moss and ivy. Elayne appeared to his left in the arch.

'I promise your horse will be safe,' she smiled.

He went up to her, she stood aside and he entered. Only one candle was burning, in a wall-fixture high above a simple trestle table that took up almost all that level's floor space. New bread had been cut. There were olives, figs, apples, half a huge, cold salmon, a flask of wine with two cups set ready. She seemed to have been expecting company.

She came in behind him, leaving the oak door open to the night and the forest. 'Eat,' she said, indicating the table, 'if you wish to.'

The candle-light was extraordinarily strong. At five paces, Lanslod could see the pupils of Elayne's eyes dilating. She was looking at him with a purse-lipped smile, knowing but also fragile.

Only later would he think of her as beautiful. As they stood facing each other across the flagstones, an odder idea occurred to him: that whereas he could imagine the features of any other woman transposed on to the head of a man, this woman's could never be. Her face was unequivocally, even ruthlessly, feminine – locking her for ever in her gender, making her equally formidable and vulnerable as a result.

She averted her eyes. Maybe unintentionally, that encouraged Lanslod to follow her gaze for the first time to the corner curtain, behind which he glimpsed stone steps leading up to the tower's next storey.

It was time to touch her, but he could not. Again he felt pushed beyond what he could see to a sense of some other presence: very near by. He reached for the bread, tore off a wedge and crammed it into his mouth. Elayne came closer to pour him a cup of wine. He smelled her musky sweetness and stepped back. Her profile was strong, wolfish. The cup she took up was made of glass, tall and stemmed. As the coarse wine swirled in, it took on the same blue-green colour as Lanslod had fancied he had seen on the external wall. When he took the glass, it was similarly cool.

Elayne poured a finger's-width for herself and quaffed it back, as if to show that it was perfectly drinkable. Lanslod followed suit. It tasted the way drenched roses smell. From the pit of his stomach it began to warm him.

He realized that he had left his baggage strapped to the horse, his sword and swordbelt with it. I'm defenceless, he thought leadenly. He swallowed more rosy wine. Elayne watched, poised to meet any new demand. He picked up an olive the size of a crab-apple and hefted it in his hand. He had to have something to focus on. Elayne's pulsing pupils were too much.

She eased herself past him towards the staircase corner, taking care not to let her dress's hem brush him. Moving, she smelt muskier still, warming Lanslod like the wine. He was glad she had moved. It made more sense to him. He wished they had both been able to circle each other since the moment they had met. At the curtain she turned.

'Please,' Lanslod said on an impulse, 'keep walking.'

She looked at him, then grinned her crooked grin. She had long, sharply-angled dimples very close to the sides of her mouth. 'Keep walking where?'

He tried to smile back, rubbing at the olive until his nail pierced its skin. He gestured with it sheepishly. 'Back the way you came? Please.'

She blushed, upwards from her pointed chin. That touched him. It made him feel stronger, as if at last he had started to move again himself. The candle-light seemed brighter, the room a little larger. Dipping her head, Elayne walked back to the point where she had stood before. Four supple dancer's strides. She turned to him with a flourish and made as if to curtsey. Her eyes flashed. 'More?'

Lanslod nodded.

She took a single step back towards the curtain then leapt the rest of the way with a gasp and tiny laugh. Swivelling on tiptoe, she then struck out to Lanslod's right along the adjoining wall. Stiffly he twisted.

She had pulled in her shoulders, splayed out her forearms, and was crabwising around the room's far corner. Her prancing steps sometimes took her knees as high as her breasts. She grinned wider than ever at the madness. As she passed in front of the entrance arch she kicked out and slammed the door shut on the night, his horse and baggage.

'Ha!' Lanslod heard himself cry. Defenceless.

On she loped and giggled, past the spot where she had started, then in front of Lanslod again. Unsteadily he finished his wine. He set the cup down on the table, placed alongside it the scarred olive, and waited for her, laughing in sheer relief at the new momentum. She had reeled him in now much, much closer. He had helped her to reel him in. He had fixed the bait to the end of her line then snapped up his jaws at it.

For a third time she snaked her way between him and the table's edge. Once his hands were around her, it was she who put up her mouth and heaved a sigh into his as their lips met.

'You're Lanslod,' she whispered into his shoulder when the kiss was over – as if the taste of him had confirmed what his earlier words had only suggested. His hands were lodged under her ribs. One of her bare feet was between his boots; her thigh pressed against him higher through her dress.

'I'm glad you're here,' she said, like someone taking issue, but only to reassure him, to dispel unnecessary doubt.

This time Lanslod took the kiss to her. There was no one

else here: only the two of them, and the candle she twisted away to snuff out, and the dress she now eased down past her shoulders for him, and the curtain slid aside as, barebacked, she drew him by his hand up the stair.

Elayne's bed was as large as the table below, dominating the space with its four carved pillars, tied curtains and canopy. There were no lamps or candles but the moon outside seemed to be refracted directly through the wall to soften the bedcover's darkness.

Elayne smiled up from the bed when Lanslod turned to her from his heap of cast-off clothes. She was removing her hoop earrings, lying flat on her stomach to set them on the floor. Then her right hand strayed to a point of no apparent significance high on her left arm. She felt the bare flesh, as if to check it was still there, before rolling aside to let him join her.

'You're Lanslod,' she reaffirmed as each of their limbs found the right space waiting. 'Sir Lanslod.'

Lanslod had not yet made love in Logres, nor was any love made that night. The word 'made' was wrong. This was no creation or collaboration, in the sense that two people might combine to make a fire. Nothing under Elayne's canopy felt put together on purpose. Hour after hour the two of them were inside something bigger. There *was* fire; but only in the way that an empty forest will burst into flame. The love was making – or remaking – them.

They took no precautions. Each time Lanslod came, Elayne gripped him harder. She was tirelessly, constantly generous. At one point, she slid from the bed and gave him a few more steps of her spoof witch's dance. Without clothes, her progress looked mechanical. Lanslod patted the mattress. But she veered out of the filtered moonlight with a teasing grin.

He eased himself up on to his elbows, wishing she would come back. For a moment she was lost in darkness. Then the area of light expanded to show her again, flapping her arms, raising her knees. The walls had become translucent; Lanslod saw the trees' silhouettes beyond. And although Elayne was performing on the spot, it seemed that the room had started to revolve, giving different backdrops to each thrust of her arm or loop of her leg.

As soon as she saw his expression change, she sprang forward and dragged him by his hair into a teeth-clashing kiss. He closed his eyes to orientate himself, and when he looked again it was as if she had never been off the bed. All was still, all the walls were opaque. The only shaft of moonlight now entered from the uncurtained stairway that led up to a higher level.

From that point, even during the lulls when they lay tangled and drowsing, Lanslod kept sensing some third person's presence. But, although this kept him alert, it brought a peppery edge to his own pleasure; and he ended up imagining not Elayne's son or father there but Arthur: the king who had maybe sent him out this far. It suited him to think that it was great Arthur's shape inside these shadows. His own defencelessness, then, hardly mattered. Armed with a thousand swords, he could not have saved himself from the king. Even so, this king looked ill-at-ease: hunched, departing, beckoning Lanslod back.

The forest birds' songs started well before dawn, trilling in triumph through Lanslod's shallow dreams. He woke to find himself alone, but he could hear Elayne's soft voice – rising from outside the wall as she prattled bits of nonsense to his horse.

He threw on his clothes and left the room. The table had

been cleared and a much smaller spread of oatcakes and cloudy cider stood ready, but Lanslod had no appetite.

Elayne was standing in the dew outside, her blue-dressed back to him. She was only ten paces away but it could have been the length of Logres. The horse came away from her towards him. Lanslod stepped out of the tower, wondering if he had left anything behind.

As he began to approach, she again put a hand to her left upper arm, then absently scratched the bare flesh. A neutral enough gesture but it stopped Lanslod in his tracks. He guessed that she had meant it to.

There was something forbidding in her stance. He thought at first she might be crying, but she was holding her whole upper body in a different way from before. Again he thought he saw through to a darker, far less accommodating woman at her core, someone as regal in her way as the king himself.

He had the shrewdest idea that she was no more truly called 'Elayne' than the land in which they were living was now called Albion. He supposed that he should have felt deceived, used. In fact he felt apprehensive.

His heavily-laden horse stopped beside him.

'You should be gone,' she called back without looking his way.

He wanted to see her wolf's eyes again but did not dare to ask. He had no wish to watch her turn an entirely different face on him. Once again he was convinced that he was being watched; maybe not from the tower but from some place closer. A space so small, he hardly knew that it existed.

'Back to Camelot,' she went on sharply; a harder voice than the night before, one that would brook no argument. 'You should go. Now.'

Again he saw the beckoning shadow-king; again he felt that tug on the thread.

The woman did not turn even as he mounted his horse. Nor did Lanslod look back at her as he made for the causeway to reorientate himself before heading south.

By that day's end, he was quite unable to summon up any image of her at all. Whenever she entered his mind it was in the shape of that dark, svelte figure stepping skywards, her child held out before her like an offering.

NINE

'Are you waiting for someone? Can I be of help?'

Dyfric's abrupt questions startled the young dark warrior. He swung around from the aisle-painting: a monstrous, fanged hell-mouth sucking in sinners. His fingers closed on his sword's hilt, but on recognizing the chaplain in the nave he dropped his hand.

Dyfric smiled patiently. 'This is the house of the Lord,' he said. 'No weapons belong in here.'

The other glared back, the pupils of his eyes turning almost black. At half Dyfric's own age, if that, he wore the mail and surcoat of a member of the Company but looked like a boy dressed up in his father's clothes.

Dyfric's smile widened. 'The king himself comes in unarmed.'

'Well, the king would have to, no?' His voice was shrill; his prominent Adam's apple bobbed in a painful-looking way when he spoke and he held his left hand stiffly to his chest, as if his arm were in a sling. 'As I've been given to understand it, the king never goes armed at all now.'

Dyfric tipped his head. *Given to understand . . .* He could only mean from the strays' tales. This wiry, unkempt youth had not shown himself at Camelot since the first Round Table. 'Nonetheless,' the chaplain pressed, 'can I be of help to you?'

He hesitated before answering and glanced back up at the wall-painting, which even Dyfric himself could still find compelling.

'When I came to the city,' he answered more steadily, 'I was told to report to the College of Arms. To consult about my . . . blazon.' He said the word as if for the first time, but maybe not entirely without pride.

Dyfric turned. 'Come, then. My acolyte will guide you. The offices you need are in the first quadrangle, next to the armourers' workshops . . .'

'I know that. I've done that. It's done. I've chosen my pretty pattern.'

Dyfric turned back. 'Not just pretty, I assure you. In combat you'll be glad of your device. A man in an iron cocoon on one side is very easy to confuse with a like-dressed warrior on the other.'

'Whatever. They're working on it now.' He jerked his head at the nearest sparkling stained-glass window as if to catch an echo of the sound of paint being brushed on to hide through all the shouts and hammerings of the mobilization outside. Then he shrugged. 'I came down here afterwards.'

Dyfric nodded as if he understood.

Wherever this callow knight had been in the past nine months, it was possible that he had not, until now, come across a chapel that was still fulfilling its original function. But if he wanted to talk about the lapse of the faith in Logres, Dyfric would disappoint him. It was a subject on which he refused to be drawn, even by himself.

'Forgive me,' he said instead, fluttering his fingers and

narrowing his eyes. 'There are so many in the Company. And with their own levies assembling as well for the campaign, it is easy to lose track of names . . .'

The knight's look hardened, but his defiance seemed more defensive than ever, as if he were being taunted and was not quite sure of the proper response. Outside, the sun had shifted and a late-afternoon shaft through the clerestory window was picking out a vague shape on the floor just ahead of him. He edged one well-worn boot towards it, then quickly drew it back.

'Please,' Dyfric persisted. 'What is your name?'

'Peredur.'

'*Sir* Peredur?'

He shrugged, acquiescent, and then they studied each other in a new way.

Peredur held the hawk-featured chaplain's eye, wondering what he might have heard about him. The strays' strange stories doubtless pulsed through Camelot as feverishly as in the region around it. For all Peredur knew, they originated here. Thanks to the stories, this cleric was already no stranger to him. Dyfric was his name. 'Archbishop' Dyfric.

He watched the chaplain's eyes fall to his own awkwardly-held left hand.

'And you are to fight, Sir Peredur?' he asked. 'You are to sail with the king?'

'It would seem that I have no choice.'

'Oh, but not all of the Company is assembling.'

'So I've heard. Brumart has not come back. Nor Lanslod.'

'There you are wrong. Lanslod arrived soon after noon today. I spoke with him just hours ago, before he too chose his armorial bearings. You yourself must have returned only recently. I certainly haven't seen you since the first . . .'

'You say nothing of Brumart,' Peredur interrupted. The scene at the end of the first Round Table was as vivid as ever in his mind – and still as obscure. He had heard strays telling their crazed, fantastical tales about many of the Company's knights but never one about Brumart. Nor about any child or woman.

Dyfric pursed his lips, made as if to speak, then stayed silent. There was no telling how much this cleric knew. Instinctively Peredur thought it was quite a lot.

He glanced past him to a side altar where only the stub of candle and a three-leaved icon stood. Apart from the striking hell-mouth on the wall and the saints' images on the windows, the chapel was almost bereft of decoration. And it felt – like every other temple he had visited in his endless circuits of the region around Camelot – as pregnantly empty as the tomb of Christ on the third day after his death.

Almost in spite of himself, Peredur decided to ask his questions. He had gone for nearly nine months without a frank conversation. And now he was about to leave on a campaign where he expected talk of any sort barely to figure. He had to speak here. That, after all, had been his main reason for coming down the slope with its pit to this godforsaken place.

'What did Brumart mean that day?' he asked flatly. 'What boy was he talking about? What woman?'

Dyfric blinked, then shrugged. Obviously he knew what Peredur was talking about. 'That was in another kingdom.' He glanced at the three-leaved icon. 'And the woman is dead. You heard, that day, what the Regent said. She has no place in Logres.'

'But who was she?'

Dyfric's eyes levelled with his own. 'The mother of the king's child. And she is dead. Both she and the child are dead.' He seemed to be steeling himself not to look again at the icon. 'And that is all I know.'

He bowed to Peredur, turned, crossed himself in front of the altar and left the building as if he were too uncomfortable to stay inside it.

Peredur followed at once, with an idea that the chaplain was wanting him to do so. Taking a last look up at the mural, it seemed now as if the beast of the bottomless pit was sicking up the sinners not sucking them in.

When he emerged into the sunset, it was like stepping out of sleep into waking. The chapel's walls had kept all the sounds outside muted. Grooms were hurrying horses up the hill while siege-machines were creakingly being wheeled down to the city's smaller postern gate. Such a muddle of colours and catcalls.

Dyfric, his hands linked loosely in front of him, was standing with downcast eyes at the still-uncovered upper lip of the abyss. The gaping hole made for a curiously raw sight amid the lush grass and splendid stonework, and just as misplaced in this paradise as all the preparations for war.

Peredur stepped down to the chaplain's side. Briefly they stood in silent communion, somehow continuing their exchange in the chapel. The shaft below them was shallow at first, then it sloped away to look almost endless. Peredur felt giddy, imagining the vacuum expand beneath them: a vast cluster of nothing at the heart not just of Camelot but of Logres too.

That was in another kingdom . . . In Albion, this would have been the spot where Arthur was said to have dug out some kind of protective talisman. He had remembered that much in the past nine months. Stories, always so many stories, but what else was there? Peredur had even chosen as his blazon a pattern of severed, unseeing heads – after the images

conjured up for him by this hole when he had ridden back
into the city.

He cleared his throat. Hours seemed to have passed since
he had spoken a word. He felt that he and Dyfric had crossed
some important boundary together, even if the 'Archbishop'
was not yet ready to accept that.

'This war,' he heard himself say with a tremor. 'Is it
necessary?'

Dyfric did not look at him. It took him some time
to answer. Everything both men said next – low-voiced,
urgent – was addressed to the gash in the ground before
them as if it were a third person, or an oracle that might
possibly join in the debate. 'There are many kinds of necess-
ity.'

'And of which kind is this?'

Dyfric shook his raptor's head with a humourless grin.
Peredur saw how hard it was for him to speak. 'Think of
it as a tree. There's so much *sap* waiting. It has to rise. There
has to be a tree for it to rise up into.'

Peredur stared into the void. 'Please, tell me simply.'

'Maybe not everything can be talked about in that way.
Not honestly.'

That, at least, was simpler than Peredur had been expecting.
He noticed some nearby men looking across at them, making
less noise now as they passed.

'"Not everything,"' Peredur echoed. 'Like the Great
Remaking?'

'No one could presume to read the mind of God on such
a matter.'

'*God?*' Peredur had never seriously considered that God's
hand lay behind any of this. He flexed both hands in frustration. 'There's so much I don't understand.'

'About the Remaking?'

'About the forgetting. Why can't we remember what went before? Why do we have to forget?'

'We have been led out of Egypt into the land of promise. Why do we need to remember the desert?'

'As a useful comparison? Or is Logres like that after-life of the old giants, where people had to drink from the river of forgetting before they were allowed to go on?'

'The waters of Lethe,' Dyfric remembered softly.

'But those people passed into an underworld! They went into hell!'

Dyfric stiffened. He rubbed at his smooth cheek. 'We forget, then, to remember. We have to forget in order to make more space to remember.'

'But to remember what? What is there here except stories? And why are there so many new stories? About the Company, the king, the queen – about *you*?'

'You have clearly given this thought yourself. What is your view?'

Dyfric was now looking up the hill. Suddenly he sounded indifferent, and newly edgy too. So Peredur held back his own uncertain answer: his suspicion that the strays' kingdom-wide cobweb of words was not so much an entertainment as a kind of propaganda, a history of Logres as it was *supposed* to have happened, a manifesto – but for whom? And against whom?

'What went wrong?' he hissed instead, cutting to the quick. 'From the very start, what has been wrong with this kingdom?'

Dyfric at last turned his head. And when he smiled levelly, Peredur knew at once that he had lost him.

'Kingdoms are like mirrors,' said the shepherd with no flock, just loudly enough for any interested passer-by to hear, 'they show you so much of what you bring to them. May God be with you in Outremer.'

Peredur watched him hurry up the slope to where the Regent was waiting – presumably having beckoned him away.

As Dyfric came alongside him, the older, taller, distinctly greyer figure turned and fell into step. Then the jostling crowd swallowed them both.

TEN

Brumart emerged from the forest and turned his horse towards the causeway.

Just an hour earlier the great natural sea-path had been hidden from view. Now the evening tide had retreated from the curved double-trail of rocks – closely aligned like a pair of thin lips – to show a glistening black-toothed grin.

Brumart himself was not smiling. Splay-nosed and slack-mouthed, he sat exhausted in the saddle, sick and stiff with travel, entirely oblivious to the sky blazing by above his head: mottley-milky, as if some old-time giant god had ejaculated against the roof of the world, shooting his wispy lake of seed across the ever-moving blue.

The haze at the end of the causeway was clearing. A tower of sorts stood there – a mariners' beacon, he guessed, although there was no sign of a port nearby. Half a moment before he urged it on, Brumart's horse began to move towards it. Then it stopped at the water's edge as if inviting him to dismount.

He swung himself down gingerly. The stallion backed away as soon as he was standing. Had Brumart been less tired, he might have noticed its pinned-back ears, raised muzzle and bared teeth as well. But all he saw was his own crude little image, an *aide-mémoire* scratched months before with the tip of a knife into the leather of his saddle.

He stretched both arms Christ-like to the sides and let his head loll. He was not hungry. He did not even want to sleep, although he felt as if he had ridden five times around the island since he had last properly rested. All he craved – all he had ever craved since thundering out of Camelot – was to track her down. Her. The king's sister, Morgan: the False, the Fateful, the Fay. The loveliest woman he had ever seen; so alluring that he could well understand why the king had smashed through taboo to have her, only to try to put her from his sight for ever – both her and his so-called 'seed sown in darkness'.

But whatever had happened to the boy, Brumart knew that Morgan was still alive. He knew that she was at large in this crazily made-over kingdom. She seemed to haunt it all, to thread its air with her blood-spattered spoor. He had sensed her from the start. Morgan with her unmistakable golden dragon armlet. When they had all been sitting at the great stone table, it was as if she had stolen into the hall, looped a thread around Brumart's neck, knotted it, then slipped away again.

From that moment – his own Ariadne at the centre of this new dark maze – she had perpetually been enticing him through the labyrinth of Logres, leaving the broken circle of knights behind him.

At first he had thought he might find her, with or without her son, tucked away in the bustle of one of the towns. Calleva, Sarras, the two Ynys Witrins, Almesbury, Dinas Bran. He had followed his nose through all their teeming streets. He had spent a month combing the docks and markets of the massive new entrepôt of Caerlundein.

In those months he sensed her surrounded by people — among them, not of them. But he never came close, never asked another soul for clues; and he never spoke her name. If he had been made to talk of her, then he would have had to say why she mattered. And he did not think he could do that. This was his own consuming dream. The longer it went on, the less sense it made, and not just because of the forgetting. She had been fading in his mind for months. That was why he had scratched the little sketch on his saddle: a woman whose figure had seemed to fatten as he rode. But he had managed to keep her real for himself; more real than much of this brand-new Logres, certainly more real than the rumours of its wars.

She called him on through hills, valleys, forests. Past rivers, lakes and streams as the winter bit, gripped hard, then let him go. Equally convinced now that he would find her far from any sort of settlement, it was relatively easy to stay clear of all roads and pathways. Great swathes of the remade kingdom were never trodden save by charcoal burners, happy madmen and hermits. And as the hawthorn bushes began to bud, whenever Brumart pictured her to himself, he always saw her alone, and near water, turning her dragon-loop around and around on her upper arm like a charm.

All he had was his hunches. Those and the pull of the thread round his neck. Which at last had led him to here: a remote stretch of western coast well north of the Wall. A place to which no logic or reason could have guided him.

But logic seemed to be in short order all round. This part of Arthur's realm was said now to be ruled by that old goat Lot. And twice up here in the previous month he had seen fishing people gathered around in a huddle listening to stories told not by strays, but by women.

The willows rustled in the sundown breeze to his left. He

trained his eyes back on the tower ahead. There had been other towers on his travels. Usually near water, too, even though those near lakes and inland streams had been oddly placed for beacons. This was the first time he had come so close. It looked like a tower lifted bodily out of some far larger castle. The last rays of the sun struck unexpected colours from its stone. Shades of green and watery-blue; almost as if it had been faced in places with some kind of glass.

Glass Castle . . . He had heard the phrase both times that he had chanced upon those curious women storytellers. It had floated out of their otherwise obscure babble like butterflies from a mess of pupas. *Glass Castle* . . . Whatever they meant, the words had a soothing sound.

'Soldier,' called a rich, female voice behind him.

The moment folded over on itself and pretended not to have happened. But it was too late. Brumart closed his eyes at the shock.

Behind his eyelids he saw Camelot's hall again, then the steps leading up to it, the steps down which he had watched her come sluggishly on Logres' first night – alone, unencumbered, chased by her own bloodied child as she made for the city's postern gateway. The son who grew ever smaller while new-born Logres continued to burgeon around them; just as one land was hatching from another, so this boy would at last grow back into his mother.

Brumart knew that he should have killed Morgan then. Killed her or gone with her. One or the other. He should never have allowed her to leave alone and find her own place in Logres. And now she had found him.

He opened his eyes and turned his head a little way; not quite far enough to catch sight of her. He was so tired that he thought he might have imagined her voice, sketched it on to the air in much the same way that he had pricked out her picture on his saddle.

'Is it you?' he asked. 'Morgan? Here?'

No answer came. His heart smashed against his ribcage. As his nerve began to desert him, he threw his arm across as if to grasp his sword's hilt but then he let it fall away. Kill her or go with her. He still did not know which was right, nor why he had hounded her down.

'Brumart,' he called back, as if this mattered. 'My name is Brumart.'

'All the way from Camelot.' There was laughter in the way she said it.

He grimaced. She had reeled him in, all the way through to the labyrinth's centre. But still he would not twist his neck to see. He dreaded to find that she was not alone; that the bloodied child was still there beside her, or even half-inside her now, and half-out. Whatever came next, there had to be only himself and her. To his astonishment, he felt tears rolling down his long-unshaven cheeks; big, mucous tears of distracted relief.

'Why won't you look at me?'

It was her voice. Undoubtedly hers: rich, alluring, almost arch. But now it sounded choral too; as if she had somehow formed a semicircle of herself around him, pinning him into this bleak crescent of land at the sea's edge. He dared not turn. That would mean looking her in the eye. The eye that had always gone with the voice. The eyes now that now went with these voices.

'Come inside,' the chorus of Morgans purred from closer, more huskily: a command he could not disobey. Brumart wrenched himself around and he knew at last why he was here. But too soon, too soon.

Again his right hand moved to his sword, and this time it

closed on the hilt. But even before he looked, everything was changing; the world had opened up before him in a rush, the world that was already inside Morgan.

He felt himself running fast towards her, towards them all, like a child himself now, his eyes shut tight but not afraid of falling – feeling, in fact, that he was far more likely to leave the ground altogether and soar like her own golden dragon into beautifully billowing clouds . . .

Nabur was combing this latest stretch of shore quite quickly. *Find the son . . . Find the son . . .*

He felt sure that he had heard a cry. More like an animal's than a person's, but not of any animal he knew. That had been an hour ago. He was about to veer up to the forest, to search out somewhere to bed down before the night closed in, when he saw the tower.

At fifty-eight years of age Nabur no longer saw especially well. He noticed the tower first – an amber light aglow in its lower-storey window – then the causeway on which it stood, and only then the armed man lying prostrate by the split stone path.

Find the son . . . It was the first corpse Nabur had seen in Logres. He knew at once that the man was dead. People did not rest like that, with their heads so near to the water, with a sword at the end of one outstretched arm.

His step slowed as he came closer. *Don't be him. Oh, not him . . .* he breathed, half in prayer but with no idea to which god. From what he could remember, this dead warrior was bulky enough to be his own son. His sodden hair was short enough, his one visible ear outsized enough.

Nabur had been walking ever since the deluge had washed him up on Logres. Nothing of the old time had stayed in his mind. He could not even recall what work he had used to do.

But he knew that he had come ashore with a son. A big bluff man half his own age. On disembarking the younger man had taken a horse at once and ridden away: for the king's court, he had said, to become a knight.

Nabur still knew little enough about Camelots, Companies and Round Tables – only what he heard from the strays he passed on the roads. Maybe his son really had found service with Arthur. Maybe even now he was fighting beside him in his wars across the sea. But somehow Nabur doubted it. And to keep on looking for him in Logres was as good a way as any for an old man to eke out his days. 'I'm looking for my boy,' he would say at one isolated settlement after the next. 'I'm trying to find my son . . .'

Tears clouded his eyes. There was no sign of a horse. No sign of the man who had done this. The tunic on the body's back was streaked dark brown with blood. Its hair was dark, too, from blood and not the tide. *Not him. No, please not . . .* And then like an island rising, his son's name came back.

'Oh, not Owain!' Nabur tilted back his hairless head to plead aloud to the barrelling clouds. 'Not Owain . . .'

And it was not. Still six steps short, Nabur could see that this was not his own child: his great, lumbering, lop-eared dreamer of a son.

Spurred on by relief, he rushed across the causeway's neck towards the corpse and pulled it over on to its back in case there was still some life left. It was warm to the touch, and limp and bloody, although Nabur could see no cuts on the skin, no slash-marks on the clothing. He had not been a handsome man, although he seemed to be smiling. And he was quite dead.

Nabur murmured what he hoped was a suitable prayer. He felt badly unqualified for this. All of this. *Blood without cuts*, kept running through his head. *Blood without cuts . . .* In his confusion he started trying to hoist the corpse up on to the causeway, afraid that the next tide would surge in and sweep it away.

With surprising ease, he levered the upper body on to the slimy stone, the unstained sword slipping from the hand's grip. Then, leaving the torso and head slumped, Nabur hauled himself up before continuing.

At that point he heard her cry.

The sound seemed to fly at him from the dusky shore. Choked, pained, deep; quite possibly a strangled version of the call that he had heard earlier.

'Please . . .' she then begged, dragging out the word into a groan.

At last Nabur got his bearings. He swung his crouched body around to the tower which, ever since seeing the body, he had quite forgotten about.

She was standing in the unlit doorway, side-on to him, her back against the architrave with her head thrown back, a mass of umber hair hanging loose. Oddly – Nabur thought afterwards – it did not cross his mind that she too might have been hurt. Even at first glimpse, she looked invulnerable.

'Who is this man?' Nabur yelled across the fifty feet or so that separated them, gripping the tunic at its drenched shoulders. 'What happened?'

'Please!' she simply wailed again, aiming her cry at the darkening sky.

Nabur peered at her harder. She was distraught but not solely on account of the dead man. Perhaps not on his account at all. She was talking to Nabur with her hands: cupping one beneath her enormously bulging belly under a shift, while drumming the fingers of the other at the top of it.

'Now?' Nabur almost laughed, turning further towards her. 'Your baby? It's coming now?'

She nodded, vehemently, and seemed to slump where she stood. Her features were vague in the poor light but he knew that she was stunningly lovely – just from the shape of her face, which was as milky-skinned as her hair was dark, and also from the size of her eyes; her lustrous, burning eyes.

Nabur let go of the corpse but with only one hand. 'What shall I do with him?' he yelled helplessly. He was too old for this. Much too old. 'Who is this man, do you know?'

She shook her head as hard as she had nodded, then clutched at herself, wincing. 'Help *me* . . .' she gasped before slumping back inside the tower.

As soon as Nabur stood to follow her, the dead man snaked backwards off the causeway and back down on to the sand. It was as if he had been pushed.

The labour was long and difficult.

Dawn broke before the child gave up the fight and, already screaming, allowed Nabur to ease the rest of him out. There was so much blood on him but mercifully none was his own; blood without cuts.

As soon as it was over, the old man knew that he was no longer wanted. He too had no wish to linger. Not, at least, in their immediate company. But he did not intend to go very far. With a last look at the bloodied yet beautiful boy in his mother's unringed hands, he backed out into the morning.

All births are momentous, no newborn seems ordinary. But only when Nabur was outside again did he realize how profoundly this particular ordeal had touched him.

He shivered as he relived the climactic passages. The infant's emergence into the world had guided his mind back to the thrill of earlier births, the details of which were now quite obscure to him. But also – more confusingly still – it had drawn him forward, to a distant night when this same child, fully grown, would be waiting to receive Nabur himself in turn.

He paused and glanced back at the tower. The fresh morning light was striking it in such a fashion that it seemed to glitter like the sea beyond it. Like the sea too, it suggested unimagined depths. The child's cries wound anthemically around the tower. And Nabur, quaking, felt tears easing down his own cheeks in response.

Find the son . . . Nothing was the same in the world now. Nothing was ever going to be the same. He tipped back his head and gazed up through prickling eyes at a sky that had never seemed so huge, nor so gently protective. It was as if the great celestial dome above him were a vast bunched fist of air, holding him safe now; redeeming him, even. And all because of the child's arrival.

He shook his head at what was, for him, such unwonted whimsy, then continued on his way.

He had to wade through several inches of water to reach the shore along the causeway. The warrior's body was gone, swallowed by the sea, never to be washed back. Nabur wished in a way that it had reappeared. For years afterwards, every time he put out in his coracle at night to fish, he was nervous that a hand might suddenly grab up at him from below.

But on that first morning his thoughts were not on the corpse. *Find the son . . . find the son . . .*

He had come to the causeway dreading that he might have lost a child. Now he walked away with the warm but awesome feeling that he might instead have gained one.

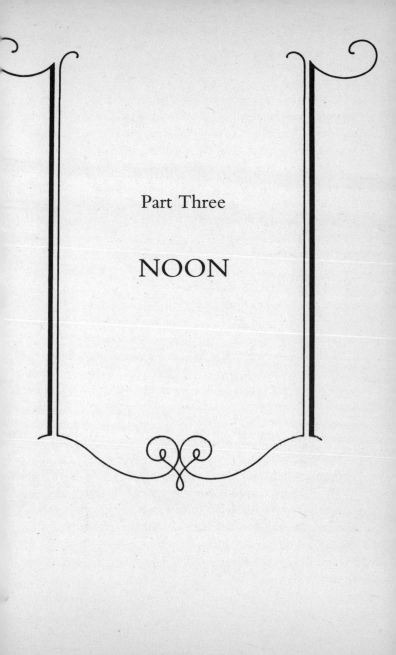

Part Three

NOON

ELEVEN

As soon as the eating was over, King Lot of Orcadie excused himself from the remainder of the evening's entertainments and left the hall.

After days of squally rain it was mild outside, warm enough to sit until the darkness closed in. Without a word from Lot, his two great wolfhounds bounded towards the rose-garden. He followed at his own sluggish pace, stiff from too much sitting, wavy-headed from too much wine with his meal.

Red, red, red, red, red: the first avenue of flowering bushes converged in the dusk ahead of him, parading its riot of single-coloured blooms. One avenue, all the avenues. Five years earlier, Lot had sat here trying to guess how many different shades of rose his garden would produce. He had not known then that only blood-red roses would ever grow in Orcadie, or at least in those few parts of it which he ever felt driven to visit.

Touring Orcadie only made Lot feel more irrelevant. Each town and village seemed so utterly self-contained. And although the shores of Logres had long been left undefended there was never the slightest threat from abroad. With less and less for him to do, Lot could only kick his heels in his rock-perched palace above his capital. At times, indeed, he was capable of little else. Over the five years, his physical condition, unlike his wife's, had not deteriorated further, but his store of energy diminished by the month.

He found an arbour with a bench and sat straight-backed.

The roses' relentless redness oppressed him. In Albion, he felt certain, there had been whites, pinks and ambers. But this was meant to be the land of promise, and for all Lot knew, every rose in history had always set out to be red, with only the failures turning out otherwise.

His dogs settled at his feet, stretching away with their bellies to the ground, their heads and shoulders vigilantly raised. He felt for a moment like a charioteer with the two beasts yoked ahead of him in frozen motion.

Lot was unsure whether he liked the dogs any more than he liked the roses. A gift from his wife three years earlier, they were devoted to him but only in the cold way that a doctor is devoted to a patient – a devotion to the mere fabric of his body, or even to his illness.

As the light palled, he stared over the foliage to the lights at the windows of his hall's long gallery. It almost sobered him to think of the number of women inside; women of leisure, women in service, women who sat listening while other itinerant women came to tell their stories. Even the lamps now seemed to burn with a girlish glow, the stone of the walls to have some specially feminine finish. At one time Lot might have thrived on that. Not now. He had certainly not reckoned on this when so many able-bodied men had followed Arthur overseas.

He envied those men now. He could see why they had been so keen to leave. Logres lacked some vital aspect, some necessary dimension without which it could offer only the trappings of an earthly Eden. Lot had never been able to put his finger on what this might be, but he had felt the absence more and more powerfully. At times he was tempted to see it as a spiritual deficit, not that he had ever been formally religious. But he felt a craving to be part of something larger – closer to others in more than his usual physical ways – even if it were only Arthur's army on the march.

Wherever that army might currently be campaigning, it was surely not sitting around camp fires being regaled by fables from females. But Lot had no better idea about the king's exported wars than he had about his own proper function up in Orcadie. For years now, no one had told him a thing.

His promotion to the kingship had plainly been a way of putting him in quarantine within Logres. He seemed to have forfeited his right to a say in the larger monarchy's affairs – or even to be told why the wars were being fought. Ruefully he regretted banning all strays from Din Eydin. In their first guise as news-bringers they might now have served some useful purpose. But nobody in the region admitted to having set eyes on a stray for years.

An hour passed slowly. A second dragged slower still. Finally Lot dozed where he sat in the blackness. He thought he heard, like many times before, a woman's voice calling out a ghostly roll of Anna's original seven handmaidens: Moronoe . . . Mazoe . . . Gliten . . . Glitonea . . .

He was stirred by the low growl of one of the dogs. Someone was approaching through the maze of avenues. The dog fell silent as it picked up a familiar scent. Lot's first reaction was to feel intruded upon. Whichever of his mistresses was coming, he did not know if he wanted her attentions tonight. He closed his eyes and waited until he sensed that she was in front of him.

'My lord,' came a quiet voice from low down. She had to be kneeling.

Lot chewed on the inside of his lip, still not looking. The dog had obviously known her scent better than he himself knew her voice.

'My lord,' she repeated, calm but insistent, and without the local accent.

Lot opened his eyes to find a young, upturned oval face that he had never before seen at such close quarters. Her eyes looked constantly shocked and wide but her speech was always measured; it was as if some kind of panic had gripped her, but subsided by the time it reached her mouth. Her name was Tyronoe: one of Anna's three remaining serving girls. In the past five years, to the queen's great distress, four had slipped away – apparently to become storytellers, or 'morgauses' as they were locally known.

'Lord,' the young woman went on steadily, 'the queen has sent me. She wishes to speak with you. Something has upset her.'

Lot leaned forward and pinched the skin above his broad nose. The girl, he imagined, was just as embarrassed about this as he was.

He had asked for little enough from Anna. Her failure to give him another child had not mattered; it surely did not matter to Anna herself – Lot had never known a woman less obsessed with reproduction. But he had expected her at least to be calm and consistent where he was so prone to mood swings. But year by year she had seemed to be losing her grip. In public and private alike she could now dissolve into tears for no reason at all.

Then with a lurch in his stomach, Lot thought of the morgause who had come into his hall that evening. Again he closed his eyes.

'A story, was it?' he asked without needing Tyronoe to answer. 'Another one of those damned legends?'

'A Glass Castle legend, lord.'

Lot snorted. She had said the words with hushed reverence, and even with the politest possible reproof. 'Glass Castle, Glass Castle . . .' he repeated with a weary shake of the head. Others in Logres obviously shared his need to engender some larger, over-arching sense of community; but this way of meeting it seemed to him to be way off the mark. 'So tell me, what happened in tonight's tale?'

Understandably, the girl stared back for a moment in silence. Lot had listened to only a handful of the morgauses' flights of fancy and had soon enough lost patience, precisely because so little *did* happen. He could not even say why the tales were so named. There had been no castle of glass in any that he had heard, just two people: a woman and a younger man.

Sometimes this man was called her son, at other times her lover – even, occasionally, both. Nameless, ageless, they often went naked, usually in deep forests. Where the trees were too dense to walk between, they flew.

The morgauses were poor conventional storytellers. They seemed to feel that it was enough roughly to describe this couple, and what they did together. There were no beginnings, middles and ends. At times the elemental pair were at war with each other. They fought, they clawed. Even when they made love, it was somehow like a fight, a struggle for supremacy.

But the legend remained essentially unformed. Here were two characters for ever poised on the edge of adventure, the rawest of raw material for a story. It was possible, Lot thought, that the listener was meant to take this and make a story for himself. Or maybe he was missing something. There was no denying that other listeners — male as well as female — sat entranced. And Anna, of course, would become upset.

Lot shifted on the bench but did not rise. Buttery-haired Tyronoe with her hooped silver earrings stayed on her knees between him and the dogs, waiting to be dismissed. Lot felt irritated and quite horribly alone.

'Stand,' he said, gesticulating. She obeyed but still hovered. 'Tell me,' he said, partly because he was too tired not to, 'why do you think that this . . . legend makes your mistress so anxious? Does she ever talk of it to you?'

The girl's enormous eyes seemed to widen even further. 'Lord,' she replied, 'it's you she needs to talk to.'

'As she needed to twice before?' Lot rapped back. 'And both times she would tell me nothing when I came.' Both times she had laughed off her tears like a bad dream from which she had subsequently awoken.

'Perhaps, lord, she thought you didn't really want to listen.'

'And she was right,' Lot barked, before he realized how forward the girl had been. She dipped her head a little, maybe in acknowledgement.

Lot reached down and rubbed at the nearer dog's haunch. He often found himself showing the animals affection in the presence of other people; it was as if he were building up an alibi for a crime he might one day need to commit. 'And the legend,' he asked Tyronoe absently, 'it doesn't stir you?'

'I try not to let it,' she answered, knitting her fingers in front of her.

'It touches you, then?'

She shrugged prettily. 'It can make me feel different. If I let it.'

'And those others of your number? Moronoe, Mazoe . . . It made them feel "different", did it?'

She swallowed. 'Yes.'

Lot nodded, still bending forward to stroke the dog. 'I think,' he said finally, 'that we have had enough of this legend now, don't you? At least within these walls?' He straightened, then staggered to his feet between the sleeping wolfhounds. 'I shall give an order to that effect. No more Glass Castle stories.'

As he said this he stepped forward, reached out and brushed the back of his hand against Tyronoe's thinly-sleeved shoulder. Her skin was icy beneath it; unnaturally so. But she did not flinch, so he slid his palm down her other arm and took the tips of her fingers in his. This was the land of promise. This was how he was meant to live in it. He bent over, lifted her hand to his lips and kissed her slender wrist. She tasted of salt-water.

'Would you come to me again?' he asked, softly enough for the dogs not to hear in their sleep. Stooped like this, he could look levelly into her eyes.

'I'm not what you want,' she replied without blinking. She could almost have been talking to someone else behind his shoulder, someone who had just made her an entirely different reflex proposition.

Lot kneaded her cold little fingertips between his own, then turned her hand pulse-upward. 'You think you know what I want?' he asked, largely to himself.

He let go of her hand but she left it poised in the air. Seen from a distance, she would have seemed to be offering him something in her palm. But there were no distances inside that small arbour. And in the darkness only Lot could see her, and what she was not offering him. 'Lord,' she said at last before smiling beautifully and leaving, 'the queen needs you.'

But when Lot went to the cadaverous Anna, it was the same story as before. She could not, would not, speak with him. Only the deeper redness around her eyes suggested that anything at all had been amiss earlier that evening.

Hardly caring either way, Lot shambled off to his chambers with a flagon. The next day he went ahead and banned the morgauses from Din Eydin.

TWELVE

Nabur knew that many babies were born completely without hair on their heads. But it seemed unusual when, after his first year, the tower-child still showed no signs of growing any.

By the end of the second year his pate darkened a little, but it turned out to be only a change in his skin's pigmentation, like a shadow on smooth stone. And a year later, already so strong on his feet that he seemed to swagger, he remained as bald as Nabur himself. But like his mother the boy was strikingly handsome. His baldness only emphasized his head's fine shape. Finally Nabur came to hope that he would never grow a mane at all.

Throughout these years, Nabur had no fixed home near the tower.

He would wander off for months on end but always come back to the coast, the causeway, the couple. Finally when the boy was four, the old man built himself a shelter just inside the forest. He made such a thorough job of it that he felt sure he must have worked with wood in Albion.

He spent little time with the woman and her growing child, but watched them almost constantly. The stark white, dome-headed boy seldom smiled. Nabur himself would not have smiled much if he had spent so much of his life in the company of so severe a woman.

He came to see the few occasions on which she left the boy alone with him as a reprieve from her, a form of compensation. And he saw it as his own duty to humour the child, to give him free rein. So if he chose to be a little fey now and then, a little precious, then Nabur was happy to indulge him in that too.

Both mother and son were enigmas to Nabur. He never knew precisely what went on between them. He asked the boy at the age of five how they passed most of their time together. 'She just talks to me,' he replied in his solemn way. 'She tells me things she has learned from the giants.'

She certainly told him a lot, most of which flew over Nabur's own head. He could speak with such precocious fluency. The way he talked about the wider kingdom, in particular, made it seem impossible that he had never left this remote corner of Orcadie and seen it all for himself.

The longer Nabur watched them together, the less they seemed like mother and child. There was too little softness in the way she spoke to him, the way she left him to sob alone and made him run along behind her. She was more like a nursemaid on constant call, or even a tutor. Someone who was seeing him through the steps of his development as quickly as she could, with her own sights firmly fixed on some far larger goal.

Yet she was not unaffectionate. Sometimes Nabur would glimpse her holding the boy's hand, or stroking his head and neck. In her own way she was devoted to him. She surely was proud of him too; of his lovely sad eyes and strength and cleverness. But there was an edge to even her fondest smile. She seemed to hoard him rather than embrace him.

She would hold him to her like an act of defiance against unseen others – as if to declare that no one could stop her from hustling him along now in any way that she saw fit.

Nabur's own feelings for the tot from the tower were simpler. He loved him. And, in spite of his own great age, he loved him not as a grandson but as a son. The boy stripped years off him and filled him up with energy. Their relationship, such as it was, was intensely active. Nabur thought this best, since the boy only ever seemed to use his brain with his mother. At four, Nabur had him swimming. Around that time he also started taking him into the forest to show him which snakes, roots and berries to avoid. He taught him to see how wolves and wildcats could as easily be encouraged to retire as to attack – lessons which he seemed to have learned already, in theory at least.

Often they wrestled on the spongy turf at the water's edge north of the causeway, and before he was five, the boy was already proving the stronger. Then Nabur began his light-hearted education in arms: mock combats with dummy wooden swords, running at each other on wild pony-back with rough poplar poles stuffed under their armpits for lances.

'You're the little white knight!' Nabur would tell him. 'You'll be the finest knight ever to grace King Arthur's court' – at which the boy would flush and look away with the oddest expression.

They hunted a little and fished a little less. The first time that Nabur took him out in his coracle, the boy soon became unsettled. He cowered and squirmed where he sat, as if he were being crowded in on by others.

'I want to go back,' he panted into his midriff, 'I want to go back . . .'

Nabur, thinking he was seasick, returned them to the shore

at once. But the boy stayed hunched in the vessel, staring around himself in horror: 'I want to go back, I want to go back . . .'

'Back to your mother?'

'Back with the giants. I can trust the Mighty so much more than any king.'

Nabur had smiled and asked no more questions. Not then. The child was young and lonely. He said lots of surprising things, maybe just to draw attention to himself. Like the time when he had spoken at the raven.

His mother had taught him to identify every bird he saw. He would gaze, wholly absorbed, at flights of gulls or lone cormorants and shags. But if he saw a raven he became restless, holding up his arms as if to attract it. 'Father,' he once dreamily called to one while Nabur was showing him how to use a hammer. Then he clapped his hands with such sudden violence that Nabur almost drove a nail through his own thumb.

Whoever the father was, he never came to visit. Nabur half-hoped it had been the dead warrior at the causeway. The mother for her part gave every impression that she needed no partner in bringing up the boy. Yet, astonishingly, she seemed to have a need for old Nabur.

He had hardly been looking for intimacy with her. He had thought his days for that were over, and with his lumpy head and stumpy teeth he would not have given himself a prayer with a svelte, full-lipped beauty like her. But sporadically she took him to her bed as if it were all a part of some secret deal that she had long ago acquiesced in: a deal that perhaps involved him never asking questions.

She was a furiously busy lover. In time she taught him all the mechanical ways in which he could please her – and she expressed her pleasure noisily. She did not ignore Nabur's own needs but her priorities were clear. She seemed to take an almost objective delight in her own physical reactions. It was as if she kept on bringing her body along for them both to play with. And, from one session to the next, it never seemed to be quite the same body.

Nabur could not explain this. Going into her was like going into a whole sea of women. At times he felt dangerously close to drowning. He guessed that she had to be using him in some way. As a stand-in for another man, or maybe for every man. From the little she ever said to him, he traced some bitterness. Even when she was thrashing on top of him, rubbing her breasts and crotch against his gaping mouth, he thought he could taste her contempt for all his kind. And she always looked at him so obliquely. Someone somewhere must have made her suffer before; given her the child, then packed her off.

'Who do people say I am?' she surprised Nabur by asking as he dressed after one of their nights together. He always left the tower before the boy woke in the room above: his decision, not hers.

He paused, tried to smile, and waved at the emptiness all round them. 'I see very few people.'

'Some pass through, though. I've seen you speak with them.'

This made him uncomfortable. Nabur liked to chat and he had so little chance to do so now. He could not help mentioning her – rather gleefully – to pedlars, travelling players, riders who had lost their way. He talked about the pair of them with such pride: his little white knight and the lovely young mother who slept with him. They rarely looked as if they believed him. Others smiled at him as if they understood only too well. One tinker, however, had speculated on where she might have come from.

'I've heard it said,' Nabur answered carefully, 'that you may have . . . known the king.'

'The king?'

'Our king. Lot, of Orcadie.'

She looked faintly amused. 'That's good enough.'

'Is it true?'

She smiled then, and sent him away by putting her cool palm to the side of his face in a gesture of the purest derision.

One of Lot's women, was what the tinker had suggested. Lot's choice. In Albion, apparently, he had been known for fathering bastards. But that was probably just a story, one of the many. Nabur had no real interest in who she was, where she had come from, or why. He had never demanded a great deal. As long as she stayed around, as long as she let her boy come to him from time to time, then he had as much as he needed from the promised land of Logres.

But still the boy smiled so seldom. And at six, with his mother's blessing, he started to spend mild nights outside the tower. He would bed down under pelts on the causeway, just above the tide-line, close to the place where Nabur had found the dead man. It seemed absurdly dangerous. Not just tempting fate but issuing a challenge, to which it could hardly fail to rise. Nabur himself never turned in until checking whether the boy was outside. If he was, he would then secretly keep a vigil from the shore until morning, when his mother would come to gather him up.

'Why do you *do* it?' he burst out at him in the end. They were sitting together outside his shelter, the remains of several spit-roasted pheasants strewn across the earth apron in front of them.

'I'm quite safe there,' the boy replied in a voice that seemed already to be deepening. 'Safer than anywhere. The giants see to that.'

Nabur picked up a sharp poultry bone and prodded his own palm with it. The giants again. The Mighty. He was not quite sure what the boy meant by these phrases. Something more elemental, he thought, than the colossal race of masons and engineers that was said to have ruled the world in its youth. Or then again, maybe not. Their stone circles and hill-figures had always had some kind of mystic significance. Even on his earlier wanderings in Orcadie Nabur had seen them being lovingly scoured and refurbished.

'You dream of the old giants, do you?' he pressed. 'When you're outside?'

'Not the old giants.'

'No?'

He too had picked up a bone and was jabbing lightly at his wrist. Nabur's heart went out to him. His face was gaunt and white without any hair to frame it. At times he could look raw, like a boy who had been boiled – or else like one of those great chalk men up on the hillsides.

'You dream of different giants?' Nabur said softly.

His lips were pressed hard to his thin, raised knee. Still he pricked at his wrist with the bone. 'The next giants,' he answered in the end. 'The Mighty that we'll be again. After this kingdom of Arthur's is over.'

'And that will be good?' Nabur was talking to a lonely boy with way too much imagination. And although they were sitting so close, he dared not dig him in the ribs, squeeze his arm, drag the fun out of him or try to put some in – the boy always stiffened at the slightest touch. 'Aren't you happy in this kingdom?'

'It's not for me to be happy anywhere,' he answered – very

slowly – into his knee. 'I'm only ever in the places where I have to be.'

Nabur chuckled out loud, but it made an empty sound. Maybe this was the price of being so bright. Maybe no infant prodigy ever took pleasure from all his knowing. But this child seemed to suffer for being so able and articulate. He was not yet seven but his soul seemed already to be old.

'Well, I'm happy to have you here,' Nabur grinned, throwing caution to the wind and hugging him hard. 'You're my little white knight.'

'You don't know who I am,' the boy said brusquely, breaking from his grip and springing to his feet. As he rose, the pheasant bone he was fiddling with seemed to sink into the fleshy heel of his hand. Nabur at once saw redness.

'You're hurt,' Nabur cried, mortified.

The boy glanced down, raised his hand to his mouth and cleaned it with a single lick of his tongue. He turned out his palm to show Nabur. 'It's not my blood,' he said with a rare and perfect grin. 'It never is.'

He was standing directly in front of the setting sun. Nabur put up a hand to shield his eyes, and for a moment the boy towered over him. In that moment he seemed to multiply, the sunshaft appearing to pierce him like a prism to make a single startling figure from a multitude of men, at least one of whom looked remarkably similar to the dead man on the causeway. And dangling from his hand, just in that moment, was no mere bone but a knife.

By the time Nabur blinked, the boy had turned and was parading in his cocksure way back down towards the causeway. Quaking, Nabur sat on as darkness fell. *After this kingdom of Arthur's is over . . .* The way the boy had said the phrase – quickly, dismissively, purse-lipped – it had sounded more like 'after this kingdom of father's'.

Finally Nabur fell asleep and dreamed of the knife that was only a bone, dripping so much blood that it was drowning the whole of Logres.

THIRTEEN

Lanslod rose fast as the alarums sounded. Two squires stood ready in his tent with weapons and armour; the grooms had scuttled off to fetch his horse.

Another night attack. Lanslod had almost forgotten what it was like to fight by daylight. Under the heat of the Outremer sun, the enemy seemed simply to melt away. Any enemy. Whichever new multitude happened to be standing in the rampant king's way. These people were not slow to learn. They knew that they stood no chance in an equal clash with Arthur. Their only hope lay in surprise. Falling on the massed tents of Logres deep in the night.

When Lanslod was ready, his squires led him forward. Outside the tent, he sized up the scale of the raid. There was no point in him assembling his retinue, talking tactics and strategy. Faced by these sudden sorties, every man had to work off his own instinct, flair and luck.

Smoke seeped through Lanslod's visor, his stallion stood waiting – caparisoned in blue with Lanslod's grey wolf's-head motif dotted all over the cloth. It took five men to hoist him up.

From higher, he saw flames away to the east. Only the sleeping army's flank had been attacked so far.

Lanslod rode hard along the avenue of canopies to where the fighting was thickest; to where the king would already be turning the tide.

Six years into this expedition, it was hard now for Lanslod to distinguish one campaign from another, each freshly-captured kingdom, duchy or palatinate from the last. It was no easier to remember specific battles than it was to remember each throw that had been made in a drunken all-night dice game. And for the past three years at least, he had been finding it almost impossible to picture their route on any mental map. 'Outremer' was clearly a catch-all phrase to indicate any part of this vast, eastward-rolling landmass which lay across the southern strait from Logres.

At first they had traversed great open grasslands, often within a few days' ride of the shore to the north. The vistas had regularly reminded Lanslod of stretches of Logres itself. The spruce, stone-built towns too were similar to those that he had seen on his reconnaissance. It was as if each territory they were passing through had been an early, imperfect version of the land of promise which finally came to flower at the Great Remaking.

But since striking south-east into drier, more barren climes, any sense of familiarity had left him. These arid landscapes looked as if no deftly-shaping hand had ever come near them. Soon enough, he felt sure, they would be approaching the region from which Christ Himself was said to have sprung. And beyond that, Lanslod's imagination could not stretch. Nor had he come to understand his leader any better. Since leaving Logres, Lanslod had been closer to Arthur than anyone in the Company. The king himself had seen to that. But still Lanslod felt no bond that was not strictly military.

He knew, however, what certain other members of the Company whispered. That Arthur was grooming him for some significant future role, maybe even the succession in the absence of a son of his own. That, they argued, was why the king had assigned him no province in Logres, and why he had not deputed him — like Gereint, Bediver and Manannan already — to hold down any of the newly-conquered territories.

Lanslod seldom let his mind dwell on all this, partly because he shrank from the mere idea of a time when Arthur would be gone. His only ambition was to serve the king, and preferably while on the move. For him, unlike those who constantly debated this campaign's true causes, the king's perpetual conquests had their own logic. He knew enough if he knew that he was under the orders of his commanding officer.

But to his surprise, Arthur had turned out to be no kind of a commander. His leadership lay entirely in what he did — which seemed to be to win each battle single-handed. His army was always ranged about him but increasingly, Lanslod believed, only to impress the enemy with its conventional size and strength. In conflict these men were virtually redundant. Arthur was amassing his empire in a series of single combats.

It was easy now to see why he had been called Lord of War. He had changed war's nature, mastered it and made it his own. He was a king not just of a kingdom, an emperor not just of great swathes of Outremer; he ruled over the entire business of bloodletting too. He came alive to battle cries, seizing the sword of whichever of his men was closest to hand. He could have fought a fleet on foot. And he would have fought it fast — because he seemed to be fighting against time as well as men.

But between the battles he barely existed – or else he lived in some separate dimension from which he broke through only to sever limbs and shatter flesh, leaving behind the vanquished with savagely-jointed corpses like overcooked chickens dragged from a pot.

Off the field he was so silent. *It's not what he says*, the men in Lanslod's levy liked to tell one another, *it's what he means*.

And while they passed their nights with drink and sex, Lanslod would often see Arthur sitting alone on the outskirts of an encampment, staring back westwards with a look that defied any description. But at those moments he could appear – in some respects like Lanslod himself – to be glad to have put paradise behind him.

It was not a lengthy contest. Little more than a brief, brutal skirmish. Lanslod killed his quota, but spent more time marvelling at the king's exhibition of blood–mastery. He always found it hard not to. Here was the essential king of legend – fleshing out the old stories' bones even as he stripped the meat from his still-flexing victims. It was like some cautionary spectacle, even if its moral remained opaque.

But that night, there were some differences. As ever, Arthur wore no helmet over his flowing, Styx-black hair. But he was fighting on foot with an axe, not with somebody else's sword; and although his great circular shield was slung round his neck like a loose-fitting carapace, he seemed to be relying more heavily for protection on the dark cloak that billowed underneath.

Time after time he grabbed a fistful of its fabric and brandished it at thick swarms of arrows that would then appear to change direction before falling harmlessly to earth.

Lanslod wondered why he bothered with a shield at all.

Any value it had was purely cosmetic. And unlike the men he led, he needed no emblem to mark him out. His hair did that; so too did the awesome, frenzied air about him. The shield was dark-blood red. On it had been painted a pale, rudimentary Virgin and Child. That, at least, was what Lanslod took them to be, which was curious since the king showed few other signs of piety. He attended none of the camp chaplains' thanksgiving Masses after each victory; he razed holy places on the march as if he were duelling with God Himself for the lordship of all Outremer.

But now Arthur was holding the shield up high against his shoulder. As he turned and turned, hacking one-handed with his axe, he flourished the great disc oddly. Less, it seemed, to defend himself; more as if to hold up the mother and son as a target to the mounted archers who in these regions always led the main line of attack.

Fleetingly, the sight of this unsettled Lanslod in a way that all the severed hands and sprays of blood did not.

Then, again, Lanslod was compelled by the sheer scope and speed of Arthur's death-dealing. A dozen men might converge on him, and at once he was hurling them all in spastic parabolas around him, each one hitting the ground already splayed apart. It amazed Lanslod that, even in numbers, they went on feeding Arthur's need for blood. He was touched by their faith in their armour and weapons. Any man who imagined that he could prepare to do battle with Arthur was almost mystically crazy. It was like taking a bath before diving into mud, then hoping that somehow the water would still keep you clean.

It's not what he says . . . This, truly, was what Arthur meant. Once and for ever. Lanslod had heard of men who fell apart under the peculiar conditions of warfare. Arthur fell together. War was for him the ultimate exorcism. Again and again he arose from the human wreckage cleansed. Purified, even.

By the time the pale sun came up, it was over. The field smouldered greyly, as if in commiseration. Out on its perimeters rows of silhouetted figures were slowly closing in. Not with any martial intent, but to throw themselves on Arthur's mercy. These were the elderly, the women and the young whose champions had just been slashed to pieces like so many stalks of fennel. Many would join the army's baggage train; more whores, cooks and story-tellers. It had happened like this so many times before. It seemed that it might go on until the end of time.

The king at last threw down his axe. He gazed around himself, still not spent. No more men could be found to stand against him. But he looked as if he might be about to dig out the squirrels and hedgehogs from their winter rest to make a new opposition. He was smothered in blood, and none of it was his. Blood without cuts. Blood from others' guts.

Lanslod thought of dismounting, of leading his horse over to the king and presenting it to him. That way, when Arthur returned to his pavilion to accept the massed surrender, he would be able to receive his own army's acclaim formally, on horseback. But something in the way Arthur now stood made Lanslod decide against it. It was not a triumphant stance. He had slung his shield on to his back again, but it seemed to be weighing him down, making him lower his head, bend his knees. Lanslod almost wanted to go over and offer to relieve him of his burden. But no one ever made that kind of a suggestion to Arthur. In his torments as well as in his triumphs, the great king was alone.

Unobtrusively, Lanslod reined his horse around and headed for his tent.

He had lost just one of his own men — a groom who had

fetched him his horse an hour earlier. Once his armour had been removed, he sat alone with his head in his hands. His mind felt cavernously empty. *Blood without cuts*, echoed inside it. *Blood without cuts* . . .

His current woman came later, and they made love twice before he fell asleep. When he woke in the small hours she was gone. The wolf's eyes on his shield glinted in the frosty moonlight that crept in through the tent flap. On arriving back at Camelot after his reconnaissance of Logres, he had chosen the wolf for his blazon without a second thought.

He sniffed and drew his covers higher. Always after sex he thought he could smell the distinct muskiness of the woman who had called herself Elayne rising through his own pores. He fell asleep counting the steps of air up which he always saw her progressing: her eyes fixed higher than the clouds, her gleaming dark hair flying behind her. And high on her left upper arm, a golden band glinted. A trinket which Lanslod had long since begun to wonder if he should have recognized.

After burying the dead and repairing the insurgents' damage, they advanced only ten miles the next day.

The sun-bleached country here was craggily inhospitable, far better suited to the myriad snakes and lizards than to human settlement. But scouts came back towards evening with news that a large town lay a further day's march ahead. Most of the local people within a fifty-mile radius had already fallen back inside it. Doubtless they had hoped that Arthur's army would pass directly through the evacuated region and leave them unmolested.

But Lanslod knew, even before the king beside him signalled the order, that this town would have to be reduced. These places could never be skirted.

Some animal instinct seemed to lead Arthur on, not always along the most passable routes, but he never backtracked. And he never left a town or city unbesieged, even if its capture was of no clear strategic value. He liked to ride in the straightest line, as if the route itself mattered most, with all the conquests incidental. The contrast between his urgency in battle and his patience on the march could not have been greater. His mind seemed to work slower when there was no scent of blood in his nostrils.

At noon the following day they arrived outside the walls and began to dig in. By nightfall they were entrenched, and ready to wait for however many months it might take. Lanslod ate among his men, then stayed idly chatting with them around their fires until the baggage-train women wandered up.

Lanslod slipped away to join a dozen or so members of the Company who were sitting in a loose circle. At its centre sat an old, cross-legged stray, telling a tale that Lanslod had heard before, about the Regent's origins. It was a thin little story, and even the teller lacked any zest for it. As a boy, he maundered on, Merlin had been seized and sentenced to death by an evil king, so that his blood could be used to bind the foundations of a castle that kept on collapsing. Lanslod lost interest before the boy's escape. His thoughts went back to this expedition's very beginning.

On the day that they sailed from Logres – the whole force falling in behind Arthur's flagship *Prydwen* – the Regent Merlin came to the quayside with four strays and watched the soldiers struggling on board with the siege machines and horses. There was true sorrow in the Regent's eyes. Finally he sent the four storytellers up the ramp, and raised his arms to the throng in a quivering salute. When he embraced Arthur, he clung on so hard that the king had gently to wrench himself free.

Lanslod, standing aboard *Prydwen* at the king's specific request, had been close enough to hear what Arthur then said to Merlin before embarking. The king's utterances were so rare that each had an inevitable resonance. But this one had a genuine ring, and it stayed with Lanslod.

'He who is head,' Arthur had said, or quite possibly quoted, 'let him be a bridge for his people.'

And maybe, after all, that was the best way to understand the past six years. The king as a bridge reaching deeper and deeper into Outremer – its fabric occasionally sagging just as the king had sagged beneath his shield. Maybe they were all in some fashion crossing Arthur rather than the land.

FOURTEEN

On the morning when Guenever finally left Camelot, Dyfric was roused too late by his serving boy to try to persuade her to stay.

By the time he had risen, dressed and shuffled through a fine dawn shower to the top of the citadel's steps, the queen's train was already crossing the plain.

Dyfric watched it disappear into the misty drizzle with a mixture of rancour and resignation. He was a realistic man. He knew that he could not have stopped her. Not with words. Too many other people had already deserted this city on its hill. It was as if, in leaving, the king had opened a floodgate which had never subsequently been closed. And underneath her cool exterior Guenever herself had been withdrawing for a long time; maybe for the full seven years since her husband had led his unbriefed fleet out of port and into Outremer's oblivion.

Dyfric returned to his lodgings with a heavy step.

He had barely known the queen. After Arthur's departure she had come to his chapel maybe half a dozen times. They had spoken alone only twice, and even then inconsequentially. But she had fascinated the older man; her constantly haunted expressions had come to haunt him too.

Often he had an idea that she wanted to talk with him. To speak her heart. She certainly seemed to have no one else to talk with. While even her own handmaidens were abandoning her in the general exodus, she had kept herself virtually confined to her quarters. And Dyfric, from the fastness of his own lodgings, had come to see the two of them as partners of a kind, keepers of a flame. So her going was a blow, and to more than just himself. He felt in his water that some far larger defeat had been inflicted.

During that day Dyfric's sense of ominousness grew. His intuition told him that around Camelot, and far beyond it, the decks were being cleared for a new struggle for supremacy. He could almost feel the ground bracing itself beneath his feet, the air slowing down in readiness.

Towards evening, he was surprised to be brought a letter by one of the Regent's staff. Unaddressed, and quite possibly unwritten by the queen herself, it flatly stated Guenever's intention to move her court to Lundein for the foreseeable future. No reasons were given.

Dyfric raised an eyebrow at the choice of words. In Arthur's continuing absence, Guenever had hardly been presiding over anything so grand as a 'court' at Camelot. 'Lundein' puzzled him too till he saw it as an abbreviation of Caerlundein, the burgeoning south-eastern entrepôt. It had, he knew, a formidable tower which offered even better defences than Camelot. But he doubted that this was really a matter of security. Not, at least, of the kind where mortared walls could make any difference.

He handed the letter back, presuming that it was a summons of some sort by Merlin. The Regent rarely gave a clear order when there was the chance to be elliptical. But Dyfric did not think that this was a[...] [...]

in Arthur's protracted absence, [...]

been losing ground. There were so[...]

that he was mad; it was easy – perhaps a[...]

see why.

The city was almost silent as Dyfric again made [...]

the citadel. Few outside lamps were burning, and the da[...]ess

seemed to make each of his steps slower than the last. He

thought he could hear someone laughing as he climbed up

to the hall: a woman's laugh, a pleasant, attractive sound.

There were no lights on in the hall but Dyfric could see

that it was empty. Even so, as ever, he eased himself through

the arch as if the whole Company were seated inside and had

turned their heads towards him.

He went to the Table and gently drummed his fingers on

its surface. He did not know whether to be glad or relieved

at the Regent's absence. He wondered if perhaps he had

been shown the letter to suggest that he too should leave

the city. Perhaps he should. But not yet. And not because

Camelot felt safer to him than anywhere else, nor out of

any residual sense of duty. He simply believed that this

was where he was meant to be. This was where he had

fetched up after the Great Remaking, so this was where he

would stay.

As for the Regent, he was neither quite in Camelot nor

out of it. Sometimes Dyfric wondered if even he knew

where he was.

He could certainly look deranged. His untamed hair had

thinned and whitened, giving him the air of a biblical prophet.

When he walked he sometimes waved his arms impatiently

like a man beating his way through cobwebs. He would

mutter too, gutturally, obscurely, as if he were addressing

someone invisible nearby. But what set tongues wagging

...his habit of holing himself up like an anchorite
...the pit below the chapel.

For years he had simply stood sentry at its lip, staring
down into the darkness – unnaturally erect, his arms folded
tight across his chest, his wild hair flailing in the breeze. On
countless evenings, Dyfric had seen his tree-like silhouette out
there. He looked as if he were locked inside himself and was
forlornly searching for the key. But then he had started to go
down, staying in the shaft for up to three days at a time.

Dyfric guessed that he was there now. He did not know
why and he shrank away from asking. He too had felt the
lure of that hole in the hill. In the first years he had spent
hours at the rim, often with his eyes closed, imagining the
vast emptinesses below, wondering how it might feel to fall
and fall for ever. Dizzily – and not entirely disagreeably – he
would sense the whole of Camelot, of Logres even, being
sucked inside this cavity.

And he had seen others – some of them outsiders – standing
in silent wonder around the gash in the slope. It was the only
reason why anyone ever came into Camelot now. Ordinary
enough people for the most part: innkeepers, tradespeople,
women with young children. But only Merlin ever went
inside. People said he was trying to look for something in
there. Maybe, rather, he was trying to hide something. Either
way, it never seemed to bring him any satisfaction.

Dyfric returned to his lodgings without going near the
Regent's abyss. He ate a simple meal, then went through to
his own portable altar to pray. He was feeling a new weight
on him. Perhaps, he now thought, the queen's leaving and
Merlin's withdrawal made it more vital than ever that he
should stay on. Perhaps some form of authority was devolving
on to him simply by default.

Standing on top of the altar was the king's icon which,

a year earlier, Dyfric had finally taken out of the chapel for himself. It no longer belonged, after all, in any Christian temple. It probably never had. The triptych seemed larger now than when he had picked it up after the king's desecration. It was possible that in seven years it had just grown bigger in his mind. There was plenty of room in there for growth: all the space created by the loss of so many memories. But the size of this thing was the least of Dyfric's concerns.

Before kneeling, he went up to it with his eyes averted, and covered the central panel with a torn-off strip of old chasuble. The other two images were still more than enough for him. Then, hesitantly, he put a finger to the rectangular left-hand panel's gilt wooden frame. Always that panel first. The feel of it made him shiver – only partly out of disgust at what the king had done to it.

This panel, left-sided as he looked at it, was less murky than the similarly-shaped one to the right. Dyfric wondered if the king's urine had made the paint there fade. On a mottled, blood-red background stood a woman holding an infant. Both woman and child were naked but nothing shameful showed. The hairy-headed baby obscured its mother's breasts. And although she stared directly out at the observer, below her waist she was twisted around so only the side of her thigh could be seen.

Dyfric let his hand fall, breathing hard. He turned his eyes to the right-hand panel, moving his whole head as if to stress that he had finished with the mother and child. From a jet-back field on this side a single male figure glowed out dully. Again he was naked, but crouching in a way that kept his sexual parts concealed. His ankles were crossed, his shoulders tensed, his hands drawn up like a squirrel's paws beneath his chin. His skin looked very smooth; even his head seemed hairless, unless – black as well – it had been swallowed up by the background wash.

Dyfric again put out his hand to touch the frame but faltered some way short. He could not do it. Not any more.

Slowly he moved his head, comparing the crouched man on the right with the baby held on the left. The posture of the one deliberately echoed that of the other, although both were facing inward. They might have been studying the central panel, peering under the scrap of draped cloth, if both had not had their eyes so firmly closed.

Dyfric shut his own eyes but the twin images were etched on the new, flashing dark. Not as they were now, but as he had seen them on that first night, just before the king's decision that he had needed to go to war. Then, the crouched male figure had held a knife. A simple kitchen tool but savage-looking all the same. And the woman had worn on her left upper arm a band in the shape of a dragon swallowing itself.

Surprisingly, it was the band that had unsettled Dyfric more. And it had been the first to disappear: abruptly, halfway through the first year – as if it had been painted over rather than faded away. The knife had taken longer to disappear. It had still been visible when Dyfric had begun to hear of the stories circulating in Logres. Stories about two people whom, little by little, Dyfric began to match with these figures on the icon.

From what he had heard, the 'Glass Castle' legend seemed to be haunting the whole island. Dyfric's own curiosity rarely took him very far from Camelot. Besides, he had no wish to see the loving way in which the ancient hill-figures and stone circles were being restored and plainly used for worship of a sort. But for years, wherever he went, he had sensed the legend.

It was like a river that had risen unannounced, then slowly insinuated itself across the entire landscape. Now it was as much a part of the kingdom as its castles and rains. Dyfric had no idea whether it would ultimately prove useful to those who lived along it, or finally burst its banks and drown them all. Either way, it seemed too strong to be confined indefinitely.

He had heard rumours that Lot, for one, had forbidden all mention of the lore in his own northern court. Dyfric doubted how effective that would be. The tales already seemed to sustain so many people, even inside Camelot. There were stories in which the pair healed incurable hurts. Others told of their shapeshifting: how to maintain the forest's balance they would assume the guise of wolf, bear or bird. Their role seemed protective. Warding off encroaching evil – as if the law of the absent king were not enough. And there lay the nub of it.

This legendary couple had established what could be called a rival court to Arthur's, a mystic parallel to Camelot. It was also, Dyfric accepted, a threat to the kingdom's official religion. The pair in the Glass Castle – whatever that construct actually was – had to be placated in some way. They were like gods; household gods on a nationwide scale. If there was a popular faith of any sort now in Logres, it was in them.

He had spoken about it with the handful of other clerics in the region. Some of them believed that the legend was ancient, that it had recently arisen after lying dormant for centuries. But Dyfric doubted that. Truly it had an archaic feel, but so too did many stories with classic contours. And this one was classic.

Even at second-hand, it touched Dyfric unawares, affected him in ways he could not begin to explain, crept up on him regularly and moved him almost to tears. The only time he had ever felt remotely like this before was during the extraordinary passage from Albion into Logres. In contemplating the cult pair, he had that same sense of vastness, of fellowship, of an endless human potential made possible by some immense protecting hand – a sense which had been all too elusive in the years since the Great Remaking.

Close to weeping now, he took a breath, put out a shaking hand, and plucked away the strip of chasuble from the icon's central image.

FIFTEEN

Lot paced restlessly around his dark bedchamber, cursing his dogs when – equally restless – they swarmed too close to his legs and made him check his step.

The night wore on, and still no one came. Dawn was less than two hours away; soon it would be too late to enjoy even the modicum of sexual ecstasy which was nowadays all he could hope for.

Outside, the dead midwinter rain gusted louder, drumming hard against the outside wall of his quarters. He had left one window open to watch for her crossing the wide inner courtyard. The floor beneath it was now puddled with water. Lot paused briefly to tip more wine from the flagon he carried with one hand into the goblet which he held in the other. Half as much again spilled on to the rushes underfoot. Lot did not notice. Setting off once more, he emptied the goblet in a single draught. One wolfhound was too slow to move aside, and with an oath the palsied King of Orcadie kicked out at it.

He felt so light now, as if he were floating on the surface of Logres. Din Eydin had always felt to him like an Ark; a refuge, almost, from the seas of spiritless perfection all around.

To him, the 'land' of promise had always been more like water. An ocean of self-regulating serenity. Orcadie had as much to do with Din Eydin as a sheet of still water has to do with a lily that sits across it. His court was no more than an adornment – pretty, cosmetic, unnecessary. A great stone flower that somehow did not sink.

He had not left it now for three years, and he planned never to leave it again. He was resigned to staying in this Ark for ever, finding tiny diversions in the form of one or other of the kitchen girls. He rather despised himself for doing so. He knew that he could have been aiming higher; seeking out the rarer sublimation for which privately he continued to yearn – even if sometimes he believed that he was achieving this simply by slipping ever closer to death. But the girls were what he knew.

They came to him on an irregular rota. Lot never knew which one would answer his signal until she arrived. The waiting, to be truthful, usually had more spice for him than what came after. Each girl always did her best but he rarely managed a response. More often than not they would end up singing gently to him until he fell asleep in their arms.

But on this night of inexplicable delay, he felt strong and ready. If no one came soon, he was even considering paying a visit to Anna.

It was years since the royal couple had slept together, weeks since Lot had seen his wife. They kept separate courts within Din Eydin's high walls, coming together infrequently for meals. As far as Lot knew, there was no animosity between them. Anna's emotion seemed to be bound up exclusively in her serving women, all seven of whom had now renounced her.

Lot understood that she spent long periods alone in the equally-abandoned chapel, bringing her own icon. If she found solace there, that was fine by him. She deserved some peace. He sometimes wondered if she might finally disappear into a nunnery, if any such places still existed in Logres.

He paused in front of the open window, winced as the icy rain sprinkled his bare feet, drank what was left of the wine and tossed the empty flagon out into the courtyard. As he did so, he spotted a pale shape edging along the grass's perimeter. Her head was bowed, and she was holding up the hood of a cloak against the weather. It could have been anyone.

Lot took one quick step back, not wishing to be seen, not wanting any of the girls to know how keen he had become; how dependent, even.

Pulling off his bedshirt, crawling back on to his bed, waiting to hear her step on the stone stair, his earlier peevishness passed. No longer impatient, he wished he could delay her arrival even longer just to relish the suspense. It was always such a sweet moment when he found out which of them had come. Often he would keep his eyes closed as she slid into his arms, and identify her only by touch.

He heard the creak as she pushed back the outer door which he had left ajar. She was slow then to ascend the steps. Too slow even for Lot. He could not hear her coming; raising himself on to his elbows to listen harder, he wondered if she had started to come up at all.

The drink must have dulled his hearing. As soon as he lay down again, the door to his room was being pushed back. Lot, uncovered, closed his eyes tighter, picturing her – nameless, faceless – stepping carefully around the sleeping dogs, casting off her sodden cloak with a flourish, then running both hands through her hair before touching him, touching him . . .

'Listen to me now.'

The words jolted Lot: low, breathy, earnest. He opened his eyes and saw the pale shape huddled in the room's far corner. She could have been a painting – framed by the bed's mattress, the canopy, and its two farther supports – but still too deep in the shadows for him to appreciate any detail.

'You?' he said. It sounded like a chuckle, but he could hardly have felt less amused. Almost as soon as he spoke, he began to doubt that this really was Anna. Whoever she was, she plainly needed him to be at a disadvantage.

'We must talk,' she said with a kind of rattle, as if even the thought of conversation exhausted her. Her voice was both Anna's and not Anna's. Tired but quietly controlled, as if she did not expect to be argued with.

'Who are you?' he heard himself asking.

'I am your queen . . .' Her voice had tightened. It was as if she were being gagged from the inside. She had sounded just this way when she had shirked from telling him why those shallow little tales had upset her so.

Lot narrowed his eyes but her hood was still up, swallowing her face, and he did not feel inclined to sweep across the room and unmask her. He reached down to pull up his bed covers but they were too far away.

'Those stories of the woman and her child,' she began, 'they were not just stories.'

Lot sighed just loudly enough, he hoped, to deter her from saying more without driving her away altogether. Her presence had started to stir him.

'The stories were only ever the surface,' she went on, the words seeming to come at Lot from different corners of the room. 'The woman and child exist. And now they have been seen. In a tower on your west coast.'

'And does this,' Lot breathed, 'please you?'

He heard her hoarsely echo the words 'please me?' Then she stormed forward, flung herself half-across the big bed and grabbed him between the legs.

Lot threw back his head in a beautiful confusion. The scent of her swam through him: pungent, damp-earthy. She had sounded ferocious but her hold on him was exquisitely deft. He thought she might even be dancing her fingertips along him. Anna had never done that. Anna would never do that.

'You let it happen before, my sweetheart,' she hissed from halfway up his body. 'You can't let it happen again.'

Before . . . Lot felt an unmistakable sting of guilt, quickly followed by relief that he could not remember, did not have to remember. No one did. He sensed her swelling up and over him and felt like a fledgling about to be fed a worm from its mother-provider's beak. He frowned, curling his legs at the continuing sweetness below. Whatever she was talking about, her mouth was so close to his penis that her hot breath swarmed all over it.

He reached down, grasped her by the cloak, and drew her up his body. He was weak but she did not resist as he pushed up her skirt and sat her astride him. He wrenched her undergarment aside and entered her with a deep groan.

He did not move. He did not have to. She was doing it all for him, rearing above him, and although he still could not see her face inside the hood, she seemed as monumental as Arthur's own queen. Her voice, too, moments before, had had Guenever's distinctive ring.

'Who *are* you?' he bayed at her again, but she disregarded him.

'A man on the coast has seen them: the woman and the child. You must bring him to Din Eydin, so that he can speak to us himself.'

'"Us"?'

'It is your duty to listen.' Something in her voice throbbed with an urgency that Lot was not quite prepared to laugh at.

His *duty*. And he knew that she wanted him to understand that the listening would be only the start of it.

'Logres,' she said, 'must not end in the same way as Albion.'

'Albion? . . . End? . . .'

'Through the child coming back. The son who should never have lived.'

That sting of guilt again. Such piercing, awful remorse. She seemed to be speaking directly to his conscience, a stratum of himself where there could be no forgetting. He ached to cry where he lay. He ached to come.

'Why,' he murmured, moving faster, 'have you not talked like this before?'

'Because I couldn't. Because she wouldn't let me.' She was speaking out of the side of her mouth, as if somebody else in the room might be listening. She ducked her head a little closer to Lot's. 'But I don't know how much longer I'll be here. She can do anything now. She knows . . .'

She broke off so abruptly that Lot lost his concentration and then, moments later, his erection. Peevishly, he pushed her off him.

She seemed to recede very fast, as if she were being dragged back bodily, so that when he focused on her she was standing again by the door. It was even possible, he thought, that she had never come forward.

'"She, she, she,"' he croaked. 'What in hell are you talking about? Where in hell would you be going?'

'Find the man,' she called in her tortured way, slipping from the room.

'Find your own damned man!' Lot yelled back, rolling disconsolate on to his side, and already wondering whether in yelling those words he had given her exactly what she had come for.

SIXTEEN

At first the sound was chillingly similar to the one that had drawn Nabur to the tower almost nine years before. But this time it was higher-pitched, and it was not a single scream. Yell after yell seared up from the shore to where Nabur was sawing wood: a whole quiverful of cries arrowing through him.

He did not want to stop, drop his work, and then lumber as best he could down through the forest to the causeway. He did not want to but he did. He had to. He had recognized the voice this time. It was the boy. His little eight-year-old white knight.

Nabur could not remember, afterwards, how he got down to the water so fast. Even though the din continued, he was driven on by an image of the child prostrate by the causeway, smothered in blood that had come from no cuts. He begged for it not to be true, closing his eyes with the force of his prayers. He had seen so little of the boy in the past eighteen months, but at least he had known he was there, had believed he would always be there.

He came out through the last knotted tree-roots on to the shore: just a stony sliver since the morning tide was high, although the causeway was still walkable. What Nabur saw made him gasp.

There was no blood. At least not on the boy. Not yet. He was crouched several steps down the causeway from the land. His mother stood facing him in her long thin blue night-dress, maybe ten paces in front of the tower. Her statuesque stance – legs apart, hands on hips, head to one side with her chin tilted up – went past defiance into deliberate baiting. Nabur could almost hear her whispering through a grin: *Come on, you can do better than that. Come on now, what's wrong with you . . . ?*

The boy must have fancied he heard the same thing. With another ferocious bellow, he scooped up one more pebble from the pile at his side and hurled it at her – with such force that he stumbled when letting it go and had to jerk back his shoulders to right himself on the slippery rock.

The stone flew past his mother's unflinching head. A second swiftly followed, a third, a fourth – each time launched by the cry. Not one of them hit its mark. Nabur now heard the tears of fury in the boy's string of sounds. He was frantic. Far too wild to take proper aim, although Nabur had no doubt that he was meaning to strike her.

His arm windmilled faster, looser, ever more erratically. His once-separate shouts slid together into a single whimpering screech. And at last the target turned away from him, folding her arms now in front of her. She was so confident. As she stepped back barefoot to her tower's entrance, she held herself even straighter than before, pushing back her shoulders, her head poised high with its unbound plume of dark hair spilling down.

In spite of himself, Nabur felt keenly for her then.

More than a year had passed since they had made love, but only now did he admit to himself how much he had been missing. Pebbles arced past her, some of them so big that they must have filled the boy's palm. And still the pile beside him was the size of a small cairn. Nabur, too stupefied to move in any direction, tried to imagine the boy madly amassing it, then slumped with relief when finally she shut the tower door.

The boy went on throwing until the cairn was gone. Simply sobbing now, he no longer stood to coil back his arm but stayed down almost on his haunches, like a child innocently skimming stones over water.

When he had finished, the boy flung himself down on to the causeway's greasy surface to thrash and kick and curse and wail. Nabur had seen these less vicious tantrums before. They could last far longer than he was prepared to wait; and he knew of old that he could not be consoled. And so, helplessly, he withdrew.

When he went back down, shortly after noon, he was startled all over again.

At the causeway's landward end, a paler grey and dry now that the tide had slunk back, there stood a fresh cairn of stones. It had been deftly shaped like a head facing out to sea. From the forest's edge, it looked in profile as if each component stone had been cut or milled to fit so snugly.

The tower's door was open. Both mother and son were sitting on the shore, and like the head made of stones they were staring out to sea. There was a space between them, and Nabur could see only their backs, but their silence was companionable. They seemed to be concentrating hard too, as if they were expecting some seaborne visitor. It had occurred to Nabur many times before that they might be here at the island kingdom's edge in order to be closer to a third person who might one day come by water.

The boy rose first and wandered with a proud step back down the causeway to the tower. Even from a distance Nabur could see that he had regrouped. There was an undeniably different air about him. Newly purposeful, adult in spite of his years.

Had he been a horse, Nabur might have said he had been broken. But the boy now looked properly made. More than that: he seemed somehow larger than himself, as if he were transcending not just his own flesh and bone but this whole stretch of shore as well. He was filling out the air like a cool, clear shout of authority.

Nabur had often puzzled over what he had meant by that peculiar phrase 'the next giants'. Now with a tremor he wondered if he might be looking at one. But with his whole racked being, he prayed that he was not. All he ever wanted to see was a carefree little child, a boy he could go on dreaming about as his own. *Find the son . . .*

He did not glance down at the cairn as he passed it on the way to the tower. After several minutes his mother followed, as if she had taken his lead. She skirted around the cairn, admiring the handiwork.

Nabur went back to his shelter with the boy's cries ringing in his head; for days afterwards they hung heavy on the air around him, like the smoke from some ill-judged sacrifice. But he felt more trepidation still when he remembered how the boy had looked in the calm aftermath; and then his words 'after this kingdom of Arthur's is over' began to swim back, sounding less like a strange speculation now than a grim kind of statement of intent.

He said nothing to either the woman or her son about what he had seen. He did not know how to. Besides, he could not afford to. Discussions about the boy were taboo. He had discovered that to his cost, a year and a half before, when he had dared for the first time to make a suggestion.

'Would he not benefit from being with other children?'

he had asked her, as if it had just occurred to him, when the boy was out of earshot.

She had not answered; just looked up at him without narrowing her lovely eyes with their huge pupils.

'Is he never lonely?' Nabur had babbled on, 'or bored?' But already her steady gaze was chewing at him.

He had never known anything like that gaze. She must — he told himself as he shook — only ever have looked at him sidelong before to save him from its full, ravenous force. Her eyes seemed to spit fire. Lustreless dark brown liquid flames — with teeth. He threw his hands in front of his face, but her shocked stare seemed to maul and eat his fingers' flesh too, and he felt as if he were drowning in a whirlpool of his own blood.

'Soon he will be with everyone,' she told him at last; which at the time Nabur had dismissed as histrionic nonsense, just as for years he had dismissed his own highly-charged presentiments at the boy's birth. 'And soon everyone will be with him.'

Nabur wanted no more of that. Nor did he wish to risk losing all contact with the pair, especially the boy. It had been easy to live largely without the woman afterwards. He did not need the sex; it was almost a relief to regard her now only as a daughter. But the boy was another matter again.

He had put the question about other children for a very good reason. Shortly beforehand, the boy had contrived a meeting with him in the forest. It had to have been contrived. Nabur was out collecting mushrooms at dawn. The boy knew his routine well; he knew precisely which trees Nabur always picked around, and had no other reason for being perched high in the alder.

'Will you help me?' Nabur had called up lightly.

'Do you need help?'

The old man shrugged then looked down, flushing.

'Do you need help?' he called down a second time, loudly enough to stir some doves above him. He was holding the branch on which he sat with only one hand. In the other he held a switch of hazel.

'I thought you might enjoy it. You used to enjoy it – picking with me.'

He said nothing. Nabur continued to stare down at the dewy fungus. He shook his head, shutting his eyes. 'I want you to be happy,' he then said through lips that were beginning to tremble. 'I just want you to be happy.'

'You never used to.'

Nabur glared up at that. The boy's eyes met his. His mouth was curved into a smile but Nabur saw only his great woeful eyes. He looked so very sad.

'I don't know what you mean,' he replied, breathing fast and shallow. 'Ever since you were born, I have lived for you here . . .'

'Oh, not here.' The boy then leaned so far back on the branch that Nabur instinctively waved him forward.

'You'll have to explain to me.' Nabur tried to keep his voice gentle. He wanted no fight, no crossed words. They had to stay on the same side.

'In that other time, that other world,' the boy said in a sing-song way. 'The time before this, the world before this one.'

Nabur blinked. How many times did he think he had been born? 'Tell me,' he urged him with a grin that he hoped would hide his deeper fears. 'Tell me how it was then.'

'You never spoke to me. You never smiled. You didn't care if I lived or died . . .' He broke off and twisted his neck away.

Nabur watched him run the switch over his lower row of teeth, fighting not to cry. The old man himself was close to tears now.

The boy had sought him out for a reason; this had to be it. He sniffed and maundered on: 'You gave me nothing. You even pretended that you were dead at the end — just so that I would have to go . . .'

Nabur shook his head. 'Does your mother . . . ?' he began, swallowed dryly, then started again. 'Has your mother told you these things?'

'How would my mother know?' His sad eyes blazed. 'She was driven away. That was why I had you!'

The baffled old man raised both hands to the boy. 'Come down, child. It doesn't have to be like this for you.'

But even as he said it, quakingly, he wondered how true this was. His mother seemed bent on shaping his life her own way; if she wanted it to be like this, then so it would stay. And that crushed Nabur. She was giving the boy so much that was special, but depriving him of the equally necessary humdrum. Nabur's greatest fear was that he might come to adulthood stunted by the shadow of his own sense of destiny: a sense which, without his mother's promptings, he might well not have had. And increasingly, Nabur felt that it was his own duty to disperse that shadow.

'You know nothing,' the boy smiled down. 'Not even my name.'

'Then tell me what I should know. For this world now. What I need to know.'

'Nothing,' he laughed. 'Except that you are the king's subject.' And with that, he dropped like an egg into the cushion of mushrooms, somersaulting as he landed, then springing straight back to his feet before rushing away.

*　　*　　*

After the day of the stones, two months passed before Nabur spoke again with the boy – briefly, impenetrably.

By then events were already overtaking them all. A week earlier a horseman from Din Eydin, Orcadie's capital, had ridden out to Nabur's shelter. It was early in the evening; Nabur had been preparing for bed. The stranger was sympathetic enough, and looked as if he had been in the saddle for a long time. He had brought papers, which he brandished rather apologetically, since he had guessed that Nabur could not read.

'You are to come to court. The queen herself wishes to speak with you.'

It made no sense to Nabur at first. But he spoke with the official for long enough to verify what he suspected: that he was to answer questions on the couple in the tower.

'Why me?' he asked, sensing danger, although he was not sure for whom. 'Why should they not go and speak for themselves?' And if Lot's queen is so curious, he thought, why does she not come here?

The official was swinging himself up on to his horse to leave. 'The queen is hospitable,' he said instead of answering. 'You will be treated well.'

As Nabur watched him ride off into the night, he flexed the fingers of both hands behind his back as if he were letting thirty pieces of silver drop to the ground. The court at Din Eydin, he thought. Lot the Lover. Was he the white knight's father after all – taking a furtive, belated interest in his own son? But why, then, should his summons have been sent by the queen?

Yet however long he delayed, Nabur knew that he had to go. And when he saw the boy sifting stones at the water's edge a week later, he said nothing at all about it. Even if he had planned to tell him, the boy's bizarre remarks would have made him wonder what was the point.

He stood but did not greet Nabur as he approached – his gaze was fixed past him, on the tower. The change in him, closer to, was almost tangible. It was as if the child had been driven right out of him. He looked so poised, so unnaturally assured, and still he was not yet nine years old.

More powerfully than ever before, the old man was smitten with pity, at least a part of which was for himself. You poor, poor child, he thought, longing to see tantrums and tears again, to be given the opportunity to try to comfort him. And then he was horrified to hear himself expressing his next thought aloud:

'You need more,' came the feeble protest. 'One parent is not enough.'

'That may be so,' the boy smiled at the tower. 'But two can be too many. And in a short time now, I will have none.'

'Your mother is leaving? Is that why you were so furious with her?'

'I was angry because I didn't understand. Now I know that the head must be replaced, that I am to be more than just my mother's son.' He turned his beguiling smile at last on Nabur. 'So much more.'

And when Nabur then watched him stride past, towards the tower, it was somehow like watching an entire army march away and abandon him.

SEVENTEEN

The king stood alone in the poppy field at sundown.

Before him sat the stump of a single, isolated cedar. Hours earlier he had ordered a score of Peredur's men to hack it down and have it tossed bodily over the walls of the city they were now encamped around.

Four months into this latest sleepy siege, it had seemed an oddly energetic move to make. Peredur, standing apart from the camp-fires' smoke with his unsheathed sword planted in the ground before him, could only imagine that the tree had a mystic significance for the besieged, some special talismanic status that the king had deduced and was trying to override.

No one, of course, had asked him to explain. Not one man in this force of ten thousand. Asking the king to account for any of his actions was as unthinkable as Arthur coming to them and asking for advice.

In the ninth year of the expedition, the king had grown more remote than ever. For all Peredur knew, he had been calling a massive bluff from the start of this enterprise, daring every man to demand of him what these wars were for, maybe as a test of their unswerving loyalty. The upshot was that still no one could be sure where they were headed or why, although a ship could have sailed back to Logres on the wind made by all the rumours.

Fascinated now, Peredur sank to his haunches, gripping his sword-hilt close to his face to keep his balance. Over the weeks, he had become used to the unlikely sight of the tree sprouting outside the city. Some of the archers had used it for target practice. Almost daily it had served as a turning-point in fiercely-contested horseback races between the Company's more restless members.

Now, from this angle, it looked as if the king was growing in its place: rising directly out of the stump, a great black trunk of a man, his head thrust back with its matted mane rippling in the crimson evening breeze. He seemed to be challenging the evening sky not to come any lower and touch him. Peredur, smiling to himself, thought of the sky assessing its options and deciding to hold off for a few moments more.

The king spent so much of his time alone like this. He spoke, when he spoke at all, more readily to rank and file foot-soldiers; to those stalwarts from Logres who foraged and reconnoitred for him, built special pavilions for him outside each new city, cut down inoffensive trees and never so much as glanced at him with a question in their eyes. He ate apart, drank apart. Then night after night he would stalk around his encampment, seemingly sniffing the air for clues, casting grim looks eastward. Always eastward, ever further from distant Logres. It seemed to Peredur and all the others hunched by their fires that not one man but a whole army was encircling them then; patrolling to keep intruders out, but also to keep themselves penned in.

At these quiet times – as much as in his rarer battle-frenzies – the king seemed truly to be legion. Just as the lizards here took on the colour of their surroundings, Arthur seemed able

to become the *number* of any group in opposition to him;
then he would surpass it. No one could be his equal. No
army either. Least of all his own.

Out in the field of poppies now, he kept his head flung
back – the head on which he disdained ever to wear any
protection.

Peredur raised his own eyes and saw, only then, the birds
swirling high above. Half a dozen of them, dark and silent
with startling wing-spans. There were eagles in these parts,
and eagles come out to hunt at dusk, but these looked more
like outsized ravens.

Watching them swoop and soar in a small patch of sky
around the king, Peredur became mesmerized. It was as if
Arthur had them all on invisible strings, and was choreo-
graphing their every turn. Inexplicably, the thought of this
saddened Peredur. These moments came and went; he had
learned to live with them. He never knew quite where
he stood with Arthur. None of them did. You could not
know where you stood with a man who was a multitude.

Peredur closed his eyes. When he next looked, all the
birds had been shot down – presumably, again, at Arthur's
command. Their pierced corpses lay like low cairns of coal
across the field.

The king was staring hard at the tree-stump. There was
fresh determination in the set of his shoulders. He could have
been intending to rip out the roots with his bare hands; or
setting himself to draw from it some specially symbolic sword
that at present only he could see.

Whatever he was doing, Peredur could not guess how episodes like these fitted into the expedition's broader purpose,
if at all. He often wondered whether even Arthur knew.
It seemed entirely possible that he was searching for any

diversion to make time lighter, any pretext for spinning out this peculiar armed progress.

But while it seemed inexplicable that a king should choose to become a virtual exile from his own kingdom, maybe Arthur thought that he stood to lose more by being inside it now? And who was Peredur to suggest he was wrong? For all he knew, Logres might have been remade again in Arthur's absence. The remaking could even have begun before the armies had left – certainly then the mood of its strangely-knowing people had been anticipatory.

Peredur had a fairly shrewd idea that Albion's shadow still hung heavily over the king; that his troubles were rooted in the time before Logres. Perhaps, unlike his people, he had not been allowed to forget. At moments like this, as the night finally inched down around him and the smoke from the fires curled out across the poppies, the king looked as if he remembered every bat-squeak that had been made since Creation.

The pull on Peredur's calves made him stand up from his squat. After sheathing his sword, he ran a hand through his own ratty plume of hair. The others mocked him for it, calling it effeminate because, unlike Arthur, he had no dense beard to set it off.

They themselves had all worn close crops for comfort since assembling at Camelot. Not because the climates of farther Outremer were much hotter than that of Logres, but because a shorn or even shaven head fitted better inside a battle-helmet. In the first five years Peredur had followed suit. But since then, as there had been so few pitched battles, he had seen no reason not to let his hair grow.

Frankly he was disappointed that this string of sieges had replaced the fighting – the sheer brute, blade-to-bone fighting that he had always imagined to be the essence of war. He had taken so smoothly to combat. It was like falling back into the mould from which he had first been cast. A skilled technician with sword, axe or lance, he soon found that he was able to improvise too, that he could think on his feet in the stormiest moments. Fighting at Arthur's side, he had never thought he would die. Nor, he learned later, did anyone else in the Company. Lanslod, the unofficial 'first knight', fought with a constant, awesome verve that Peredur would not have believed possible; even so, the king seemed to attract the heat of any battle. Yet Peredur never saw an enemy draw blood from him. He has no blood, the others would grin. It's fire inside him, just sulphur and flame.

But to Peredur it all came to look less elemental. Everything Arthur did on the field seemed calculated, even down to the detailed mutilations he carried out on long-dead corpses. Eerier still, by the third year it was beginning to appear to be a part of some broader collusion with the men he slaughtered. The sallow-skinned hordes did not exactly queue up to feel his blade pass through them. But nor did they flee from him in forgivable blind terror.

What was missing from the entire operation was a sense of panic among those who invariably came off worst. It seemed as if their every move had been agreed in advance; destined and accepted before the king's dust even showed over the horizon. The battles and sieges seemed more and more like showpieces, albeit with real blood and death and splintered bones. A game of chance with the numbers forever weighted in the king's favour.

To Peredur, by this ninth year, it was seeming like a dream, a great collective dream of irresistible advance and consolidation. When he lay still under the smoke-veiled stars at night, he thought he could hear the click and hissing not of insects but of new unfurling narratives. A great carpet of words being rolled across the expanses of Outremer, delivering episodes to each awaiting station. This armed royal progress felt so stately, so measured; even – crazily for a business in which so many died – so gentle.

And in each of the new-won territories, crowds of the defeated would flock to the king's standards. These more than compensated for the men of Logres who were left behind to hold the new lands: Pelles, Agravain and all the rest. At times it seemed that whole adversary armies were awaiting the moment when they could turn their coats and do homage to the king; that a show of opposing him was only a ritual for admission to his ranks.

Maybe, Peredur thought, Arthur's relentless advance could not end until everyone in his original force had been replaced by men from the growing empire. He fully expected, in time, to be granted a fiefdom like the others. Probably one of the farthest-flung from Logres. He was one of the youngest in the Company, after all; his reward would have to come later.

'Lord,' called a voice close behind him; it was one of the younger grooms. 'Your food is ready. Will you eat in the tent, or shall I fetch it to you here?'

'Bring it,' barked Peredur, surprised to see how quickly the night had thickened while his thoughts had been wandering.

But the king had stayed rooted beside the tree-stump. And now he too was being approached. Peredur peered harder. The figures crossing the field to him were female. Young, palely-dressed camp-followers: three of the hundreds who now swished like a raggedy tail behind the army wherever it went.

As they approached, they picked up the bodies of the ravens.

One girl carried a small torch. By its light, a metallic object glinted in another's hand. Seeing them, the king nodded and sat down on the stump.

The groom came back and set down Peredur's platters, canteen and goblet. Game, pastries, ripe citrus fruits. Another excellent meal. After each successful siege, the army always provisioned itself for months ahead.

Gnawing on spiced venison, Peredur supposed that the king must have summoned the whores. Unasked, they would not have presumed to come so close. There were as many rumours about Arthur and women as there were about the purpose of the war. But, so far, no one had ever reported on him making love in public.

Reaching behind him for wine, Peredur became aware that more spectators had come up quietly. From Peredur's own retinue among others; two chaplains, and some members of the Company too. Dinadan, Pellinore, Balan. He exchanged a blank look with the second of these, then turned his head back.

The women had ranged themselves around the seated king. The skin of his face was virtually all that could be seen of him now in the dark. It took Peredur a moment to be sure what the women were doing. By the light of the torch held by one, a second was combing out the king's hair while the third had begun to cut it with the scissors she had brought.

They worked slowly, doubtless terrified of making a wrong move and angering him. The cutter seemed to be stuffing each chopped hank into a pouch she wore round her waist. If any fell to the ground, the comber would retrieve it and put it with the rest. No one behind Peredur was making a sound. What they were watching seemed prosaic enough, but everything around Arthur had its own drama. Because he spoke so little, his slightest move was sifted for significance. *It's not what he says, it's what he means.* He certainly said little – and nothing at all about this expedition's goal.

Peredur again remembered what the chaplain at Camelot had said. 'Think of it as a tree.' A tree . . . An empire was being amassed on this expedition in the way that a tree-trunk gathers moss as it grows – giving the tree its distinctive appearance but having no real bearing on the tree's own purpose, which is simply to grow as far as it can. Quite possibly this tree of theirs would keep on growing until at last it reached its own highest point. A point measured not by their closeness to any goal, but by the distance they had put between themselves and Logres. A tree, after all, is measured by its height from the ground, not by its distance from the sky.

Peredur drained his goblet of the smooth wine and turned to pour some more. As he did so, he noted a muted commotion near the city's front gatehouse. There were no cries of triumph from Arthur's advance sentries – quite the opposite – but Peredur knew at once that this was another surrender. Whatever chord Arthur had struck with his treatment of the tree, its resonance now rang throughout the region.

A more stupefied kind of hush than before passed across Arthur's army as it waited for the inevitable procession. There were always twelve wizened city fathers. Always patently unarmed. And always dressed in white, dangling sprigs of olive from their loosely-folded arms.

Peredur swallowed hard as the first of the six pairs came into view, weaving their way between the fires. Ash-coloured skins, fluffs of duck-feather hair, nobly erect, by no means starvation-frail. The others followed closely. They looked – like the wraith-women attending to Arthur – as if they had been conjured up out of the night. No one spat or jeered at them as they passed. No one under Arthur's command felt that he had the right. This was a victory, to be sure, but not their own to celebrate.

The twelve knew where they were going. They stepped out into the poppy field and made directly for the place where Arthur sat. Once in front of him, they each went down on bended knee, then finally lay prostrate.

The newly crop-headed king gave no sign that he saw them. The women fluttered on around him, grey fireflies in the dark. Again Peredur felt the surge of sadness that had surprised him when the birds had been wheeling overhead. Sadness for the king whose shearing appeared more and more like a sacramental gesture – and not one made from a position of strength.

Soon they would be investing the city. Within a week they would be marching east again. The battle here had been won but Arthur seemed to be fighting his own personal war now. Perhaps he had been all along. A war that might not be winnable by him, at least not outside of Logres.

However closely Peredur watched, however hard he speculated, it still made so little sense. Something told him that it was not fathomable. That he was trying to guess the shape of a log by staring at the smoke it sent up into the sky when it burned. But he simply did not know where else to look. He turned, tossed the goblet to his waiting groom who caught it at the second attempt, and returned to the isolation of his tent.

EIGHTEEN

Nabur was received in a private inner courtyard at Din Eydin.

The equerry took him as far as the archway that gave on to it, then stepped aside to reveal a slight man and a spectral woman sitting under an awning, their seats turned in a little way towards each other. A third seat stood empty in front of them.

'Their royal highnesses,' the equerry whispered, just as Lot caught sight of Nabur and beckoned him across the closely-trimmed sunlit grass.

Nabur kept his eyes down as he ambled forward, partly out of deference, partly in wonder at the turf's impossible greenness. Already he had seen enough in this city to keep him stupefied for weeks after.

'Sit. You must sit,' he heard Lot say, a little testily but not without concern for his age and obvious frailty.

Nabur tipped his head to the beautifully-shod feet of both, then lowered himself into the high-backed settle. Only then did he look into Lot's face. A heavily-bearded but fragile face, slant-eyed under beetling brows, his skin coloured drinker's

crimson across the nose and cheeks. He merely glanced at the
queen. Lot looked unhealthy enough but she was seriously ill:
hollow-cheeked, bulbous-eyed. Nabur thought at once that
she seemed to be wearing her body, not inhabiting it.

The king smiled. 'You have been a long time coming.'

'Lord, I have been unwell.'

'Yes.' He drew out the word, and smiled again, thinly, as
if he guessed that Nabur had been unwell only with worry
at the prospect of coming here, which had some truth in it.
'But now you are cured?'

Nabur stared back. He had not been expecting to be
quizzed by the king as well as by his queen, and they were
sitting just too far apart for him to keep both in his vision
simultaneously. 'Lord,' he said, attempting gallows humour,
'I'm unwell with age. There's no cure for that.'

'The boy, then,' Lot went on, briskly, maybe in case Nabur
folded up and died on him then and there. He shifted his
bony body in his seat, as if to distance himself further from
his wife. His eyes were dark and glassy, the kind of eyes you
saw in stuffed and mounted animals. 'Talk to me about this
boy of yours.'

His smile was broader now. His teeth were large and regular, and seemed to belong behind different, more generous
lips. Then he met Nabur's eye, for just a little too long. He
seemed to be suggesting that a tacit, secondary conversation
had already begun between the two of them.

'What do you wish to know, lord?'

'Your woman in this castle, I hear, has a boy with her.
Tell me about him.'

'With respect, he is not my boy. Nor is she my woman.'

'But you have slept with her? Have you not spoken of this
to others?'

Chastened, Nabur nodded. He had talked so often about

the pair, to whoever had seemed ready to listen. There appeared to be little point in him being here now. They knew it all before he said a word; Lot already sounded suitably bored.

'And so: the boy? The one you call your knight?' He raised an eyebrow.

'He is nine years old now, lord. He is,' Nabur shrugged, 'a boy.'

'He looks like other boys, behaves like other boys?'

Nabur hesitated, then shrugged.

'And he lives alone with the woman?'

'There are just the two of them, yes.'

'Do you not find that odd? That they have no staff, no servants?'

'It's not a large place. A lodge rather than a castle. More like a hunting lodge.'

'On a causeway? What's to be hunted from there – seals?'

Lot turned away, as if to acknowledge applause from a host of shadier figures behind him. He seemed very keen to establish that, in spite of all his questions, he had little personal interest in the matter. In fact he gave the strongest impression that nothing in the world could hold his attention for long. He looked physically tired of being alive. With those inert eyes he also kept darting unreadable looks at his queen.

Nabur was beginning to find it hard to breathe. His throat felt parched; pinpricks of pain blossomed on his chest. Then he became aware of the queen leaning forward. Her thin-fingered hands were turned palm-up on her knees as if to invite him to dump a confession there.

'They are different, this woman and her child, no?' Her voice sounded far tighter than Lot's. She could almost have been pleading; and now he knew that they were coming to the real business, Lot having merely made the overtures. 'Different?'

Nabur kept his head down and made as if to shrug. Different? Of course they were. But the boy's differences still mattered far less to him than the ways in which he could be mistaken for any other lad of his age. Without his mother's coaching, he would surely not have been 'different' anyway.

'How do they support themselves?' Lot cut in. 'Do you provide for them?'

Nabur frowned. He began to shake his head but then stopped. He did not know the answer. Truly he did not. The couple were somehow self-sufficient. In the boy's own language, *the giants meet our needs*. Nabur met Lot's eye and again found that odd look of collusion. Nabur wondered then whether he was here to provide Lot with an alibi. Was the king wanting him to claim all responsibility for the child – conception, birth, unkeep – and thereby exonerate himself entirely in front of his suspicious wife? Lot the lover. Lot the lecher. But he looked way past caring about the effect his behaviour had on anyone.

The king widened his eyes at Nabur, apparently inviting him to make some clinching statement. Yet Nabur also felt that simply by saying nothing, he was telling them everything they needed to know. His guilty confusion was precisely what they wanted.

The queen then rummaged under her voluminous skirt to produce what looked like a book. She stood, stepped closer to Nabur, stooped, and unhinged the object in her hand which turned out to be a diptych.

'Do they look like this?' she asked confidentially, almost as if the king were no longer with them. Nabur gauged from the way her voice and hands trembled that a good deal rested on his answer. He looked at the image to which she was pointing. It appeared to be a Virgin and Child.

'Maybe they did,' he said, peering closer, 'at one time . . .'

'Maybe, maybe, maybe!' Lot erupted so unexpectedly loudly that his queen started and stepped back, taking her icon with her. 'And only you would know, wouldn't you?'

Nabur looked up bulbous-eyed to find Lot stabbing a finger in his direction. 'Only you would be in a position to say. Isn't that so?'

Nabur touched his temple, panting now. 'Lord, I don't quite follow . . .'

'No. You don't follow. You lead – with all your shameless fantasies! "Knight" indeed. And you, no doubt, were his squire – when you weren't servicing his sweet young mother!' He guffawed unconvincingly. 'It's true that men here are few and far between nowadays, but even so . . .'

He broke off to appraise him scathingly, then beckoned behind himself.

Nabur looked in appeal to the queen, who sat back down as if she were being pushed. She in turn looked at her husband for an explanation.

'Some might accept your stories at face value,' Lot went on, directing his words more to the queen than to Nabur, as two liveried men padded up to the awning. 'I sent out to have them corroborated, when I was told that you were to come.' He waved at his retainers, the older of whom had a lazy eye. 'Speak.'

'Lord, we followed the coast for a week to either side of where this man has his hovel. We found nothing. No dwelling. No couple.'

Nabur gaped at them. They were indeed familiar. Twice he had seen them from his shelter; perhaps he had even spoken to the one with the eye; the usual boasts.

Lot dismissed them. 'This woman and child do not exist. No one else in your region has ever seen them. There is not even a tower. Why in Christ should a tower stand on a causeway? You are a laughing-stock, man. People encourage you to speak about these things only to amuse themselves.'

He glanced once more at his wife in dead-eyed triumph. She clutched the diptych close to her throat, as if he might be about to snatch at it. This was plainly as much of a surprise to her as it was to Nabur.

The older man strained forward. It was all too far away from what he had been anticipating. Too far away from the truth. But he could see that Lot had been made rabid by more than the fact of the boy. He seemed affronted by, or possibly even envious of Nabur's devotion to him, his boastful but life-affirming pride in him, his *belief*.

Nabur's breath ballooned inside him. He felt stoppered at every orifice. And when at last he managed to part his lips, nothing approaching a word came out. Lot saw his difficulties and his expression softened.

'These tales have been going round for years,' he elaborated, 'although, as far as I'm aware, no one has ever claimed to have taken part in one. They mean nothing. Less than nothing.' He clenched and opened his fist to illustrate this. 'They meet a sort of spiritual need in the more simple-minded, that's all. Woman! Child! There are even some who refer to them like royalty . . .' At that, he paused and knitted his brows. 'Do you need water? Your colour's gone.'

Nabur shook his head vehemently. His mouth already felt full of liquid. Fantasies. Tales. No tower . . . Lot went ahead and signalled for refreshment to be brought up.

In a daze Nabur watched two butlers arriving with an array of wineskins and drinking vessels. Then the queen stood, shuddering.

'You can't leave it like this,' she rasped at Lot, still holding the hinged altarpiece to her throat. 'Won't you see that there could *be* no stories if the pair of them weren't alive? Somewhere, here, among us now. The stories are like their shadows, like smoke from their fire. Oh, they're real enough. People sense them, talk about them. But he,' she flung out an arm at Nabur, 'he has seen them. He's been with them! Real real, real.'

She took a step towards the startled Lot before continuing. 'It's her, don't you see? Won't you remember? Morgan.' She shook her head, grinning at the sheer brute obviousness of it. 'And the boy – again – it's Mordred!'

On the last word, one of the butlers lost his grip on the wineskin from which he was decanting. The contents gushed out, spattering the seated king's shin and foot. Lot paid no heed.

Nabur watched a cloud pass over his face as he stared up at the queen. Her lips were still pulled back in a rictus from having said the second name with such strenuous emphasis. Nabur sat transfixed. The strange name's two syllables seemed to string themselves out and hang like black bunting between her own head and her husband's.

Then, just for a moment, the courtyard felt impossibly crowded; the queen's face changed, and Nabur was looking into the eyes of his woman in the tower. And when the queen's features reappeared, a bead of blood was standing on a scar he had noticed before, just below her hairline.

The butler, muttering, was fussing over Lot's sodden leg. Lot brushed him away. 'Leave me,' he ordered a little shakily. 'Both of you, all of you. Leave us now.'

The butlers withdrew, and only then did Nabur realize that he too had been sent packing. He began to rise, but the queen intervened.

'He must stay,' she cried, but the fight had gone out of her. 'He's told us nothing yet.'

Lot waved Nabur away without looking at him. 'Go. Now. Damn you, go! And you, lady, sit.'

The queen gazed forlornly at Nabur as if she expected him to argue, or force the king to listen to whatever else he had to say. The blood had begun to dribble down her brow. This, Nabur knew, was the wrong place for him to be. He continued, gasping, to rise, found his balance, then headed back across the grass to the arch.

He knew that – by speaking, by not speaking, by coming, by going – he had betrayed someone that afternoon. And he prayed that it had been only himself.

At the lawn's perimeter he paused, ostensibly to catch his breath. He glanced over his shoulder. The queen was seated again under the awning, Lot stood above her. The words Nabur heard gave a clear indication of what he was telling her. 'No son . . . No child . . . I'll belive in no child . . .' But the language of his body was what stuck in Nabur's mind as he shuffled on to where his horse waited to take him home. He was gesticulating so leadenly, once even raising his knee, then stamping with the other foot. It was as if he had been deprived of some vital all-purpose limb which left him with only the normal – hopelessly inadequate – four to work with.

Mordred . . . the old man repeated two, maybe three hundred times on his slow, distracted ride back to the coast. And eventually it began to hit him on the quick.

When the queen had said the name, it felt like someone at the start of the world letting all the captive winds out of a bag. 'Morgan' meant nothing to Nabur, but the other name was different. When he said it even half-aloud, it seemed to glow darkly on his tongue, to leave its own ashy aftertaste. And when, towards evening, his mouth felt over-moist again and he spat, he saw black streaks of blood in the spittle.

By the time his shelter came into sight he was feeling faint. But he had to go down at once to the tower. Still seething with the idea of betrayal, he felt that in some way he owed it to the couple to talk about his inquisition at Din Eydin. He had to tell them everything. What they might then tell him in return was purely up to them. As before, he would ask for nothing.

No light showed from the tower when he reached the forest's edge. The night was so dark, he stumbled twice over rocks on the shore as he approached. Already the tide was close enough to dampen his ankles.

Struggling for breath, he forged a long way along the shore. Too far. He knew that he had passed the point where the causeway began. But the water never usually swept in to cover it. In panic he turned and began to stumble back the way he had come, squinting out through the blackness to where the tower should have been.

But there was no tower now. No causeway. Just as Lot had trumpeted.

The grimly nihilistic king of Orcadie had sent out men to look for the landmarks. Had he perhaps then sent another party afterwards to dismantle them? Or had he by sneering at 'spiritual needs' simply wished them out of existence – and Nabur's beloved child and its mother along with them? If so, then Nabur had his own obligation to wish them back into being.

The queen in her way had also helped to make this happen. They are different . . . no? Different, different; tangling them up in the mystic, giving them a spurious otherwordly veneer. Yes, the pair was different but only as different as others – queens, rumour-mongers or whoever – might desire them to be.

Nabur fell to the stones and curled up on his side. He was so tired that he slept without moving until morning. He dreamed of being with his woman and boy, that he was lodged tight and happy between them on a shore that stretched out into eternity. He knew that they lived, that they were real and somewhere near. For him, the boy in particular had been so much of this world that he could have been hacked out of it like peat. 'Stories' were neither here nor there.

On waking to their absence, Nabur knew what he had to do.

Find the son . . . Find the son . . . His search after the Great Remaking now showed itself to have been little more than a rehearsal. His true quest was about to begin. He swore that he would not rest until he had found them: two flesh-and-blood people; a woman and a boy; a boy he now found hard to think of as anyone's son but his own.

NINETEEN

'. . . Betray . . .' said the king through the hubbub. He made it sound as if he were clearing his throat, as if it were not really a word at all.

It was always this way when Arthur spoke. His talk seemed to bypass the ear and make straight for his hearers' insides. Peredur felt the churning at once. Like everybody else, he stared stunned at the king's wide, unaccustomed smile.

The pared down Company was seated at its tenth Spring 'court' since leaving Logres. Every May-time, if the advancing army happened to be occupying a suitable city, a crude approximation of Camelot's Round Table would be hacked out and sat around. If the army was on the move or encamped, the two dozen knights would simply sit in a circle on the ground.

Annually they would then pass an hour in solemn commemoration, although of what or whom, Peredur had no idea. Often he wondered if the king was again testing their loyalty, daring them to question his grander strategy, and privately despising their subservience – because as a rule the

Company would sit in unbroken silence, like so many cairns of stones around him.

It was possible that the ritual had originally been religious. But not any more. Like the strays, although perhaps less surprisingly, the expedition's chaplains had all long since slipped away *en route*.

Years earlier, some of the knights had speculated that Arthur was leading them on a kind of crusade to shore up the Christian faith. The opposite now seemed truer. As they drove on closer to the land of Christ's birth, each new region of Outremer seemed more intensely Christian than the last. In every seized settlement there were always plenty of chapels, churches, even cathedrals – all in regular, popular and apparently unthreatened use.

Even here in this huge desert city-state, invested only days before with its throng of urbane, brightly-dressed citizens, there was a towering, domed Holy of Holies. Inside it, the local clergy were already preparing for a service of thanksgiving to its new, barely Christian masters.

Meanwhile here in the citadel, the customary vigil was being held by the current Company: those few original knights who were still following the king, plus newcomers like Palomides who had been raised up along the way, with a leavening of elevated commoners from Logres. As ever, a place in the circle had been left empty directly opposite Arthur – the space filled by Brumart at the first Round Table.

The strays used to call this the 'perilous seat'. None in the Company took any real notice of that. They were less concerned about danger than sheer boredom. The king would sit in a silence so deep that they could hear their own hearts sinking, with a look so remote that his eyes could have been two stars. But this year, the tenth, was different. This year at last the king had spoken. 'One of you will betray me,' he had said to their stupefied faces. 'One of you,' he repeated, slowly looking about him, to show that he was not simply pronouncing a seasonal biblical text.

A moment's pause followed, while the enormity of this sank in. Then a storm of protest erupted.

Peredur was as vociferous as anyone, but even while he yelled and banged the cedar Table, he also looked hard at the crop-headed king: wrapped around in his increasingly shamanistic-looking cloak of hair, now bristling too with ravens' feathers.

Inside it, he sat oddly on his makeshift throne, his body uncharacteristically slumped, as if his head had been disconnected from his shoulders, then poised precariously back on top. And the tone of his statement had been peculiar, sounding less like a conviction or a prophecy than a weary kind of plea. Almost as if he were asking one of them, there and then, to come up and kiss him on the cheek.

Peredur was shaken by this sad, resigned self-pity. More shockingly still, he also sensed that here, for the first time, he was hearing the true voice of Arthur. His mind went back to the countless times when the king had eyed his captains with what, in a lesser man, would surely have been called suspicion. He had looked at them all with such deep mistrust, as if afraid that, inexorably, they were being seduced from their allegiance to him. Maybe that was even why he had never shared the secret of this expedition.

But Peredur doubted that anyone present had been turned. Who else was there to follow except Arthur, especially so far away from home? But he could see that the king's concern was real – and quite possibly based on the conviction that for some reason he deserved betrayal. The image of a ruler in flight, living on borrowed time in self-imposed exile, again struck Peredur forcibly.

The king's eyes scanned the Company. Peredur looked around himself too. Lanslod, he noticed as the din of denial subsided, was staying silent.

Arthur's glassy stare fell on his first knight. Lanslod met it levelly, but Peredur could not be sure of the expression on his face. He thought he detected disappointment rather than defiance; and some fear as well, not of any reprisal, but of his once god-like monarch's abrupt reduction.

'You,' Arthur nodded at Lanslod. 'You say nothing to me.'

'What would you have me say, lord?' Lanslod's voice was low but steady.

Arthur nodded again, indicating the still-echoing tumult. To Peredur his every movement seemed stiff and difficult. He looked very old, although he was still only fifty, and besides, Arthur had always aged differently from other men. Lanslod finally tried to smile, to shrug off the incident. But Arthur's eyes stayed on him, mortified, pleading.

'Can you say nothing to assure me?'

Lanslod stared back. This was so unlike the Arthur that any of them knew. Peredur could plainly see that Lanslod – loyalest of the loyal – was refusing to answer because by answering he would only dignify the question. And it was impossible for him to acknowledge insecurity in his king. Arthur – for Lanslod, for them all – had to stay undiminished, above the petty panics of ordinary kings. Peredur began to smart at Lanslod's treatment. He resented the king for putting him through so pointless an ordeal.

'When?'

Peredur heard the word almost before he realized that he himself had said it. He flushed as it died on his lips, but even when the king's eye moved back to him, he felt invigorated. He would speak. Someone had to. They had all been craven for long enough. And perhaps, finally, the great warlord's insecurity was justified and needed to be exposed.

Arthur crushed his eyebrows closer together and narrowed the already slitted eyes beneath them. Peredur leaned forward in his chair as if he were being tugged bodily by the Lord of War's inquisitive look. The younger man had never known such a look. It seemed to make any normal kind of conversation irrelevant. The king was reading his beating blood.

'When, lord,' Peredur stammered on regardless, 'when would you be betrayed?'

'On our return now.' The king's retort was quick and sure. The hush around him spread out until even the hall's stone walls seemed to be listening.

'To Logres?'

Arthur widened his eyes, scathingly, as if he were inviting Peredur to suggest some alternative destination.

Peredur swallowed, aware that everyone's eyes but Arthur's were fixed on the impromptu Table. At a word from the king, any one of them would have risen, seized Peredur and hacked him apart. The majority would probably have found it easier to do that than let the tension caused by his questioning continue to mount. Peredur swallowed again.

'The wars then, my lord, are over?'

In his nervousness he spoke too loud, and sounded – he thought – like a honking goose. But under his nerves he was quite clearly calculating: so this is where he will leave me; this will be my own little fiefdom, here, ten years on from the land of promise.

Arthur closed his eyes, blinked them open, then closed them again for what felt like an eternity. Crazily Peredur wondered if the king might be struggling to hold back tears

– or, more crazily still, that he was trying to force them out. He appeared to be dredging up an answer from so deep inside him, that years of his life had been spent concealing it. But at length, with his eyes still clamped tight, he merely nodded.

A rustle of wonder passed round the Table, although no one dared speak out.

'We have achieved our goal then, lord?' Peredur had to press on. The 'we' came out – unconsciously – with a sceptical edge. It was as if the words as well as their tone were saying themselves. But more than just the wars seemed to have ended here.

With a sigh Arthur hunched himself lower in his seat. He had turned his face away from Peredur now and towards the shadows. But wherever his eyes were looking, he was searching inside himself too; here was a man cut open and trying to read his own entrails. 'What do you ask?' he said absently.

'If the aims of this campaign have now been met.'

The king smiled, quietly, inwardly. At that point a new voice cut into the silence from Peredur's left.

'These questions are inappropriate.' It was Lanslod. It could only be Lanslod.

The younger knight turned to him and managed a smile. His heart felt faint but his tongue took him on: 'Inappropriate to what? To whom? To all the men who have died in the fighting? To everyone we left behind in Logres? You speak only for yourself, Lanslod, and maybe with good reason. Maybe you know already the answers to these "inappropri-ate" questions . . .'

'I know enough,' Lanslod growled, turning aside in his seat as if to speak outside Arthur's earshot, 'if I know that I am the king's subject.'

'Ha!' Peredur, warming further, waved a hand at the

Table in frustration. He could not understand why he felt so invulnerable, at least in this gathering. And to all intents and purposes the Company now consisted only of the king, his first knight and Peredur himself. For all the difference they made, the rest could already have been shipped back to Logres.

'Say, then,' Arthur called across to Peredur. 'What do *you* believe was the aim of these campaigns?'

Peredur bit his lip. The word 'aim' seemed absurd. To have an aim, they should have been looking forward, but all the while they had been looking back. *Think of it as a tree* . . . A rose-tree, maybe; a tree whose roots stretched right back to the Eden that was Logres. As they went along they had been pruning the branches – specifically so that countless more blooms could come through to be cut, an endless supply to be slashed at.

Peredur ran a finger down his thin nose. A single phrase rang in his head. Blood without cuts, blood without cuts . . . When he answered he looked at Lanslod. Even now he could not say this and keep his eyes on the king: 'I don't believe that we have fought *for* anything at all. Nor, truly, have we been fighting against anyone. This hasn't been warfare – not as war is usually known. There's been blood, yes, but it's been blood without cuts.'

He paused, so dazed by the sound of what he had said, that he repeated the phrase which had come to him from nowhere, turning at last to Arthur with a madly conclusive smile. 'My lord, blood without cuts.'

It was so quiet in the hall that Peredur heard his king take a breath, then lengthily exhale through his beard. Everyone else but Lanslod sat rigid, each man having made his own decision to hear no more, in case the mere fact of having heard it might one day be held against him.

'Blood without cuts,' Lanslod echoed in a voice unlike his own: high, lilting, almost feminine. And when Peredur glanced his way he frowned back ferociously, as if someone had spoken through him, used him as a medium.

Meanwhile Arthur began to nod. The nod of a person who has heard the worst confirmed. So powerfully ordinary a response that Peredur brimmed with pity. The talk of betrayal could well have been a ploy, simply to bring matters to a head. Here was a man who had admitted to himself that he had come as far as he could. Whatever — or whoever — he had tried so hard to escape from in Logres had reached out and reclaimed him.

But while the immediate hostilities might have ended, the king seemed to have entered a state of undeclared war against himself. With each moment now his aura seemed to be dimming, the extra dimensions of him to be shaved away. A fist inside Peredur tightened, suggesting that he was responsible. But he knew in his heart he was not that important. All he could do was watch, think, ask, press.

'Lord,' he said hoarsely, leaning so far forward across the Table that he could have been trying to reach the king with his outstretched fingers, 'where is the real war being fought?'

Still nodding, Arthur beckoned behind him to one of the foot-soldiers who stood guard. Puzzled, the man stepped forward. He paused within the king's speaking range behind the throne, but was then waved closer still. He stopped at the king's right side, his jutting jaw visibly twitching.

With awesome speed Arthur shot out his great hand. Through the surcoat and mail, he grabbed a fistful of the soldier's sexual organs. The man doubled up in silence, seeming almost to drape himself over the king's extended arm. 'There?' Arthur hissed at them all with flashing black eyes. 'You think that there is the real battleground? Is that what you think?'

When he took his hand away, the man began to fall helplessly but Arthur managed to grip him again, first by a twisted-up hank of his hair, then by clamping his huge hand around his head.

'No. It's here.' He shook the head as if it were disembodied. 'Here!'

Then he dashed the man down and rustled to his feet. The whole Company stood.

'You,' he said to Peredur, 'and you' – he pointed at Lanslod without looking his way – 'will ride on ahead to Logres, with the news of our return.'

As soon as he had spoken, the life seemed to go out of him again, and he drifted from the hall like smoke from a fire that was sullenly refusing to catch.

TWENTY

It took them much longer than Lanslod had expected to return to the north-western shores of Outremer.

The army's outward journey had taken ten years. But then they had travelled only as fast as their slowest siege machines, and spent countless months reducing the towns and cities on their route. Lanslod had thought that he and Peredur alone would tear up the ground. He had hoped to be setting sail for Logres within six months. In the event, it took a year.

Part of the blame lay with Peredur. Not because he rode too slowly; on his day, he could easily outstrip the older Lanslod. But time after time he contrived delays – because, Lanslod knew, he was afraid.

Lanslod had doubts of his own. Like Peredur, he could not know whether Arthur's sending them on ahead was a punishment or a privilege. He guessed it might be neither. In the first months Peredur often tried to draw him into talk about what might lie waiting in Logres. He seemed to think that Lanslod had answers to it all: the war, the king's condition, the nature of the Great Remaking, that last enigmatic Round Table, even Lanslod's own implicit status as heir apparent.

With regard to this last, Lanslod had threatened Peredur with violence if he brought it up again. It was something he tried never to think about, just like the king's own senseless notion that he was going to be betrayed.

Finally Peredur learned to keep his peace. But this made him all the keener to linger at every provincial court in the new empire at which they stopped on their way – sounding out other Company members. Although Lanslod thought these conversations had no useful end, he did not force the pace. In truth, the closer they came to Logres, the less eager he too became to reach their journey's end.

He had no picture of how the kingdom might have changed. So many years had passed since he had made his reconnaissance, he could barely remember what the remade land had looked like. There were times when he wondered if it would even still be there. It had been proclaimed as the kingdom made for the king. What then happened if the king was never in it?

The queen, though, would surely have maintained a form of status quo. The queen with the Regent. While away on campaign, Lanslod had rarely given a thought to either. But mile by mile on this protracted journey back, the images of both grew sharper in his mind. It was as if in forging closer to home, he was being washed by the farther tides of their authority. And he began to see their faces fused, always in an expression of deep anxiety.

By the time they were nearing the north-western coast, Lanslod's dreams were full of the queen. On the day when at last they arrived at the port, and they were waiting for the cargo-boat's master to prepare them quarters, Peredur asked Lanslod if his sleep had been recently troubled. Lanslod denied it briskly.

'But have you dreamed differently in the past few weeks?'

Peredur pressed, his meal and drink untouched in front of him in the master's lodging. Like Lanslod, he had worn only simple riding gear since departing from the army; yet wherever they went they were greeted by name. 'Have you had dreams, recurrent dreams, that you've never had before?'

Lanslod looked into his earnest eyes under that riot of uncut hair. After so long, he knew that Peredur rarely expected him to reply. Lanslod had come to treat him like an over-active pup: a shaggy, ill-disciplined infant of almost thirty. 'Have you?' he surprised the younger man by asking.

'Well, yes. I keep seeing myself in a particular stretch of the kingdom, of Logres. A stretch that I don't think I've ever been to . . .' He went on to describe, at great length, a region of rolling hills and valleys that sounded curiously similar to Logres' western peninsulas known as Galles, although Lanslod merely tilted his head and widened his eyes.

'And are you happy there?' Lanslod smiled, pushing away the bones of the roasted bird that he had picked clean. 'In your dreams?'

'I'm not *un*happy . . .' He tailed off, blinking in puzzlement.

Once aboard the boat, Lanslod left Peredur to yap at the master, a taciturn Logretian himself, but responsive enough under questioning.

Lanslod could not help noticing that he, like everyone else they met on their route, asked nothing about the campaigns. It was as if their sequence of successes had been taken for granted, or that it just did not matter in the broader scheme of things.

When Peredur quizzed him on the state of Logres, he shrugged and claimed that he seldom now travelled far inland from the port of Dubris where he docked. But he mentioned in passing – as if Peredur already knew – that the queen now had her court in Lundein, not Camelot.

Lanslod wandered out of earshot, patiently pacing the decks as if that might bring him back to Logres quicker. An hour or so later he overheard Peredur in further conversation, this time with the helmsman, whose answers again were respectfully curt. The subject now was the 'Glass Castle'.

On his southward journey to Camelot before leaving Logres, Lanslod had several times heard mention of this fairytale. Each time, the 'Castle' was said to be located nearby. No one ever seemed to care when he said that in other communities, elsewhere in the kingdom, there was similar talk. It seemed to have no specific place of origin or belonging. It was almost possible that it moved around Logres like a flight of birds with the seasons.

Peredur was feigning ignorance, his usual gambit with the credulous. '. . . So what property does it have, this castle, other than being built of glass?'

'All who approach it become a part of something larger.'

'Just by approaching? Not going inside?'

'Yes.'

'So who lives there?'

'The lady and her boy.'

Peredur nodded. 'And is it true that the Castle is there at some times, but not at others? I think I heard that once.'

'No. It is always there.'

'Then why does no one go inside?'

'No one has any need to. We find all that we need at its perimeter.'

'All that you need?'

'Yes.'

'And there is a lady, with a child?'

'The boy is growing. He is close now to becoming a man.'

'What do they do?'

'They are there, for us. That's all. That's everything.'

'Would I be able to see them?'

The helmsman pointed. 'Can you see that mast?'

Peredur turned, saw it and nodded.

'Then yes.'

'And they can be seen anywhere in Logres?'

He nodded as he moved aside to let his night relief take a turn at the helm. 'Most clearly,' he said over his shoulder as he stepped down for some rest, 'when you look to the skies . . .'

Peredur glanced at Lanslod. The man had given every answer without a flicker of humour. At some level, he had to believe in what he was saying. And curiously, his belief had struck an unwanted chord inside Lanslod himself; a chord which resounded more loudly, the closer he came to the rearing white cliff-faces which marked the shores of long-abandoned Logres.

Their disembarkation at Dubris was anticlimactic.

Lanslod had guessed that word of their arrival would have travelled on ahead, and a party would be waiting. But only the night received them home.

He looked around cautiously from the quayside, unsure quite what else he had been expecting to find, and at a loss to describe quite what he was feeling.

This was the port from which they had all originally left for Outremer. The nearer narrow streets which he could see looked unaltered – but why, he asked himself, should they not have done? Peredur was strangely quiet. Lanslod glanced his way and saw that his ear was cocked.

Lanslod turned and listened too. The sound of song was drifting from a steepled church. Slowly it gathered in volume, although the words remained unclear. It was no hymn that the two knights knew; and this seemed to be an unusual hour to be holding a religious service.

The port workers knew both 'Sir' Lanslod and 'Sir' Peredur by sight and were duly deferential. Neither man had heard that particular honorific in over a decade.

'That singing,' Peredur said to one, 'what is it?'

'The celebration of the Son,' came the answer at once. And the gesture which the stooped old man then made before scurrying off – a touch to his left upper arm – could just as easily have been a form of salutation as the scratching of an itch.

Belatedly a senior port official rode up as they awaited their own horses' emergence. He welcomed them without dismounting, and directed them to a suitable hostelry for the night, several miles up the main road to Lundein.

'In the morning,' he concluded, 'you can then go your separate ways.'

'Separate?' It was Peredur who spoke.

The official half-grinned. 'You to Galles, and Sir Lanslod to Lundein where the queen is now in residence. Is that not your plan?'

'We thank you,' Lanslod intervened, before Peredur could speak. He urged the younger man away to where their horses had appeared.

They spoke only after riding a mile or two inland. A scatter of lights in the distance marked some houses, among which stood the hostelry. It was so dark that Lanslod could not see his companion on his black stallion.

'We ride together to Camelot in the morning,' he said with such finality that Peredur did not even reply. They continued on their way for some distance, found themselves a different inn, and turned in immediately.

Lanslod lay awake in his room until shortly before dawn. At the foot of his bed was a small portable altar, but instead of an icon of Christ, a hinged diptych stood upon it. One panel featured a naked Virgin and Child; the other showed a hunched young figure with a knife. Unsettled by it, even in the darkness, Lanslod finally rose and snapped it shut.

Because he had not yet seen Logres by daylight, he could not fully believe that he was here. Nor had he recognized the atmosphere since their arrival. Plainly the kingdom had remained intact in Arthur's absence, yet its air felt subtly alien – as if it had been invaded from within, somehow occupied from the inside. The singing at the port church, which still resounded in his head, seemed to be intimately bound up with this.

And the port official's remark also continued to trouble him. The man must have been confused by some old story of the strays. It was true that in Albion Lanslod had briefly been assigned to Guenever; and he knew that Peredur's own origins lay in the west (hence, he had earlier presumed, the younger knight's dreams). But what did this have to do with the present, in Logres?

Lanslod drifted off to sleep imagining the past seeping slowly up out of the earth to claim them. Not just their personal pasts but something larger: the past of the island itself, the return of that old dark night, seeking vengeance on the bright new day of Logres by which it had been eclipsed.

Then he dreamed, of a woman.

For a moment she looked like Elayne, but only because Lanslod wanted her to. In truth she was darker, more statuesque, altogether more forbidding. *Morgan* . . . he thought, from deep in his own lost past; and as soon as the name had come to him, it vanished again.

She was floating past this inn on a bier, laid out as if she were dead. Lanslod watched her travel fast upstream, surrounded by wild flowers, lit by her own inner glow. A golden armlet decorated her upper left arm. No one else was with her.

Lanslod followed, trampling the rushes along the bank, planning to dive in and swim after her, although he was not sure why. Then a boy called out, close by. Little more than a whisper: 'You've returned.'

Lanslod let his eyes veer away from the bier. He went to the boy on the bank, and sat next to him.

The child was as old as the wars had been long. War-child, Lanslod thought, quickening. He was smiling, hairless, his limbs smooth and soft-looking, his flesh very pale where it showed.

Lanslod remembered the woman he knew as Elayne when he had left her. Standing with her back to him, holding herself oddly. Heavily pregnant, even then. Pregnant by some other man but still this war-child was Lanslod's son. Suddenly he needed this to be his son: the extra presence he had sensed when he had spent his night in the tower. In the dark he almost shone; here was everything that Lanslod had always forfeited, simply through being the man that he was. A son, a son. This was what he most wanted for himself.

He began to speak about the campaign. And only then did the last eleven years gather meaning. It poured from him like a story, as if he had not been involved himself. The pacing, the rhythms. It was as if he had been telling it all his life. Not living it. Telling it. And Lanslod realized that the boy to whom he was now so close had never been far away. This boy – and to a lesser degree his mother – had always been somehow at hand.

'And you,' he wanted to say, 'how has it been with you? With your mother?'

But he knew that was pointless. All this child had ever

done was wait for his return, so that this could happen now
– just as the whole kingdom had been in a busy kind of
abeyance during the absence of the king. And the child and
the kingdom were inextricably linked, he felt sure.

Lanslod talked and the river flowed past, bringing the
story and taking it on. So much was happening here. Such
a vast transaction, and Lanslod did not know if he himself were one of the hagglers or the item being haggled
over.

As the words tumbled out, he looked ahead. He would stay
with the boy. He was free to do that now. It was as if he had
proved himself on the campaign; won an empire for Arthur
and this freedom for himself. He badly wanted to stay; being
with the child made him feel so much bigger. But already
he felt one burden of guilt slipping away and another being
strapped on in its place. A new and potentially crushing sense
of responsibility.

The boy was so attentive, his knees raised to his cheeks
while he plucked at the dew-soaked grass between them.
Plucked without tearing it from the ground. It was as if he
could not afford – or was not meant – to leave any physical
evidence of his presence. His footfalls doubtless would leave
no imprint in the wet river earth.

He was so beautiful. Lanslod wanted to know him by
a name, and the name which came to him first felt so
smooth. Galaad. He knew that was not his true name, just
as 'Elayne' had been no more than his own appreciation of
the mightier woman behind her. But for Lanslod's purposes
alone, to assuage all his own personal longings, this boy could
be Galaad.

Then Lanslod became aware of how his monologue sounded.
As if he were offering this young Galaad an alibi, a story made
up to cover his own tracks. But there was nothing to be done

about that. In a way, all along, he had not really left Logres. None of them had.

'. . . It was a journey,' he said, remembering what Peredur had suggested at the last Round Table. 'The fighting almost didn't matter. It was the travelling that was at the heart of it. A journey that went all the way from here to there, then back again to here . . .'

The war-child Galaad put out his hand and brushed the back of Lanslod's wrist. The king's first knight realized that he had been weeping as he spoke. The hair on his arm was glittering with tears. He thought he should stop weeping in front of the beautiful boy, but he made no real effort.

And still he went on telling. He had gone away like the outline of a man and come back dark and solid. Before, he had sieved experiences, now he was crusted with deposits. And he shied away from none of the grislier aspects.

The boy seemed to coax his speech into the right channels just by sitting so quietly. At times Lanslod thought that he was not so much telling Galaad things he did not know, as presenting to him a report in which the boy might point out errors.

His splendid head moved occasionally, not in time with any obvious point that Lanslod was making. He had a knife in his hands with which he toyed absently. The knife looked familiar to Lanslod. It seemed to belong in the same story that he was telling, but he could not think where. And again, the mighty woman's name momentarily surfaced: *Morgan* . . .

Then as if in an answering echo, the marvellous child's true name too began to sound, a name which went with the knife; but it faded away, because Lanslod would not, could not, hear it yet.

The boy seemed lightly to be drawing a shape with his knife on the grass. Lanslod was seduced into following the calm, deft movements of the blade. His own voice continued to sound, but as if it were issuing from the ground or the air, or even from the river itself. Lanslod had no control over it. He had ceased to be interested in it, or in the story it was telling.

All that mattered was the slow, deliberate motion of the knife. And when Lanslod glanced up, Galaad had gone – as Lanslod had dreaded that he might – but the knife still moved. Making a shape, making a shape . . .

Lanslod woke up in the dust outside the inn.

His head was resting awkwardly against a water-butt. In the grey dawn light two tiny girls were watching him from a doorway, giggling together. Stiffly he stirred and at once they turned and scrambled away.

His cheeks and beard were damp with more than dew. Wiping himself on his sleeve, he noticed a figure etched very delicately into the earth near his feet. A circle with a line across it. He knelt and peered closer. The circle was in fact a dragon devouring itself. The line was a perfect representation of the knife that he had seen with the boy in his dream.

He rose, carefully avoiding the emblem, remembering nothing of what he had said to his dream son, but already feeling shrunken to have lost him all over again.

Part Four

NIGHT

TWENTY-ONE

Lot had to wheedle, plead and even weep before his own lowliest servants finally agreed to load him like a sack of brittle sticks into a litter and carry him out to the rose garden.

'My lord,' a chambermaid gasped as he passed through the doorway, preceded by both his excited dogs, 'the physicians forbade this.'

'Physicians!' Lot wheezed behind his hand, which by instinct he then turned over to see how big were the blood flecks in his spittle.

He had allowed no doctor near him for months. They did not know what was killing him, and their attempted remedies were just too painful to go on enduring. The credulous common talk at Din Eydin – which from an early stage had circled well within Lot's earshot – was that he was paying the price for setting his face against the so-called cult of the Reborn Son.

The medical consensus was 'consumption', a stock diagnosis for any illness outside the doctors' experience. But at times as Lot had lain on his bed, too weak to rise unaided, he felt as if he really were being consumed: eaten away from his core, organ by organ, bone by bone – but soon, he felt sure, he would be reassembled in a far better place than this.

The servants manoeuvred the curtained wooden frame inexpertly. Twice on the spiral stairways, harassed by the dogs, they came close to tipping Lot out. Two years had passed since last he had left his quarters. The late-summer sunshine felt like heated metal on his neck but he welcomed it, and pulled back the litter's curtain further.

Shifting stiffly on to his side, he let his bed-gown slip to uncover one shoulder, then kept an interested watch on the yellowed, papery skin in case it started to smoke and catch light. He would have been quite content to expire out here in a fireball, just as long as he saw his roses one more time.

Members of his depleted household hung back in the shadows of each cloister and courtyard that he passed through. Some had not set eyes on him for the whole length of his confinement. But if they thought his eyesight had failed along with virtually every other part of him, they were mistaken. He saw the undisguised expressions of horror and alarm, and each one raised his spirits. The worse he looked, the nearer to the end he must surely be. He thought of the litter as a bier, of all this as his own funeral.

Words rushed into his head: *Blood without cuts, blood without cuts* . . .

At the approach to the little labyrinth of rose-trees, he managed to ease himself up on to his elbows. The lawns here had once been so neatly-clipped and green. Now they straggled, unkempt and strawlike, like so much tinder set out in the hope of a spark from the sun.

The neglect did not disturb Lot. It was almost reassuring. He was convinced that he had lived somewhere like this in the old buried world of before. The world that was now rising to gather him back. That world of Albion which, although forgotten, he had never quite been able to leave behind.

He fell into his cushions, then for several of the litter-bearers' steps, he lost consciousness. When he looked again, the dogs had gone but a child was skipping alongside him, her small head level with his own.

Lot knew this girl. She had silently been flitting in and out of his vision for three years, ever since Anna had died. In some sense, she *was* Anna. She had the same small scar at her hairline; the wound which had bled when that bald-headed dreamer had come with his fables. Lot had no idea if she was real or just another delirious illusion. *The child coming back . . .* poor Anna had said that day. This little child always looked so much happier than her.

As for the Anna Lot had married, she had gone from his mind as well as from his side. Whenever he tried to recall her face, all he ever now saw was the steely glare of Guenever – a woman who, in some sense again, Anna had also been. Some subsidiary aspect of her, perhaps; a wan northern echo.

At around the time Anna died, Lot had overheard that Arthur's queen was touring in the region under Lanslod's escort, but only as far as Orcadie's borders. It may have been true. But nothing beyond Din Eydin's walls was certain. Lot was even unsure whether, four years before, Arthur and his armies really had come back from abroad. He had heard it said. He was prepared to believe it. Either way, it had no bearing on himself.

Logres must not end in the same way as Albion . . . Lot closed his eyes and smiled. *The son who should never have lived . . .* So many words, so much urgency; and none of it mattered any more. None of it, for him, ever had.

'Where are you going? Where are you going?'

Lot stirred. These were not the usual words, nor coming to

him in the usual voice. He looked, and saw that the girl beside him was speaking for the first time. Her face was bright, her lips moved fast. 'Tell me where you're going.'

'To see the roses,' Lot snuffled, his palm all but pressed to his lips. 'It's so long since I've seen the roses.'

'I can't understand you,' the little girl laughed.

Lot tried to smile, blinking slowly in a resigned kind of apology. He thought he could hear someone calling to her, urging her to come away. *Anna, Anna* . . . She paid no heed and Lot was glad. Her freckled little features and mop of red hair appealed to him. Suddenly her feet were where her face had been. She had turned a cartwheel, and she looked very pleased with herself when she reappeared, still bobbing along.

The calling went on, but it was not her name that was sounding. Other names filtered through now, an entire roll call: '. . . Moronoe, Mazoe, Gliten, Glitonea, Cliton, Tyronoe, Thitis . . . Morgan.' The last name sounded loudest, as if to catch and enfold each of those that had gone before.

Lot shut his eyes and saw the women dancing and skipping near his litter: some of them old, some no more than infants; and around them all was the shape of great Morgan, so huge that all Lot could see was the hem of her garment, along which the lovely dancers moved like animated braiding.

'Anna?' Lot turned and murmured to the child who stayed beside him. 'Are you Anna?'

'I've gone across,' she answered laughingly. 'From Guenever to Morgan. I'm where I want to be now, and soon you will be in a similar place. Soon you'll be delivered too, even though you don't believe. It's where you've always wanted to be, if only you'd known it, where everybody wants to be: inside the Mighty . . .'

Lot coughed, keeping his lips sealed, in order to clear a

passage in his throat. But before he could question the girl further, she drifted away and the men set down the litter next to the wooden seat in his favourite arbour.

He readied himself for his bearers to squat down, reach in and remove him. He may even have blacked out again briefly in anticipation of the strain. But no hands came in. He could not even see the men's feet. Just the wolfhounds racing each other down the avenue ahead. He chuckled.

He had been abandoned; his request to be brought out here had been obeyed, but only to the letter. Too weak to call out, or even to hoist himself into a sitting position by gripping the frame, Lot struggled to twist himself on to his back. Then he peered through a gap in the curtains above his feet at the nearest rose-trees.

There were several bedraggled blooms, long past their best. But the branches had all been hacked at carelessly, and few of the dead-heads severed. The green swellings on the stems looked painful, as if they might be about to explode with rot and fungus.

Lot closed his eyes, almost sadder at the lapsing of this garden than at the loss of his wife or his own deterioration. He fervently wished the little girl would return.

An unmeasurable time later, he jolted awake in his litter. The afternoon had quickly cooled with the sun's going down. He wondered how long it would be before the men reappeared to take him back inside.

He shifted himself sluggishly. He was so thin, less than half the man he had used to be. But the root cause of his enfeeblement interested him as little as the constant reports of cloud men in the skies that came in from Orcadie's far reaches. He had never felt anchored in Logres, just becalmed in this Ark of Din Eydin. Now he had come unmoored inside himself too. He was rising up through this disease to float on his own life's surface. It was as if the waters that once had drowned all his memories of Albion had risen again. As his flesh failed, they swept him along from day to day, hour to hour. He took it for granted that a route had been mapped out, that some destination awaited.

And without recognizing any landmarks, Lot knew he had been this way before; hugging the shore in the vain hope that he might finally swim back to land. Yet if he got there, he would drown more surely than if he stayed on the waves. This was still his Ark – just like Noah's after the first great deluge of forgetting. This was where he belonged. And just as old Noah had taken on board pairs of animals, Lot too had come in a double version of himself: the man he was in Logres as the echo of the one he had been in Albion – both fated to live their lives far short of any true understanding. But soon it would all be over. And Lot could hardly wait.

Shadows had crept up over the end of his litter. Still no one came, not even his dogs. He did not try to call for attention. He doubted that he could make a sound, and besides his staff presumably wanted him here. It was where he himself had asked to be taken.

But the roses were such a disappointment. A sorrier sight than ever in these ragged evening shadows. But the harder he stared at the tree with its few poor blooms decaying on it, the less like a tree it began to look. He saw it as something far solider: a stone mound balancing on the thin trunk, perhaps. A cairn of stones even, with the frayed red roses turned to blood-smears on its flank. The image chilled him. He drew in his breath then coughed, and coughed again. Deep darkness followed.

When next he roused himself, the little girl was back at his side. Lot's head had lolled off the cushion. Blood-streaked saliva coated his beard. The girl, humming lightly, was pushing her fingers through it, smearing his nose and eyes with his own discharge. It felt like a kind of anointment.

'Soon,' she whispered in his ear. 'Soon now, my sweetheart . . .' And it sounded like a chorus rising around him. 'Blood without cuts,' all the women in Morgan chanted. 'Blood but no cuts . . .'

He had heard these word before, many times, but only in his dreams. Other words too, that were just as turbid: 'Replace the head, replace the head . . . The Son will come, the Son will come . . .'

'Hold my hand,' Lot pleaded in vain with the small girl, fluttering his tremulous fingers. At last he was afraid, and unbearably alone. He had always been so alone in Logres. And no one now would take his hand.

Then it began. The tree before him, that had looked like a cairn, had swelled into a mountain, looming vast above him, blocking out all else.

'Anna . . .' Lot tried to cry, but no sound came. He closed his eyes but the same dark image was etched on the insides of his eyelids. A sweep of mountainside, and picked out across it, a disconnected figure.

The limbs of the figure came clearer, stark against the darkness. Lot had slipped beyond speech, touch or vision. All he had left was this giant, gathering now on the mountainside. Wildly he blinked but it made no difference whether his eyes were open or closed, whether he was looking up, ahead or to the sides. The clean-lined perfect giant was all in all.

The Son . . . The Son . . . The words were like water coursing through him. *Replace the head, replace the head . . .*

The giant was whole, his limbs linked to his torso, his domed head secure on his shoulders. Lot watched in awe and recognition as his right-hand fingers flexed. And he knew this young giant, from Albion not Logres. He knew those flexing fingers. *The Son, the Son* . . . His hand was shaping up to offer a greeting – or to clasp a sharp weapon.

Lot knew what the weapon would be. A knife: bone-handled, two brass studs for the grip, a blade that seeped blood of its own. *Blood without cuts, blood but no cuts* . . .

Lot was rising through his own surface. He recalled how it had been: the black-maned boy in the hillcamp, great Arthur's son of incest. The child who came back, then went south with his knife, *sent* south by Lot. *Logres must not end in the same way as Albion* . . . But it would. It had to. Logres, like Albion, would pass from father to son, from Arthur to Mordred.

The giant too was rising, its right-hand fingers beckoning. The boy who came back, rising once again from the world behind the world. The giant was Mordred returning, and beckoning to Lot, bidding him rise and be received with all the others: circle on circle of waiting others, believers and non-believers alike, the dead indistinguishable from the living.

Lot shut his eyes, and then there was nothing. But outside himself now he was running. Racing blind towards the Mighty. For the first few moments he was afraid. He felt horribly vulnerable; as if his face and chest might suddenly break against some hard, huge, rough obstacle. Then came a short, sheer bolt of joy. He was running even faster towards the new oblivion.

A hot new surge came next. A gorgeous rush like birds breaking cover. Lot's face ached with uncried tears. His feet no longer pounded the ground. His body still made running shapes but now he was higher, tearing through the air, climbing the skies to where Mordred waited, to where all the masses in Mordred were hauling him.

There was blood now but none of it was his. Lot flew through seas of blood to the world where he belonged, in the time beneath all time, where no one was alone.

TWENTY-TWO

Nabur saw lights inland and only then accepted that it was too cold to sleep rough again. His horse, too, needed feeding. Coaxing it around, he headed away from the shore-path towards the small settlement.

He would be glad of a pallet that night. From experience he knew that it was unrealistic to expect a bed in this latest western peninsula. Galles, the local people called it, ruled by a prince named Peredur. It was as naturally threadbare a region as any that Nabur had seen in Logres, but its natives were not unfriendly. Far from it. They always listened attentively to his questions. They answered him as best they could. They allowed themselves to laugh only after he had continued on his way.

This was his sixth year of searching. For the past three, his progress had been especially slow. His pride would not let him beg for food and drink, for his changes of horse and new clothing. So he was working his passage around the coasts of Logres, doing whatever work in wood was wanted.

Sometimes he stayed at a settlement for as long as a month. Mostly he knew that people were more concerned for his welfare than in need of his carpentry. But he was in no particular hurry. And he seldom let himself speculate on what might happen, if and when his quest should end.

The first hut he knocked at proved empty, although lamps were burning behind the oilcloth windows. This was repeated at the second and third. Walking ahead of his horse, Nabur turned into another unpaved street where a stone-built chapel echoed with the sound of accompanied singing.

In a different world this would have been the Christmas season, the song would have been a paean to the new-born king. But here, as in so many other towns and villages, a different Son was now being hymned.

Nabur slipped inside to find a festival in full swing. It no longer astonished him to see a Christian temple serving an alien kind of faith. As he had often been told, the buildings were just shells; the sites had been sacred for centuries before the Christ's time. This honouring of the land itself – of its earth, air and water, through the Son upon whom they waited daily for deliverance – was a reversion, not a revolution.

Nabur was familiar with all the arguments and he saw no reason to resist. He still did not fully understand what was meant by 'the giants' or 'the Mighty' but he knew that the ideas made people behave no worse than before. Indeed, he was always impressed by the new faithful's true sense of community; the way they appeared to move in shoals, in constant harmony not only with one another but also with the elements around them.

It made him wonder what more their keenly-anticipated deliverance could bring them. When once he had asked, an orchard-owner had told him with a nod: 'His hand will come down and gather us all in. Our hearts and our souls will be one in him. Then the time of kings will be over, and we will live in this island as we were meant to.'

That left Nabur little the wiser. But in their own serene fashion, they seemed to be focusing less now on what they might gain than on what still had to be stripped away: namely, the élite and distant regime of Arthur. A regime which Nabur had experienced only in the shape of Lot the sceptic; one that had so seldom impinged on his own life in Logres that perhaps there was truly no further need for its existence.

Nabur stood unobtrusively in a corner as the songs soared on. Occasional phrases sliced through his tiredness: 'Replace the head . . .', 'Heal the stone . . .' and even, unless his ears deceived him, 'Blood without cuts . . .' Exactly the same words had entered Nabur's head on finding the dead man at the causeway. But all these words seemed to surge straight out of the island's air. Each breath a person took became an act of worship.

When the feasting began, Nabur was shown to a bench and served with food and drink. No one asked him his name or business. Then he watched with a smile as the tables were cleared, the musicians took up their instruments again, and a series of stately reels was danced by the older people present.

Earlier in his journeying, he might at this point have made enquiries: 'Have you seen him?', 'Have you seen her?' 'Have you seen their tower by the sea . . . ?' But by now he had learned to bide his time, to select perhaps the single person least likely to confuse his own little flesh–and–blood knight with the sacred Son of their lore.

While he was still looking, a child came across, dragging its feet, and holding a wedge of black bread.

He stood in front of Nabur, raised the bread to his mouth and bit into it. He ate it so deliberately slowly, and with his eyes so firmly fixed on Nabur's, that he seemed to be making some kind of silent statement. Nabur smiled, trying to hide his toothlessness – he did not want to frighten the boy.

He was ordinary enough to look at – wiry in his blue smock, clear-skinned, tufty-headed, his solemn eyes a little too close together under heavy eyebrows. Swallowing the mouthful of bread, he at once tore off some more. His eyes never moved from Nabur. He looked implacable, rocking to and fro where he stood, plainly trying to work out whether Nabur was the oldest living thing he had ever seen. He himself looked impossibly young: four or five years in the world, so small and golden that Nabur felt awkward just to be breathing near him. Then he dipped his free hand under a flap in his smock, pulled out a coin and offered it.

'Please,' Nabur said, shaking his head, 'keep your money.'

The boy continued dumbly to hold out the coin, then shuffled a short way forward.

Nabur showed both palms. 'No, no,' he grinned, 'I don't want your money. That's not why I'm here.'

Ignoring him, he flicked his little wrist and lobbed the coin over Nabur's hands and into his lap. He looked delighted with his shot, and gave no sign of moving away. Maybe, Nabur thought, he only wanted him to look at it. Dutifully he took it up and, still holding the boy's gaze, hefted it in his palm. Then he lifted it up to inspect it.

The coin looked fresh-minted. Even under the poor rushlights, it dazzled. Nabur nodded his appreciation. The image on the face was of a hill-figure: several strokes to show a man. Nabur turned it to find a less-familiar symbol. A circle made by a dragon consuming itself; and, laid across its diameter, a knife.

'It's splendid,' he said softly to the boy, taken aback to hear a catch in his throat as he said it. He offered the piece back to him.

'No,' the child said forcefully, stepping right up, 'look at this.'

He pointed with a grubby finger at the slew of letters around the coin's perimeter.

Nabur shrugged. 'I'm sorry. I can't read,' he admitted. 'Maybe you should ask someone else.'

'No,' he said again, coming around the coin to look at it from the same angle as Nabur. 'You see, here, it says M-O-R-D-R-E-D. Mordred! You see?'

'Mordred,' Nabur nodded. 'I'll have to take your word for that.'

Again his voice faltered as he spoke. He did not need this now. He wondered why the boy had singled him out, who might have sent him across. He glanced around to see if there was a knot of onlookers watching.

'And this too,' the child went on, brushing Nabur's palm with his hot fingertips as he flipped the coin. He pointed at another inscription.

'So what's that all about?'

'It says he is the Reborn Son, and he will be the Head.'

Nabur widened his eyes at the abstruse marks, as if this might suddenly make them speak to him. But they seemed simply to float up off the metal, to curdle across his line of vision and melt into the misty lighting.

'That's good,' Nabur told him. 'I'm glad.'

'When Logres is over, Mordred will be Head.'

'Yes. I understand.'

But Nabur did not understand, nor did he care to. The Mordred of their stories did not interest him. Their Mordred lay huge on great hillsides inland, etched between the land and sky. His own dear knight was a creature of the coast, surely to be found at some point where the land met the sea. Nabur could not think of him away from waves and tides.

He went with the water. That was where he belonged. But more than that he belonged with Nabur, his surrogate father, and Nabur belonged with him.

Again and again on his travels he had asked himself why he needed so badly to find the boy. Perhaps, like the devotees of the cult, he too was looking for deliverance; but deliverance of a far less apocalyptic kind. Without his little white knight, he felt hopelessly incomplete. It was as if a part of his own body had been chopped away and hidden. As a man without a son he made no sense to himself. Only by seeing the boy, touching the boy, reclaiming the boy, could he hope to be whole again.

The child in the smock had relaxed. He leaned easily against Nabur's knee and played with the coin in his palm, tossing it this way and that as if he were playing heads or tails with himself. 'Mordred will be Head,' he sighed, his high voice entering a softer, more intimate register.

There was no telling how much the child knew, how much he was making up as he went along. Nabur had begun to tremble, partly from the conversation, but maybe more from the boy's trusting closeness. The peppery smell of him took Nabur back to that other infancy beside the causeway at the forest's edge. *You don't know who I am . . .* Nabur's eyes prickled at the memory.

'Why did you come over to me?' he asked finally.

'Because you're the man who looks for Mordred. You go all over looking for him, asking people. Isn't that you?'

Nabur felt his throat tighten. The man who looks for Mordred. His quest had gone before him – even if it was not the quest that they all imagined it to be.

A small, attractive woman appeared on Nabur's other side. He released the boy at once and made to push him away but the woman's expression was genial. Always, everyone was so genial; everyone since Lot had raged at him so wildly. She offered her hand to the boy as if inviting him to dance. He stepped out to take it while saying goodbye to Nabur with his eyes. There was a medallion on a thread around the woman's neck. From where Nabur sat, it looked like the dragon-loop-and-knife design which he had seen on the coin.

He closed his eyes wearily and felt a disturbance deep inside his head, like a phalanx of great black birds, all flapping moodily.

He was offered a good enough pallet to sleep on after the feast. The next day, he carved a set of ash figurines for the children of the house to play with; there was no more substantial work that their father wanted done. As always, Nabur fashioned a little family set: mother, father, son.

The children accepted them with warm smiles, stroking the two smooth heads of the males as if they were alive. But when Nabur gathered up his tools before leaving, he noticed that the boy figure had been placed on the hut's small portable altar – just in front of the usual hinged diptych. He did not peer closely at its two painted panels. He did not need to. They always looked the same. The hunched young man with his knife; the parody Virgin presenting her child. It passed his understanding.

He clicked his horse forward from the settlement without even mentioning the couple he was looking for. He saw no point. There were no towers on this stretch of the coast. If he got into talking now, he would only have to listen again to fables about the new giants' advent, the cloud-pictures in the sky, this kingdom's true reversion to the Island of the Mighty.

It was past noon when the sun showed. The day seemed to be warming up from the south to greet Nabur, like a low fire left to glow in an empty house where guests are later expected.

The mood of the fisher-folk he passed was one of glassy, self-sufficient calm. Some of them smiled, not many spoke, even among themselves. Nabur found them as foreign to him as ever. They could have been preparing themselves to undergo a siege, or equally to pass through a gate in the wall of paradise. But whatever lay ahead for them, Nabur thought as he forged on along his own solitary road, at least they all had one another.

TWENTY-THREE

Peredur, the purely honorific Prince of Galles, rode alone
out of Dinas Bran and turned his horse towards Camelot.

No one marked his departure. Nor, in the whole of that
late-April day, did anyone show surprise at his passing. For
five years now, his industrious subject people had seemed to
know his every move in advance. From the moment that
the Dubris harbour-master had directed him to Galles, he
had felt sure that every Logretian had been at least one step
ahead of him.

At the converted cathedral in the Marches where he spent
the night, he was treated with unfussy courtesy. Everyone
knew who he was − if not from his lank mess of hair,
then from the pattern of heads on his surcoat. Most of the
Company no longer wore blazonry on their accoutrements.
As a fashion they had faded like the fables of the strays. But
Peredur clung to his as if to prove that once, at least, he had
been a man of action.

Towards the end of his second day's ride, he left the ridge
road to follow a newer track across some rolling downland.
He had seen a crowd assembling on one of the shallow slopes

below. In spite of himself he felt his heart rise. There were two, maybe three hundred people. A number which fitted with ease into the centre of the large white shape cut out of the turf. The shape was of a man. They usually were. A gigantic warrior armed with a proportionately tiny sword. In Galles this figure was known simply as The Son. Elsewhere there were horses, or circular, self-swallowing dragons. Both of these, Peredur understood, were referred to as The Mother.

He reined in his horse and wheeled it to watch. His eyes were trained not on the crowd but already on the sky above their heads. The day had been bright and blustery. Just the right kind of clouds were massing for a spectacle. Peredur found the silence of the celebrants eerie, even threatening. A part of him longed to dismount, to run and stand among them in the outline. But he had never quite dared. And he had never been quite sure why. Plainly these amazing shows had more force if witnessed in a group. But Peredur was not even convinced that he would be allowed to join in.

In his five years back in the kingdom he had watched the gulf irrevocably widen between country and court, between the lesser people of Logres and those referred to as its rulers. At each soporific May Round Table, his colleagues from the more distant provinces whispered much the same thing. There was no true tension, no open animosity. But Arthur's lower subjects seemed increasingly to be pursuing their own path, some dreamy destiny that ran in parallel to Camelot's. That was maybe another reason why Peredur still hung back. *One of you will betray me* . . . He still flushed when those words came back.

He heard a collective sigh as the clouds above scudded faster, blowing in suddenly from several directions at once. He swallowed hard, impressed as ever by the sheer inexplicability of it all. Already he was trembling too, leaning back in the saddle with one hand tight around its pommel.

The evening light began to change. As the sun set behind him, the sky above turned a darker shade of pale, accentuating the clouds' whiteness. It was as if this section of the heavens had been hived off from the rest, enclosed in some transparent, artificially-lit structure that reached right down to the ground and altered all sense of perspective.

The crowd sighed louder; Peredur rocked in his saddle, high up there on the giant's shoulder. It was the most extraordinary sensation – like being connected directly to the sky. The compacting clouds looked close enough to touch, yet the copse close by, the scatter of farm-buildings and the few browsing cows all looked impossibly distant. Everything that mattered now was in the ether. Then it began.

Peredur had heard reports of half a dozen spectacles before watching one. Monosyllabic accounts drawn from reliable servants of his own at Dinas Bran. At first Peredur had been sceptical. He had thought it was like looking into a fire and finding any shape there you wanted. If one persuasive man thought he saw a face, he could easily enough make ten others think that they were seeing one too.

But finally, one sunset, he had watched from his battlements as his staff trailed out of the palace. Even from so far away, the shapes in the sky had clearly been those of an armed male figure, mutating into a larger woman holding a child, and finally into a larger man still, with two smaller figures apparently eating him away. It was like a complete public play in three acts. Beginning, middle and end. And no part of it made the slightest sense to Peredur. 'You watch and you feel it,' his steward had said with a shrug. 'When you're watching all together, you go into it. And it feels good . . .'

Obviously its effect went beyond words. To try to speak

of it was like trying to clap with one hand. The Glass Castle tales had gone before it much as John the Baptist had gone before Christ. While Arthur had been out of Logres, they had prepared the ground. But now there was no more need for stories. The pictures in the sky were enough – even, at times, for Peredur.

Since that first show, he had seen moving-cloud images of a ship full of thrashing creatures that seemed not to be fish; of a man shrinking into a foetus then growing back again; of the same man on horseback drawing up a weapon from what looked like a rock. The images had all spoken to Peredur in their own soothing language. It was as if in those few moments, the world had opened up at last and let him in. But when it was over, he was again alone, watching his people trooping entranced through the gateway, many of them embracing as they moved along like some many-headed monster.

Now he stiffened as the new form took shape above him.

It was one he had previously neither seen nor heard of. The clouds were forming a huge head, long-haired, slow-eyed, scruffily bearded. Peredur would have sworn later that there were colours: shades of red and black as well as the usual white. It looked so massively real that when its lips parted, he braced himself to smell its breath, to hear a voice.

But no sound or stink came; only a long, lascivious tongue. Peredur knew then that this was the face of Merlin: the former Regent of whom he had seen nothing since disembarking for Outremer. Some said that he had long since withdrawn from Camelot to become a hermit. Others, more fancifully, that he had fallen for an unsuitable woman who had then imprisoned him in a tree. Even as he gazed up, Peredur thought he saw the face's skin texture coarsen – with mottles, ridges and pits just like tree bark.

Then the features seemed to tighten, as if the face were being inflated from within. The cheeks swelled, the eyes and mouth narrowed, the ears – behind which hair had been hooked – seemed to flap. And suddenly the whole thing burst and began to fragment. But each of the gently floating components was not a nose, a cheek, a chin. Each was a small, naked wild-haired man. Perfect cloud-replicas of the vanished race of strays.

Peredur felt the crowd's gasp wash over him where he sat in his saddle, pygmy-like, on the shoulder of the giant. He almost cried out too at the wonder of it. But there was more. Even as they floated, the men became women. A smaller number of svelte, clean-limbed girls who reached, clawed and somersaulted until at last they pressed themselves back together.

The new face was familiar at once. Strong, hard-eyed, high-cheeked, her unsmiling lips like a great bloody gash: Guenever.

But most marvellous of all – way up high and a thousand times its size in life – the queen's face seemed suddenly to fit. Her face, Peredur saw, was made to be stretched across the sky. So too was Merlin's – into which Guenever's again mutated, before turning back to her own, as if to show that both were merely halves of some greater whole. A whole both more and less than purely human.

And then the cloud-mass condensed to show a young, mounted knight approaching. Slowly at first but gathering speed. Coming with the sunset behind him, so that his shape was bathed in triumphal glory. He looked softer inside his aura than any of the earlier sights. Altogether less forbidding. As he came up through the place where Merlin and Guenever had stared down cold-eyed, his horse became a dragon. Flying on its back, he started to spiral downwards.

There were screams then. Of longing, not terror. Glancing down, Peredur saw a forest of arms reaching skyward. And just as the cloud-knight seemed likely to hurtle through them all and into the earth, he dispersed in a raindrop-fountain that left no one wet and no one wanting.

Peredur straightened, his eyes shut tight.

His body seemed to be singing to the rhythm of what he had seen. He could not afford to think how he might have felt if he had been among the crowd, nor even to look down at them before easing his horse around and setting off on the last leg of his solitary ride to Camelot.

After the spectacle, the Round Table could only seem tired and uninspiring.

Every year Peredur arrived believing that Arthur would at last have devised some new peacetime design to absorb all their energies. But every year the emperor seemed to have slipped deeper into his torpor.

He looked little different from the ragged captain who had fought abroad to such brutish effect. His body was still lithe, his eyes unclouded, his strength – in the few jousts he chose to enter – undiminished. Yet he had also clearly been winnowed down, diminished in mystique. And that year Peredur found him more densely surrounded by silence than ever. A wholly unrestful silence, the kind that any man broke at his peril.

As a result, during the full seven days no one in the Company spoke to him. Arthur was beyond reach even when he sat with them to eat or be entertained. The session around the Table itself was farcically uneasy. The assembled circle – with a new space left vacant for the recently dead Lot – applauded Arthur warmly on his entrance, sat for an hour in his silently vigilant presence, then clapped again when he rose and left.

As ever, his gaze was fixed on the circle's other space: the unoccupied place on the bench which the strays had called the perilous seat.

There was a perfectly good reason why this was always vacant. No one sat there because it was directly in the emperor's sightline to the entrance arch. His eyes never wavered from it, narrowing and widening as if already he could see the figure which, the Company presumed, he constantly awaited.

Peredur had sometimes wondered with the others who the emperor might be expecting. The consensus seemed to be Merlin. No one had ever quite fathomed his role in the Great Remaking, nor his later relationship with Arthur, although both had obviously been vital. But it was possible that the emperor missed his guidance now.

As Peredur lay awake on his penultimate night in Camelot, he kept seeing the Regent's great cloud-face fragment into a myriad smaller figures, then reform. He had spoken to no one about the spectacle. He would not have known how to. The tacit consensus among the Company had always been that 'the cult', as it was called, should not be mentioned – maybe because, Peredur sometimes suspected, a number of the knights had already been drawn into it. The only person he felt that he could have talked with was Dyfric, but the chaplain had seemed to be studiously avoiding him all week.

Why, he wondered, had Merlin's face interchanged with Guenever's? The queen herself was another enigma: care-worn, distracted, forever glancing around herself at these annual gatherings. She remained elegant, if a good deal thinner with each year, but she lacked her old composure. She appeared to Peredur like a woman who had lost all her bearings.

Oddly, she was still titled queen although everyone spoke of Arthur now as emperor. It was as if her own writ ran only as far as the coasts of Logres. When Peredur watched her closely, he remembered how her sky-face, like Merlin's, had seemed so naturally to be over-arching the island. In person, by contrast, she had no raw, physical presence. For all the sexual signals it gave, her body could have been made of stone, or sculpted from the clouds. She transcended her gender: less a woman than a wonder of skin, bone and scent that had found a female shape. You saw that she was a queen, then that she was a woman. It was almost as if she *was* her office.

And she spent so little time at Camelot now, visiting only in May, just like the members of the Company. Nine years before, she had begun to keep her own frugal court at the Tower of Lundein. On Arthur's return from the wars she had continued to live there, effectively estranged from him.

According to reports, she would stroll the teeming wharves and markets unattended, passing unremarked among citizens who knew full well who she was. She took boat trips alone downriver, paying the ferrymen with coins from her own pouch. Occasionally she would ride out into the fields to the north and west, staying away for days and nights on end.

There the reports grew less reliable – and Lanslod began to figure.

Of the Company, only Lanslod had ended up with no land to hold for Arthur. Maybe he had never wanted it. He spent the larger part of each year kicking his heels in his quarters at Lundein, occasionally escorting the queen on her longer forays. Like Peredur, he had stayed childless and unmarried.

None of Arthur's knights now led an especially gainful life. The postwar sub-kingdoms and provinces needed no real governing. Peredur always thought their rulers were like scabs that had come detatched from fully-healed wounds. But Lanslod's existence seemed emptier than anyone's.

There had once been talk that he and the queen were lovers. Peredur had been unconvinced. He had guessed that the rumours began and ended with the strays: that old kingdom-wide cobweb of words, the history of Logres as it was supposed, by them, to have happened.

Whenever he saw Lanslod and Guenever together at Camelot there was no sense of intimacy. Close to her, Lanslod was always awkward, not as a man in love might be awkward, more like a child left with too young a stepmother.

On the last evening, Peredur stood alone in the feasting hall's minstrels' gallery and stared down at the dancing below. Some of the knights had brought their wives or daughters with them; others took their annual chance to pick up with old mistresses. It made a convivial enough scene. But the longer Peredur looked, the more remote it all seemed. Far more remote than the pictures he had seen in the sky on his way here. It was like watching a show performed by puppets under water, each of their choreographed movements decided long in advance elsewhere. However hard they imagined that they were running this empire, the empire was more truly running them, using them purely as a focus for its lighter entertainment. Camelot itself was turning into a Glass Castle: a court-shaped goldfish bowl into which any outsider was free to peer and tell tales.

Later that evening Peredur slipped away from the heat, sweat and din out into the city's deserted avenues. He had more than half a mind to call on the chaplain, who had left when the dancing had started. He remembered the first time he had wandered like this, at the time of the Great Remaking seventeen years before. Since then, the queen and Regent had not been the only ones to withdraw. Domestic and commercial premises lay boarded all along Peredur's route. A skeleton staff mainly of young men remained to Arthur, but either side of his annual May court the emperor appeared to haunt this dream city almost on his own.

There were no lights on in the chapel or Dyfric's lodgings. Peredur, his head full of clouds again, stared at the great gash in the hillside below. There were those who said that Merlin had now made his home in there. But that was not why Peredur suddenly flinched from the circle of deeper darkness. He had remembered the old stray's story. In the time before time, a head had been buried here. A giant's head: Blessed Bran's, to protect the old island for ever. And Arthur in his pomp had dug it out.

Peredur's eyes widened. Superimposed upon the pit he pictured the stone Round Table in the hall, then vividly recalled the presiding emperor's deep concentration. He sensed a link between hole and hall – or an opposition.

It was almost as if the Company, by sitting in its own circle, was answering this circle here; resisting the emptiness of the one with the fullness of the other. But the Company's circle was not full. Brumart's perilous seat had been vacant from the start. Now Lot's death had broken it further.

Peredur shivered and turned on his heel. Once he had dared to ask Arthur where the real struggle was. Six years on, he was starting to find out – not from any man, but from the clouds. The spectacle, he saw at last on his way back to the hall, had shown him a battle in some mystic struggle raging above and around them all. Here was the elusive but beautiful truth that this island's people now were telling themselves *about* themselves. It seemed both new and impossibly old – and all of it bypassed Arthur. *One of you will betray me . . .* Just by being there under those clouds, Peredur felt as if he had already agreed to his own thirty-piece payment.

TWENTY-FOUR

Lanslod rose slowly, slipped into a loose-fitting doublet and descended from his chambers via the small back stairwell.

Once outside in the still, pre-dawn air, his heart beat faster. Although known simply as the Tower, Lundein's high stronghold by the riverbank was an array of several keeps and permanent blockhouses. A pennant had been raised to hang limply on the citadel. It told the city's people, if they cared to know, that the emperor had arrived among them for another of his brief stays. It also gave a far more personal signal to Lanslod.

He paused between the gatehouse towers looking west. Threads of smoke rose from the warren of surrounding streets, from the wharves and jetties where all manner of cargoes were daily shipped in from Arthur's overseas empire. Lanslod thought about the people who rested easy in their beds down there, the self-sufficient masses who would later wake without shame. Once, he knew, they had told stories about him; the current truth eclipsed any fiction.

He stood on the impregnable walls, aware that now they could be brought down only from within. Like Arthur,

Lanslod had thrived on external threats before. Now the threats had to be contrived on the inside. Such insidious threats and tests. The wars had been cryptic enough, but the challenge ahead of him here was purely personal. *One of you will betray me . . .*

He turned, descended the inner stairway and headed slowly towards the royal quarters. His duty led him on. A duty that for the fifth successive year, step by reluctant step, was merging with desire.

This courtyard was cloister quiet. Lights burned at some of the windows giving on to it. It was the thick of the night; few would be awake. The darkness in the king's outer chambers told their own story. The ravens were absent from their perching places. Dung smells wafted from the stables.

Lanslod did not look around before pushing back the door to the appropriate stairwell. He never did this furtively. He longed to be seen, stopped, questioned. But no shout ever came. No guard called his name. The Tower seemed to drug itself for him, for her, for the three of them.

The stone steps felt soft. On his feet he wore the simplest leather slippers. The spiralling walls were painted with scenes of May sports but Lanslod saw none of the detail in the light of the guttering candles in their brackets. He closed his eyes for the final flight, shivering in his doublet although the summer was still at its height. And in spite of everything, already he was eager.

Her bedchamber door was ajar. Golden lights burned low inside. He pressed his shoulder to the oak, hoping it would not yield. He always made this show of forcing his way in. He knew that it was expected. The choreographed ritual: more like the steps of a dance than a show of desire.

Her chamber was ill-lit, sparely furnished. She lay on her raised bed with her back to him. Such a long thin, animal's back. No one could have guessed at the fullness of her front. It was as if only on that side had she grown to become a woman. From behind she was still the girl who was yet to meet her man; from behind she was virginal. Their eyes so rarely met. Sometimes he yearned to speak, but words were never a part of this.

This was the fifth time, the fifth year. *One of you will betray me* . . . It was as if Lanslod came here year after year across Arthur's own body. Coming breathless on tiptoe, lest a wrongly-placed foot should rouse his sleeping lord. With every soft step Lanslod trod deeper into him.

She stirred as he pushed the door to again. It could have been a flinch. Lanslod could never tell what moved her. On these nights with him, she shook and stiffened and went soft; that was all. If this were in fact a dance, she could have been dancing quite different steps from his own, steps perhaps that women only ever danced with one another. At the critical moments she could truly seem to be not just one woman but a crowd of them. Making love to her was like hearing in a shell the whole sea's vastness.

She turned a little way. The mass of one breast showed in outline against the lamp's tawny glow. Lanslod hesitated. He wished she would be dressed when he came to her; wished, in a way, that she could be dressed all through. But it was always like this when he arrived – the bedclothes kicked back as if she had already started the ritual between them.

As he undressed he stared at her twisted torso. She lay on her back now but her legs, slightly bent and together, pointed away from him to the wall. The sight of her skin shocked him. It was good, unblemished skin; soft, smooth and pale. But he was shocked by the fact that she had skin at all.

He preferred to think of what he saw by day: a dazzle of fabric and jewellery; the office she held rather than the woman. He still did not quite believe in her as a woman. In bed she could have sprouted antlers, become liquid. He saw her as capable of being anything. And she was so far away from him. During their previous four times together the distance had somehow grown greater. It was as if, even as he caressed her, he was being dragged back by his feet, sledged off the bed and across the floor.

This was how it was. The more he explored her, the less he got to know. She was so unmappable, like a small rock at sea that below the water's level spreads to form a sunken continent. Each time, Lanslod felt himself running aground on her, his hull splintering, the waters rushing in until it was over and he was left as a mess of broken planking and torn sailcloth.

The room closed in on him as he stepped across to the bed. Its fittings were not lavishly embroidered. It was not a big bed. Barely room for two.

He saw her profile, her head tossed back, her lips already parted. He looked only at her as he approached, never into the room's shadowy corners. In truth his eyes could not have fixed on anything else. His neck was rigid, his teeth grinding. Naked now himself, already he was rising to her.

She turned and presented her back to him. Her back, her buttocks. When he folded himself against her, she let a small sigh break. He held her by the shoulder, barely able to breathe. He kicked down the remaining covers so that they were bare on the crimson sheet, distinctly pale against its dark.

At once he was splintering, choking on his own ripped rigging. She moved with such economy to show where he was to touch her next. She encouraged him over her body like the devil tempting Christ in the desert, but Lanslod could not see what she was tempting him to do, where the taboo began. Maybe the temptation was purely to go past his own self-imposed limits; his resistance to the idea that, in essence, he somehow *knew* this woman.

At first he stayed outside her. She responded fast, shuddering faintly as the spasms gathered in intensity, finally opening her mouth cave-wide as if to let out a horde of possessing demons to be swallowed by the lamp smoke.

Now and then her hands would alight on him – almost as if by mistake. She gave nothing, or only by default. Nothing of herself. Her hands brushed his thigh or gripped his calf; her mouth grazed his neck or the small of his back, but only as a part of her own readjustment. She arranged herself like a target in a butts, perfectly positioning herself for the arrows of his attention. Not once did it seem to occur to her that she might fire at him.

Time fell against itself and blocked its own path forward. Lanslod went through eternities of her quivering. He could not imagine a moment when he had not been on this bed, or would ever be anywhere else. As he was kissing her inner thighs she gripped his calf so hard that he almost reached out to beat her away. It had to be a test. Yet another test.

He reared hard against her side. She would not take him in her hand. He saw her indifference as a form of contempt. Her goal, if anything, was to show that she could do all this without him, without any man perhaps.

Then time shifted on again. Soon she would guide him inside her. He thought he heard late-August rain freshening the chamber's outer wall but it could just have been the blood in his head. His mind ran on to the emptiness that would follow. In between these nights they were such strangers. She was more remote from him than she was from even his lowliest groom. No warmth, no contact, not even a hint of their collusion on this bed.

She eased herself over him. As she stretched her long leg,

he saw a smudge of blood on his thigh. Not his blood. Then he saw the drizzle coming from her. It was as if a knife had been taken to her there. He put up his hand. The blood did not seem menstrual. Thin, abundant, it dribbled down his fingers. She did not, as usual, take and put him inside her.

They continued to touch, kiss, knead. Lanslod tried not to smear her body back. Soon that became impossible. She needed his hands on her – her throat, breasts, hips – and he could not keep wiping them dry. The covers grew damp and twisted. The longer it went on, the more blood seemed to flow; the more he handled her, the redder her flesh became. Not smeary red but dark, deliberate-looking strokes of colour. It was like painting a human canvas, daubing her until she looked ready for war – or one of its sorriest victims. *Blood without cuts* . . . It came in a viscous cascade.

Excited though he was, Lanslod dreaded the moment when he would have to enter her, push himself into the waves of blood. That one part of him would drown inside her, the part which had somehow ceased to be his already.

He shut his eyes tight underneath her. That did no good. The stuff seemed to wash all around him, the usual seas turned bloody and thick. But now the blood did not seem like hers. *Morgan*'s, he thought with a convulsion. The woman behind Elayne. The woman who was now surely animating Guenever too.

Lanslod was swept back to the time of the Great Remaking. A dreadful memory surfaced: Morgan's son on the citadel steps visibly shrinking, his body bathed in blood from no inflicted cuts. This blood was from the child's own birth, a birth he was careering back to.

Then his name came back; the name which Lanslod had tried to smother before with 'Galaad': Mordred.

This was the blood of Mordred. The boy who had brought

down Albion in the deluge, only to be sacrificed so that Logres could be founded. Even as Lanslod drowned inside this blood from above, it was still the blood of that sacrificial Son, the stuff used for bonding all of Logres' foundations, yet it was also older again: this was giants' blood, somehow drawn by Arthur . . .

For a moment Lanslod might have blacked out. When he opened his eyes, she was asleep, pressing only on his arm, which was dead to all sensation.

He eased himself free. Still, below, he was hard. Hot and shamefully aching. Her breathing was a settled purr. Lanslod was thankful at least that she had not needed him inside her. He looked only at the underside of the bed's canopy. It seemed higher now, the walls a little further apart. Faint daylight was fingering its way along the window's far side.

He should go. Go before the darkness went. Her sleep meant his dismissal. Until the next year's signal, he was as free as he would ever be. His eyes began to water. He was hearing the city's dawn sounds below the Tower walls. Children's voices. Always children first thing, as if to remind him with each new day of what he had left behind. Little dairy girls, kitchen boys, stable urchins. He tried in vain not to picture his own lost Galaad.

Thrusting himself up, he reached blindly for his clothes. He would not weep in public. Not for anyone. Still carrying the armful of clothing he crept to the doorway. This was the hardest part. Keeping his eye only on the space he must go through. Not letting it wander, even for a glance.

But this time the shadow shifted as he reached out for the door. The great bulked-out shape in its darkness on the floor – the lamp was too far away for any detail to be clear. Lanslod saw the hand come up; saw it come slowly, as if through deep, deep water.

He paused. He had to. All he could be was obedient.

The hand was thick-fingered, the back of it shining with hair. It gripped Lanslod hard between the legs. He gasped, afraid that he might suddenly come.

He shot a look down. The whole of the face beneath him had gone into its eyes. Two eyes, a hand, and such a grip. A cloaked king hunched like a dog in the corner. Always there, a faithful dog that had learned how to give out the signal, a dog for whom the two on the bed had been made to perform. But who had trained the dog in the first place? How had the trick been beaten into him? And why was he being made to suffer so? What ancient wrong was this cycle of humiliation meant to be righting?

The great shape gave a half-rabid bark. Lanslod heard a stirring behind him. He looked down again. There was nothing in Arthur's eyes that he recognized. 'Back,' came the sound from the man in hair and feathers, although his throttled voice sounded almost female. 'Finish it.'

He shook Lanslod brutally, then thrust him again towards the blood.

Stumbling, Lanslod turned and dropped his clothes. He broke his fall by clinging to the nearest wooden upright.

The queen, fully woken now, rolled on to her back and put her clasped hands over her garish pubic area. Then with crossed wrists, she pushed apart each thigh to spread her legs. The hands were Guenever's, but not their moving spirit. Her body had been invaded, possessed, usurped.

And Lanslod guessed then that this was what he was here for: to see the different, mightier woman inside her now, as well as to assist her in the king's own abasement.

Her eyes were open and staring without expression in the direction of Arthur as Lanslod lowered himself towards her.

TWENTY-FIVE

Nabur jerked awake with a cry of surprise.

For several moments more, the dream held him tight. He thought he was on water; not out at sea but struggling to find his balance on a boat still moored to a wharf. Stepping deeper into darkness, his leading foot seemed to touch flesh. A holdful of limbs, some twitching, some not. The arms and necks of babies. All the babies of May. Silent, waiting, helpless, hoping. Slowly Nabur stooped, thrust his hand into the mass, and started to sort for the one that was his; the one that would make him complete . . .

Again he gave a faint cry – this time with relief – which was enough to awaken him fully.

He blinked until his eyes came alive. The narrow roadside ditch into which he had wedged himself on the evening before stretched endlessly up to the pale night sky. He was a year south of Galles now, but he had no name for the place where he lay, nor for any of the others he had passed through. He had spoken to no one for months – asking no questions, trusting only his eyes.

And now his eyes were telling him something new. That he was not alone. That someone was standing a soft shout's distance away, where the road cambered down. A black silhouette, male, hands on hips.

Nabur rocked himself on to his elbows and craned his neck incredulously.

The figure was slim, tall, young, chalk pale – his head as smooth as marble. Again Nabur blinked and again, curiously, he felt that he was on board a ship, as if the whole ditch beneath him had suddenly flooded but somehow he was being buoyed up.

'Come closer,' he called hesitantly, 'so that I can see you better.'

He half-expected the figure to dissolve into the night at the sound of his voice. Instead it seemed to grow more solid where it stood. Nabur could see the folds in his only garment: a white loincloth, but he kept his hands on his hips and came no closer. And Nabur, weakened by shock, could not rise.

'Is it you?' he called up again, straining to discern the features on the face. 'Is it really you? Here? Now?'

Even if he had been able to see, the face might not have told him much. Not after so long. Yet this person looked the right age: sixteen or so – twice the age he had been when Nabur had last clapped eyes on him. The older man floated in the ditch, dashed this way and that inside himself.

'Speak to me,' he cried, his voice breaking uncontrollably. 'Please.'

At that, the young man let his hands fall and took several paces forward along the ditch's side. It was then that Nabur knew for sure who he was. From his easy, rolling gait. That had not changed in the slightest.

He came to a halt half a dozen steps from where Nabur lay. Then he twisted his neck to look away, back across the road, offering a profile which was quite clearly that of Nabur's white knight. His nose was longer now, curved and assertive, his lips fuller, his chin not exactly strong but nor did it detract from the overall nobility. He held himself with grace, poised in his slightness, as if he were about to take a leap back up into the skies. But this was no figment, no story-boy made of clouds. His outline began to blur, but only because of Nabur's tears.

'You've come,' he murmured. 'I've looked for you for so long . . .'

The head above turned again. Now he was looking directly down. Nabur wiped his eyes with the back of a hand. The waves roiled on beneath him.

He leaned forward and threw off the ragged turves that he had fitted over his lower body to stop his legs from stiffening in the night. His hands trembled, his tears flowed on. He had to fight to catch his breath. But he could not stay down here.

'Give me your hand,' he croaked, limply offering up his own. Now at last he would be fully restored to himself. Now he would be delivered.

The young man stayed looming above him, motionless, high. His arms hung at his sides, a little away from his body, his hands half-forming fists which to Nabur suggested indecision.

'You know what to do,' said a new voice from the bank behind Nabur.

He knew whose voice it had to be. Cool, female, authoritative. As she spoke, Nabur felt those eyes of hers swarming all over him, opening him up again. He tried to twist around in the ditch, but he could not bring her into view. It was as if she had spoken from thin air.

'Take him,' she said. 'Let it be over.'

The words spilled directly from the darkness. They came like sticky rain; Nabur's face at once felt painted, as if he had been sprayed with somebody else's blood.

When he turned back, his knight had moved closer. Suddenly Nabur took fright. He remembered the little boy's fury when he had hurled all those stones. Finding some unexpected life in his legs, he drew his knees up to his body for protection. The young man's fingers flexed.

'Why do you wait?' the woman's voice came again, this time purring up out of the earth to the side of Nabur, the voice of a lover now, not a mother. Nabur rocked away bodily from where he thought he had heard it.

'She wants me to repay you,' Nabur's young knight said with an unfamiliar deep drawl, in a flat but collusive way.

Nabur curled smaller, his heart sore to breaking. In the extremity of the moment, he found himself on the point of inexplicably protesting: *But I saved you.* Instead he said steadily, 'Why should she want you to do that?'

'I know enough,' the figure above replied lightly, 'if I know what the queen's wish is.'

'Queen?'

'Queen.' The female voice coiled around Nabur, dampening him all over. The smell of her came back to him from the times when they had made love: heady, almost nauseating. 'Your emperor's first consort, his only true queen. The mother of his son . . .'

Morgan. She was, after all, Morgan. The mother, the mother. *When this kingdom of father's is over* . . . Nabur felt the ground slopping around him. He had curled up so tight, he was like one of the babies he had dreamed about. But that had been no mere dream. The stickiness on his face thickened; it was as if his own eyes had gently been thumbed out and somebody else's inserted: Morgan's.

And again, through them, he saw the dark, milling hold as he had descended; the boat heaving beneath him in the disturbed water. He had *been* there. He had sunk his hands into the sickening catch and dragged out a living child. One among the many whose death great Arthur had demanded. The son that Nabur had believed to be his own, but who proved to be the child for whom that slaughter had been launched. The king's son. Sired on his sister.

And Nabur had saved him, reprieved him, nurtured him through to adulthood in his own embittered way. *In that other time, in that other world*, he remembered the boy telling him years before. *The time before this, the world before this one . . .*

'I don't understand,' Nabur protested in his eerily level voice. 'I don't know any of this. All I wanted was to find you again . . .'

He longed to roar at him, grab his ankle, spit, scream. But when he closed his new eyes he clearly saw how it had been at the end in Albion: the same boy before his rebirth – with a mane of black hair, just a little older than this – standing in a doorway, wanting Nabur his foster-father to ask him to stay but not being asked. *You never spoke to me. You never smiled. You didn't care if I lived or died . . .* It had happened. The scene was real; more real than the ditch Nabur now lay in. *You gave me nothing. You even pretended you were dead at the end – just so that I would have to go . . .*

Nabur screwed his face up tighter, hiding it under his crossed, clenched fists. And he saw, as if from a high ridge, his own naked, bloodied body surrounded by a crescent of quiet men near a river. And the black-maned boy was being blamed, driven away southward by Warden Lot, back towards his true father, to the place where he would unleash the deluge. The king had tried to drown his son, so the son had then gone back to drown his older kingdom . . .

And as the image dissolved, Nabur was unsure whether the woman was speaking or if the savagely inhuman sentiment was coming back to him from that other time, that other place with its boat and its babies and body: 'A seed sown in darkness will surely blossom in an evil way . . .'

He let out a racked groan, clawing at his own face in torment. He quaked at the thought of waking again, somewhere quite different from this and far more alarming. A place to show him that the whole of his life in Logres had been a kind of deep sleep, seventeen years of searching in slumber.

'I remember some of it,' he hiccoughed. 'I know that I saved you but then I sent you away. But was that so bad? Was the ending of Albion such a terrible thing, if Logres then rose up from it . . . ?'

He made no answer. *It's not for me to like being anywhere*, Nabur remembered, *I'm only ever in the places where I have to be . . .*

'Take him.' The implacable woman had seized back her eyes. Now the sound of her was remote, fading, as if she were already withdrawing to let her lovely son do what he had to.

Nabur sobbed up at him. He could have been in two minds. Nabur, crushed like a foetus at his feet, braced himself. The younger man seemed equally likely to leap in and stamp him to death as to wander out of his life for ever. 'I'll do anything,' Nabur pleaded. 'For you, anything.'

'Believe me, then. Believe everything that I've ever said to you. More importantly, believe in the coming deliverance.'

'Deliverance, yes. I do. I will.' And Nabur meant it, the ever-faithful squire. 'But is it you? . . . Were you always the Son they all spoke of in those stories? . . . And when they say they see the shapes in the clouds, is that really you too?'

'You don't see these shapes?'

'I want to. Truly, I want to. I'll shift the earth to do it.'

'Soon,' came the woman's distant voice, as if from behind the sky, 'no one will need to look up any more.'

'Are you Mordred?' Nabur hissed, and as soon as the syllables passed his lips, all trace of both disappeared into the darkness. Then Nabur knew, as truly as he knew that in some other world he had saved this boy, that this was indeed the Reborn Son of the stories and the spectacles.

Then he saw Mordred's hand move, clutching at his thigh as if to grasp the hilt of some knife that was not there. A pathetic little weapon, Nabur abruptly remembered – from the life of long before, the life that he had thought had been drowned. A tarnished old meat knife, short, bone-handled. Mordred kept clawing, as if to remember how the thing had felt in his fist.

Nabur slowly raised one hand again. His own fears were beginning to subside. Mordred made no move to take his hand. Nabur knew why. He imagined the young sky-knight's hand coming down to meet his own but passing clean through it, again and again. He was there but not there: Nabur's own white knight, and once Arthur's bastard, but the people's Son as well, reborn as more than mere flesh and blood. This now, truly, was a giant.

'I used to be so concerned for you,' Nabur said, but only because his concern had now gone.

'I was a child then. I've put away childish things.'

'You're not a child now.' Nabur said it in wonder, as if he were addressing a rainbow in the night. He was cold without the turves on him, but too spellbound to cover himself again.

Mordred's outline blurred and then, for two salt blinks of an eye, came clearer but radically transformed. Where formerly a person had stood, now there was the silhouette of a mound, a cairn like the one at the end of the causeway on that awful day of his breaking and making. Again it looked like a great stone head — and lodged in its crest was the hilt of a sword, which shrank to a knife's dimension, then swelled again to a sword.

Finally it became a distant hillside, and on it had been etched the pure white figure of Mordred. The hill figure moved. It beckoned to Nabur, not white against dark now, but black against white.

'Come back,' came his voice, sounding no more remote than the boy had been before, 'come back now and be with us.'

Nabur rocked himself to his feet. His legs felt surprisingly painless. *Believe everything I've ever said to you . . .*

Nabur grabbed two tussocks of grass and hauled himself up to the road. To the south it ran down to a fishing-port. But his eyes were fixed to the spot inland where the great hill-figure beckoned. Invisible ravens overhead encouraged him. He felt exhilarated. *Soon no one will need to look up any more . . .* Nabur knew that the true queen had been speaking of more than just the sky.

The spell, for him, had stretched and broken. He was staggering inland to be taken, towards the deliverance he had so incredulously glimpsed even as the boy had been born.

Back, come back . . . Back in his body. Casting off years with his tears. There was snow beneath his feet. With every snowbound mile he felt younger; just as being with his infant knight had made him feel younger, but more tangibly now. He was not almost eighty, but twenty years less, thirty . . . a man whose flesh had been refurbished, whose bones had been new-burnished.

The hill reared in front of him. The hill from which

Mordred was beckoning. A hill with a fort like a squat toad on top. Nabur shut his eyes and saw the truth. His feet smashed through the crispy drifts: up, up, back, back . . . The night here was calm, the moonlight full. He was running higher but also ever-deeper into the figure.

He felt as he had felt on entering the mother: as if a whole world was waiting inside. But this was so much better. These, now, were his own people.

Back. At last he was back. Back with the masses. The world behind the world closed over him and however hard he looked he could see no telltale crack.

'Logres,' he murmured through teeth that he had not had at the start of this flight. It was like a farewell salute.

Then none of it was left, and as if from the underside of time, he heard the first cry of welcome. Truly now he had been delivered. Logres, for him, was over. Albion too. Here there were only giants. Nabur was back in the Island of the Mighty.

Two small girls from the fishing-port found the body later that day. They ran at once to fetch their older brother.

'Is it him?' they asked excitedly. 'Is it really him – the man who looks for Mordred?'

Their brother took one look and nodded.

'So now he has found him?' asked the younger sister softly.

Her brother knelt at the ditchside and pointed down.

'Look,' he said, 'he's smiling. He was glad to be gone from Logres. He knew what he was going to. He knew, at the end, who was waiting.'

TWENTY-SIX

Dyfric kept as low a profile through that May-time's Round Table as he had through the previous five. He knew that by doing so he was ostensibly failing in his duty. Every year he could see one Company member or another longing to speak with him, to unburden concerns and plague him with unanswerable questions.

Last year it had been the prince from Galles. From his darkened lodgings Dyfric had watched him come as far as the lip of the abyss before turning away. This year it was Lanslod who kept trying to catch his eye. The first knight had looked quite helplessly distraught, as if his soul had risen up inside him and was beating against his skin to escape. But Dyfric wanted none of it. No talk, no debate, no speculation. He knew that the Company felt beleaguered, but alone here between the May-times he too had undergone his own form of siege, and fallen.

When he felt confident that all the knights had quit the city, he emerged soon after dawn from his lodgings and crossed to the chapel. Clutched to his breast was the three-leaved icon which, since Arthur's return from Outremer, the chaplain had never let out of his sight.

Once inside the chapel he took three steps towards the altar. As he did so, the door was slammed shut behind him.

He turned to find wild-eyed Lanslod, dressed in a doublet, his back and hands pressed to the door as if he expected it to be battered from outside. He was breathing so hard that he could have just run in from Marathon with news of his army's success. But even before Lanslod closed his eyes and gushed out his piece, Dyfric knew that he was about to hear of no victory.

'The emperor makes me sleep with the queen. In Lundein, when he comes. Five times. This year will be the sixth. He makes it happen and he watches.'

In a daze Lanslod watched Dyfric turn slowly, then step away.

He launched himself forward, rushed past the chaplain, then the narrow altar, and turned to face Dyfric across it.

Dyfric remained composed. Apparently looking through Lanslod, he opened out the triptych he was holding and set it down between them, with its face towards himself. But as he did so, his wide sleeve knocked over a small pile of mouldering communion wafers. Slowly, methodically, under the blaze of Lanslod's eyes, he began to gather them in with the edge of his hand.

'You heard me?' Lanslod barked. 'You heard what I said?'

Dyfric exhaled. Without looking up, he surprised Lanslod by asking very softly: 'Does the lady not please you?'

'I don't let myself think of that. That's not the nature of it.'

'Yet you manage well? You never leave her . . . wanting?'

Lanslod balled his fists at his sides. 'It's not desire but duty! If the emperor put me on a horse and set me in front of a charging enemy, I would fight. He puts me in his wife's bed and I respond there because I have to.'

'And the lady? She shows no more liking for this than yourself?'

Still Dyfric's eyes were on the wafers. Lanslod stared at the top of his balding head. He had never been sure where the chaplain stood in relation to Arthur. Quite possibly he was privy to the entire elaborate ordeal. This conversation could yet become another aspect of the test. 'She performs,' he answered, more carefully.

'Performs?'

'She provides for the emperor what it is that he needs to see.'

'And does her performance convince you?'

'Surely it's not me who matters? The emperor is the one to be convinced.'

'Even so?'

Lanslod gasped. 'I can't believe that she would have any such pleasure with me, when she already has the emperor.' It sounded like a formula but he was glad he had said it. Tremulously he was measuring out every word now.

'So you think it is a test?' Dyfric went on. '"I have refined thee but not with silver. I have chosen thee in the furnace of affliction"?'

Lanslod counted a beat. 'I have considered that, yes.'

Dyfric put the flats of his small hands together. In spite of himself, Lanslod was impressed by his calmness. It was as if no depth of depravity could shock him, as if he expected to hear the worst every time a man opened his mouth. 'And would you,' he asked, propping his steepled fingers under his chin, 'have preferred some other man to have been chosen?'

Lanslod hesitated, thrown. In some abstruse way it did seem like an honour, but one that he would never have wished for – like the honour of being deputed to carry a beloved kinsman's coffin.

'I would prefer,' he said very slowly for emphasis, 'to have been granted one of the provinces, like the others in the Company. They all received *lands* to keep watch over for the emperor, whereas I . . .' He tailed off.

'So you think that the emperor has made a mistake?'

Lanslod closed his eyes. Mistake? Who was he to pronounce on that? Plainly Arthur was struggling. He had become becalmed in himself. But he had done so before, in Albion, and then he had risen up from its wreckage to lead the way into the promised land of Logres. *One of you will betray me . . .*

Mistake? It was possible that this time Arthur really would withdraw, that he was grooming Lanslod for the succession in more than just his marriage bed. Always preferring deeds to words, had he been trying to show Lanslod how strongly he wished to divest himself? Suddenly Lanslod felt crushed.

'Or do you perhaps,' Dyfric pressed, 'see this as a ritual of humiliation?'

Another blow. Lanslod had, of course, thought this, too; it was where he had sensed the vengeful hand of Morgan. Not just a humiliation of himself but of all three principals, and also of the wider realm, the empire, the very stones on which the whole vast construct had been built.

'Are you afraid because you are coming to enjoy these rituals? Or even that you are beginning to depend on them?'

Lanslod glared at him. 'I am not afraid. I am . . . unclear.'

At last Dyfric met his eye fully, with the faintest purse-lipped smile. 'So what does your heart tell you? What do you think is the true explanation?'

Lanslod looked away. The words were simply not there for him. The moment had arrived but he could not speak in any coherent way about Morgan's role in all of this, or about his fears that in a way Arthur had been cursed, just like his kingdom from the day of its birth. 'I think a different thing every day,' he said weakly. 'A different explanation.'

Dyfric nodded. 'Well, consistency is the consolation of the mediocre.'

Lanslod eyed him sharply. 'Do you really believe that?'

The chaplain smiled. 'Sometimes.'

Then he went back to corralling the communion wafers. 'Could it be a kind of retribution, do you imagine?'

'For what?' Lanslod's voice fell. 'What have I ever done against him?'

'Maybe nothing,' came the unexpected reply, 'as yet.'

Lanslod frowned. This was all so wrong. It had taken him the best part of six years to reach this point, but he had never seriously thought about what he would need from the priest after confessing. *One of you will betray me* . . . Already he felt more steeped in guilt than ever before.

'How do you propose to go on?' Dyfric asked distantly. He had formed all the wafers into a shape now. A man's shape, like a hill-figure. Lanslod saw him look down on it fondly, almost childishly. From the first he had seemed to have only half his mind on everything that Lanslod had told him.

'It's not for me to propose anything. I do as I am bidden.'

'Even if it makes no sense to you? Even if it offends you?'

'I said nothing about being offended.'

'Did you not imply it?'

At that Lanslod stepped forward. He had come here to share his problem with this glib priest but now he had merely multiplied it, and by far too large a factor.

'What offends me is your damned good humour!' he cried, reaching across the altar and, more in sorrow than

anger, grabbing the chaplain by two fistfuls of his vestments.

In trying to defend himself, Dyfric jerked out a hand, which
hit the flagon of long-stewed wine and tipped it over.

Lanslod watched in horror as, thin and rancid, it spattered
the little man made of hosts. At once his mind became flooded
with images of the blood that had stained his last night in the
queen's bed.

With a snort he thrust Dyfric away from him and stalked
out.

Dyfric stared through the open doorway for an hour after
Lanslod's leaving.

He was not proud of the way he had conducted their
exchange. A man had come to him in torment and then left
him unrelieved. But startling though the revelations about
Arthur had been, Dyfric could not see them as significant.
Render unto Caesar, had been running constantly through his
mind as Lanslod had agonized, *Render unto Caesar* . . .

He turned and looked down at the figure he had almost
unconsciously made with the scraps of bread, glutinous now
with the spillage. 'This is my body,' he murmured as he
pushed his fingers through the mulch to disassemble the man.
Then, abstracted again, he coaxed the fragments back together
again. Many into one. Masses into a single greater whole.

He lifted his fingers and peered at their tips. Blood red. He
rubbed them together. Blood's consistency too. Obscurely
this satisfied him.

Whatever response the emperor was making to the quiet
crisis of Logres, any measures of his were surely irrelevant. In
the cult of the Reborn Son, Arthur faced a phenomenon far
larger than he himself had ever been. How, after all, could
even so splendid a monarch hope to turn back the oncoming

clouds? How could he compete with the couple – semi-regal, semi-divine – who had entered the fibre of the minds of so many of his people?

Dyfric closed his eyes and felt the surging current.

Once he had seen the cult and its lore as a kind of river. For better or worse, a sub-stream now flowed through his own veins, soothing, consoling, safeguarding, explicating.

Shortly before this last Round Table, Dyfric, the erstwhile 'archbishop', had at last understood why he had fetched up in Camelot and why he had felt compelled to stay. The hole in this hill mattered so much more than the church that stood sentry above it. The place was holy, but not on account of the young Christian god.

Reverently he picked up the icon. Some spots of wine had splashed as far as its central image. He smiled at that too. Dark though it had become, he could look at it now without difficulty. It showed three figures. Those to right and left were clearly the Reborn Son and his mother. Between them, being eroded by them, was an older man, crowned. All the wine-spots had fallen on him; two ran down from his brow in rivulets, like the blood drawn by Christ's crown of thorns. This central figure was as faithful a reproduction of Arthur as Dyfric had seen.

But most arresting, and exhilarating, of all was the fact that – together – the three figures made up the shape of a single severed head.

TWENTY-SEVEN

On the night of the sixth signal, Lanslod left his Tower rooms by a different doorway.

He fell, rather than jumped, from the window. Had he jumped, he would have chosen to land on his feet and not his side. The resulting pain was so great that he could barely straighten up before continuing his cramped, occasionally four-legged getaway. Already he felt himself reverting.

He guessed that he was being watched as he careered through the network of Lundein's illuminated streets. He wanted to be seen and known in this wounded-wolf state. He stumbled on, barking in anguish, accentuating his new animality, until sooner than he expected the city of his torment petered out into open fields.

He tried to feel that he was betraying himself in deserting. It had not been planned. When he had risen from his bed, he had been screwing himself up to face the queen yet again. Then, quite suddenly, the lapsing inside him had begun. Now, as he found cover in the first stretch of forest, he felt vindicated.

He had been too long away from the dirt and the mud.

This suited him so much better than being on a horse's back: crouched, twisted, hustling himself along, ducking under thicket branches rather than overleaping them. It was almost as if he had been deliberately driven to this in stages, culminating in chaplain Dyfric's apparent indifference months before at the last Round Table.

He had torn off his clothes as he went. Already his shoulders were whipped and cut. He craved the feel of blood on him; dried, uncleaned away. He hid himself in filth. And so it went on, day after day, week after week.

Within a month, deep in that damply smoky autumn, he started breathing easier. He had come so far from the city and his spoor now seemed to stripe the whole land. It was as if his soul had broken free and been blown like a handful of sycamore keys all over Logres. He rubbed his face in the needly tilth, let crumbled soil slip between his lips, stripped bark from the trees and chewed it to pulp.

Everything was his. He had never felt so safe in his surroundings. This was not so much an escape from human life as a conscious flight into a world more elemental. For ten weeks more, he travelled further west and north. When he emerged from one belt of forest he soon found a route back into the next. His instinct led him infallibly away from all the beaten paths.

He swam through rivers, forded streams. Whenever he was seen, most usually by children, he caused no shock. On his great reconnaissance, almost two decades earlier, the people had known him wherever he went. Still, he felt, they knew him, but in a wholly new way. When he passed close to communities he often found food, drink and, later, wolf-pelts left out. Camouflaged like this in his own insignificance, he was ceasing to feel spurious. Whereas before he had always seen himself in relation to the needs of others, now at last he was shifting towards the centre of his own world. It seemed absurd that he had ever been part of any Company. The word itself was a travesty. Every man within it had always been so alone. The spaces in their circle had always been greater than any sum the men might have made. But here, he kept thinking to the rhythm of his running, here I can come closer. Here I can belong.

By the time winter bit, Lanslod – wrapped in the pelts now – felt as if he were travelling deeper into the land's layers, not farther across it.

Logres seemed less like a kingdom in which they were all living than a story that someone had been telling. Someone whose voice had slowly been dwindling away until now it could scarcely be heard. Sometimes he lay very still at night in his hollows and, straining hard, he thought he could just hear the low, faltering swish of sound through the air.

When he put a face to the whispers, he saw first a stray, then the Regent, then, more cryptically, Guenever herself. These had to be the makers of the map he had known since the Great Remaking. Arthur did not figure at all; Arthur's air it was, but only as a grant. And through that air the strays had strung together their own brand of truth about the island.

But now Lanslod's blood was starting to pulse to deeper, more insistent rhythms. They beat up from below, bypassing Arthur, extolling an older authority.

He had scoffed with Peredur, on returning from abroad, at the cult of the Reborn Son. For years afterwards he had blithely ignored the practices and beliefs of all this island's people beneath the élite. Now he watched intently from his shelter as crowds scraped snow from the hillsides to form huge loop-and-knife images, or to redraw male figures lost in drifts. Then they would gather inside them, silent, waiting, reverent.

Lanslod never saw any of the cloud shows of which he had once heard so much and thought so little. Maybe that time had now passed, just as the time of the Glass Castle tales had passed before it. But he felt moved by their massing there. He felt the rhythms most firmly then, as almost literally he was consumed by emotion.

Years before, he had asked a Lundein merchant why even the leading citizens sometimes went out into the nearest valley figures. 'Is it,' he had cynically suggested, 'to have a better view of your gods in the heavens?'

'No,' the man had answered with a steady gaze, 'it is so that they may have a better view of us.'

Lanslod could no longer laugh. The cult of the Reborn Son had not faded as he had anticipated. Its foundations seemed to have been laid during the emperor's campaigning in Outremer, almost as an alternative allegiance. It was easier now to see why. Arthur, little more than a legend himself, had barely existed for his people. However hard the strays had promoted his regime, his feats were all on foreign fields. He lacked warmth, colour, a visible human dimension. Vitally, too, he had no child.

The Glass Castle legends with their mother and son had largely passed Lanslod by. They had been too raw and unformed. Unlike the stray's older tales, they had not been prescriptive, and Lanslod had resisted the idea that each listener was being invited to use them however he or she saw fit.

It helped him now to see all that lore as a river. There is, after all, no large meaning to a river. It rises, it runs, it meets the sea; but a man could live his life beside just one bend, never knowing where it came from or went on to, and it would be no less of a river for him. Only from high in the sky could the whole course ever be followed, the larger meaning be seen.

Then scenes from the shapeless stories started to revisit him, rising into his mind like a fragment of tooth easing itself out of a healing gum. Most persistent of all was an image of a woman and child in a transparent tower, lodged in some dark forest like a fallen comet. It felt so personally familiar, as if he had been refusing to admit to it all his life, although it also seemed to spring from some highly public future. But because he could not yet bear to think of them as anyone else's, he gave the woman the shape of Elayne, the child that of Galaad. Just to think of them with him was intoxicatingly sweet. But still his loss of them stood in his mind before the having. For weeks they seemed to be defined for him only by their absence.

Then more and more forgotten detail spilled up from the night he had spent with Elayne, his dream-talk with Galaad. The short time he had spent with both began to swell, further intensifying his feelings. His waking and sleeping dreams teemed with the three of them together. From those two fleeting encounters he fashioned a kind of family chronicle; a history which he hoped against hope had not yet been completed.

Winter went over into Spring. Lanslod found himself prowling through coastal regions, and remembering landmarks from his reconnaissance.

Until now, he had seldom been reminded of that earlier journey. Although the landscape was the same, it was as if he were seeing it with younger eyes. Similarly, little of his life in Lundein or Camelot had stayed with him. If ever he had looked backwards it was always with shame, at having rooted his life in duty, with no regard for truth.

Sometimes when he broke his forest-cover to gaze out over the western seas, he would wonder how the emperor's court had continued to eke itself out. As the season of the Round Table approached, he tried in vain to picture the Company assembling. It seemed impossible to him that it still existed. It was like imagining a ruling clique in some completely different dimension. He was so relieved to have escaped, not least from his own mounting obsession with the succession. For despite his denials of interest, and threats to men who mentioned the endless rumours, he had finally hankered to be named as Arthur's heir. It had been his only way to justify the emperor's attitude to him over the years.

Now his dreams of empire had quite vanished. But increasingly as the days grew milder his thoughts turned to Camelot. He even began to track southward again along the north-western shores.

Each day, he felt that he had no personal say in what routes he took. During the winter his own instinct had been overlaid by some other guiding principle. A different kind of thread was leading him. Regularly at nights he dreamed of the tower, with a regal figure shimmering inside it, beckoning.

Finally he came awake as one of these dreams was ending, and through the trees ahead he saw white light. He rose at once and rushed towards it.

The pillar of light was blindingly bright. Several times Lanslod collided with branches and tripped on overgrowth: wild white rose tendrils that lacerated his arms and face before he broke through into the clearing.

His heart was already sinking. Suddenly he felt gross with hidden guilts, with derelictions of a nameless new set of duties. His dream-woman clung to him. He was sure she awaited him here, to call him at last to account. Madly he picked up a hazel switch and stripped it, as if in self-defence.

'Soldier,' drawled a soft, enfolding voice which sounded, if it were any one woman's, most like Guenever's – but only in the way that any woman who might wear Guenever's crown would be seen and known as a queen.

Ahead of him, the pillar briefly darkened into the shape of a stake but there was no one there for him to release. Not any longer. Lanslod looked around himself but now he was inside the glare: the pillar had become a corona. He had forgotten how to speak, how to narrow his eyes, even how to be afraid.

A figure gathered substance in front of him. A fine young man, ready. At first he looked more like a cloud than a man; he seemed to have been painted on to the light with lime.

Then Lanslod felt pressure on his shoulders. He knelt, falling forward on to his knuckles as well. When he looked up again – doglike, wolflike – the figure was whole and familiar. The hairless head, the solemn eyes staring above Lanslod into the south, towards Camelot.

Galaad, Lanslod pleaded through his knees and knuckles; embodied here in front of him was all that he had never had. *My perfect boy* . . .

Lanslod craved him only for himself, but he knew that every other person in Logres needed him too – all with their own secret names for him, which finally would be merged in the name already rising from the light. In what was to come, there would be only one name, one head, one vast guiding hand.

The figure stood with lightly clasped fingers, angelic, as if awaiting his assumption. But he was dressed in the plain shift worn during the pre-dawn vigil of a man about to be knighted. *My son . . . my own . . .*

As he watched, the young man sank smoothly to one knee; and Lanslod felt himself being drawn back up to his feet. The whiteness around them both blazed brighter, and Lanslod accepted then that the light was not Elayne's, although she and countless others were a part of it, and that soon it would take the name of the light which it had rightfully eclipsed.

The beautiful youth was waiting. Lanslod looked down at the hazel switch in his hand. He understood, and found his voice.

'I am to *knight* him?'

Despair welled in him in front of this child whom he would have to lose again. Duty and truth grew too confused. 'Why does he need to be a knight? And I have no sword . . .'

No answers came. He expected none. In the first and last resort, he was always speaking to himself. He was Lanslod, alone, and he had left nothing yet behind him. The thread that had led him here had wound around his legs and trussed him tight. Never had he felt less rooted in this ancient land's pageantry, nor more essential to its sickeningly cryptic inner workings. One name, one head, one hand . . .

Slowly he went to the boy – a boy in Lanslod's mind even if he had the strength and size of a man now. He wanted to touch him, stroke his cheek and feel the grain. Lanslod nodded. Tears glazed his eyes.

This was the son of everyone. His true name was pulsing now with the light, beating out its rhythm through the soles of Lanslod's feet. But still – in these last few intimate moments – he was Galaad.

Lanslod put out a hand and dared to touch his face, running his thumb along his cheekbone, brushing his temple with the tips of trembling fingers. The name pounded harder. Lanslod feared that this young god might fall apart where he knelt, disperse too soon into his masses. He raised the stripped stick, and took his last, loving look. *One of you will betray me . . .*

'Arise,' he said brokenly after dubbing both his shoulders, 'Sir Mordred.'

And in that instant he felt the first flexing of the great hand around him, and around all the countless others who would join him at the end.

The new knight stood. Lanslod watched him turn and knew that he was to follow. In file they stepped out of the circle of brilliance.

As they walked westward out of the forest, day came up behind them. Lanslod's head was bowed, as if he were being led on a leash. Blood and brown earth and verminous old skins made him dark against the daylight, while all around him the roses were opening white.

A ledge was up ahead. A high, sudden end to the land. Beyond it stretched the glittering morning sea. Lanslod half-expected to be made to jump, or be offered all the kingdoms of the waves — as if there were anyone or anything left for him to betray in return.

The knighted youth stepped aside and ushered Lanslod past him. He came to the cliff's edge and looked down. Not so very far below, at the foot of a slanted path, lay a small, busy anchorage, dwarfed by the emperor's ship *Prydwen*.

Frowning, Lanslod looked behind him. He was alone. Nor was there any forest for as far as the eye could see. He turned to gaze down again, as the first surprised cry of his own name wafted up.

TWENTY-EIGHT

Peredur took little notice of Lanslod's rehabilitation.

Until the moment he appeared – high above the anchorage like some stunned troglodyte – no one in the party from Camelot had even known about his flight into the wilds. No one save possibly the emperor himself, from whose tiny train a spare set of clothing was then hurriedly brought up.

While half a dozen stable-boys bathed, dressed and fed the errant knight, Peredur stayed close to the great ship, far more concerned about what lay out to sea than what was going on inland.

The hammer blows rang on; *Prydwen's* emergency refitting continued through that morning and well into the afternoon. The emperor, wrapped in his cloak of hair and feathers, drifted from crewman to crewman, watching the work, saying nothing, visibly keen to get the voyage under way.

In truth, Peredur had been more surprised by the vessel's sudden appearance than by Lanslod's. For almost a decade Arthur's ship had stood in its southern dock like a monument to his completed conquests. But now with its skeleton crew, each man of whom looked suspiciously like a stray, it was here – from which point no expedition of any sort had ever been launched.

The western seas off the coast of Galles had always been a mystery. In the six years of his nominal rule, Peredur knew of no ship that had arrived from there. His people sometimes spoke of 'adjacent isles', less than a day's sail away. Beyond that, there had only ever been strays' tales of sunken kingdoms or sunset islands of the blessed: Lyonesse, Ierne, Avalon. Soon Peredur would be finding out whether or not they existed, along with the rest of this odd, unarmed *ad hoc* squadron.

He had sought out and joined the other two dozen riders almost by default. News had reached him at Dinas Bran that the emperor was passing through Galles on a progress. This had sounded unlikely, especially so close to the May Round Table, but Peredur had felt bound at least to show himself.

Fully emblazoned as ever he had set off, surprised to see groups of his own people taking to the roads which led eventually to Arthur's court. But when from the opposite direction he found the emperor heading up a train of Camelot's scullions and animal-handlers, he had fallen in at the rear with less curiosity than concern.

It was the group's extreme youth that still troubled Peredur most. The majority were little more than boys: sixteen- or seventeen-year-old sons of the court's original servants who had long since abandoned Arthur. Clearly they had no idea what kind of a journey they were making. On reaching the coast and discovering the ship, their own unease became equally apparent. Some of them, perhaps, had hoped that Lanslod would be able to put their minds at rest. Any such hope had been dashed. The re-clothed first knight now sat cross-legged on the quayside like a beast set to guard the ship, glaring inland with a mute, forbidding mixture of ferocity and confusion. He had not said a word since arriving. When

Peredur had finally ridden over to where he sat, he had seemed not to see him, let alone recognize him.

Evening fell, the work on the ship continued, and Peredur heard whispers among the scullions that as soon as the caulking was complete they would set sail, in darkness or in light.

Under the first stars the anchorage looked so small, the seas beyond it so vast. The old stories kept on surfacing. Bran the Blessed was said to have mounted a raid from here. After a costly victory, only his head had been brought back, safely to be buried in that hill where Camelot now stood.

Replace the head . . . Replace the head . . . All year Peredur had been hearing the refrain from his people in their gatherings. Presumably like *Heal the stone*, its meaning was symbolic. But something must once have stood inside Camelot's mound. A head even, although not necessarily one of skin and bone. Probably, only the emperor could have said now what it was. But the emperor had not been open to enquiries ever since Peredur had dared to question him at the end of the Outremer wars.

As night darkened, Peredur could see him stalking the decks of *Prydwen* again, his perpetually empty scabbard flapping on his belt. For hours he had been lost from view. On his reappearance, an audible rustle of dismay passed through the waiting boys on their bedrolls.

Arthur was muttering, but not to any man, as he touched every oar-lock, stroked the base of each proud mast, clucked at the ship as if it were alive. He seemed to be priming the vessel for what would come. He had never looked more merely human, nor less a part of humankind: this ruler who relied for all his consolations on his ship, his scabbard, his cloak.

At least, Peredur thought, he had roused himself from his virtual stupor of the past six years. This was animation. Maybe it signalled one last-ditch, quite possibly ritualistic, attempt to revive his regime before it fully gave up the ghost. But Peredur remained pessimistic. It was just as likely that Arthur was on the point of abandoning Logres altogether, removing himself bodily, having already slipped out of the minds of the indifferent mass of his subjects.

Peredur let himself doze in the saddle. What seemed like only moments later, he was awakened by the downbeat shouts of embarkation.

Forlornly he watched the young men leave their mares and ponies behind and troop aboard. Lanslod was nowhere to be seen. The emperor stood counting in each of the fledglings with his eyes. His black hair had grown long again; hair bristled too from his nose and ears, as if a second cloak were beginning to ease itself out of him.

He turned away and disappeared below deck when the last boy was aboard. Peredur wondered whether he had even noticed his own presence. On an impulse he spurred his stallion forward and up the gangplank. Thus he arrived on the ship in some style. The boys who had clustered in the hold looked up at him wide-eyed. Their trusting expressions told him that they believed he knew what this was all about, maybe that he would protect them.

He dismounted and allowed his horse to be led away. As the anchor was weighed, Peredur looked back from the stern wondering if he would ever again see Logres. He thought of those crowds of his own people who had been travelling eastward, and of Camelot, virtually evacuated now save for Dyfric. If he did come back, he fancied that it would not be to the same kind of island. Deep changes had, after all, marked Arthur's previous absence.

The stars burned white through the dark velvet sky as if through rips in fabric. Soon the torches at the anchorage were invisible, and a wind got up to allow the crewmen a respite from their rowing. Closer to, they looked even more like strays: long-haired, leather-clad, with skins so wizened that they looked as old as the sea itself.

The emperor stood at the prow, his hair and cloak streaming behind him. If Lanslod was with them, he had to be below decks with Peredur's horse. He was not with the young men huddled together in the cargo hold, many of whom eyed Peredur constantly. The further out the ship drew, the younger they looked. Each of them was only as old as Arthur's Logres itself; neither they nor the kingdom now seemed destined to grow very much older.

After an hour, Peredur could hold himself back no longer. The emperor plainly had no intention of addressing his men. Once again, it fell to Peredur to approach him in the hope of teasing out some answers.

He smiled as he picked his way through to the bow, not wishing to dent the boys' confidence in him. He felt such a sense of responsibility for them; each one could have been his own son.

A few steps short of the prow he halted. The emperor was not alone. A second figure sat at his side; so small, stooped and frail that at first Peredur failed to recognize him. The threadbare black soutane gave him away. It was the Regent.

Peredur shivered. He had not set eyes on Merlin since leaving him behind at the launching of the Outremer campaign. But he had always assumed that somewhere he was around, that he was as integral as Camelot's hill to the kingdom. Thus it seemed all the more unreal, now, to see him outside Logres; and at once it occurred to Peredur that he, not Arthur, was the instigator of this expedition.

'Lord,' he called into the wind to Arthur.

Only Merlin turned, apparently unseeing. He sat in a strange cramped posture, as if any words that came from him would have to be relayed from deep inside him – and maybe even then they would be coded. His fingers, gripping his cape at the neck, looked like luminous talons in the moonlight. The material billowed in and out so far that his body must have been stick-thin beneath it. He had lost so much ground that he seemed to be little more than a drape, a mantle over some aggregation that was not – in any generally understood way – a body at all.

Peredur blanched at the idea that their fate might now be resting squarely in this virtual phantom's hands. 'Lord,' he called again, tilting his head as if to aim his words' trajectory past the Regent.

It did no good. Arthur was like a carved figurehead to the vessel. Peredur also had the very strong impression that he was weeping into the wind.

'Rest now,' Merlin spat back surprisingly. His face had come alive. From where Peredur stood, it looked like a swarm of outsized maggots.

Peredur wiped the windspits from his eyes, carefully, as if they were the emperor's tears. Then he turned away, to meet the expectant upturned eyes in the hold with another forced smile.

He went below, to search for Lanslod. But on finding his horse, he stayed with it for the rest of the voyage. The animal, at least, was calm. He pressed his face into its silken flank, drinking in the heady stink. It was fully caparisoned, the pattern of heads on its saddle-cloth matching that on his own surcoat. He was glad he had come dressed in this way. It felt right, offsetting the wild disarray of the emperor's own appearance.

He slept briefly beside his horse, then returned to the stern.

It was neither quite dark nor truly light overhead. A sliver of land now showed on the far horizon, which the ship seemed to be approaching at inordinate speed. Most of the boys were on their feet, eyeing it with uncertainty.

'Soon now,' came the Regent's low voice, as if from inside Peredur.

He turned to find that awful, mobile face close behind him. Its skin was like an all-but-transparent wrapping, but surely not around bone and muscle; it was impossible to tell whether the eyes were open or shut.

'What is this?' Peredur challenged him, softly enough for the others not to hear. 'Is this all your doing? Why are we here?'

'We are going to replace the head – in as far as we now can.'

'Which head? Whose head?' Peredur was haunted by the notion that everything might depend on whether or not he asked the right questions. 'And what purpose will that serve?'

Merlin appeared to grimace. 'That is what we will discover. Maybe we shall be able to construct a new Logres, a brand new kingdom for the king.'

Peredur narrowed his eyes. King, he noticed; not emperor. This creature was refusing to be frank or else he was genuinely clutching at straws. Either way, Peredur had little faith in him.

'What's wrong with the Logres we have?' he demanded. 'Didn't Arthur call it the land of promise? Wasn't it meant to be a kind of paradise?'

'The wall of paradise is built of contraries,' Merlin chewed out, as if in mimicry of an old stray's answer. 'No one can enter, save by overcoming the highest spirit of reason who stands guard at its gate.'

Before finishing he convulsed inside his cape. A kind of
death-throe that served only to suggest how implausibly alive
he still was.

Peredur flinched, wondering how long he and his brood
had been festering on this ship. Months? Years? 'So what is
this place?' he asked, nodding at the oncoming shore.

'The place where all things begin and end.' Another typical
stray's answer.

'Tell me its name, damn you!'

'Avalon?' Merlin drooled the word with a smirk, and for
a long moment it bumped around in Peredur's head like an
echo in search of its shout.

Again he glanced at the shore. If day had truly broken
through, it was still no more than a hairline crack. The murk
refused to grow any clearer, but it showed a shingly stretch
of coast with cliffs banking up behind.

Peredur thought he saw a villa overlooking the shore.
When he blinked it was gone. There was no port but he
heard the anchor dropping. Two of the stray-crewmen had
already leapt into the shallow water and were wading ashore.
More followed. Many more than Peredur had reckoned to
be on board.

Closing his hand over his sword hilt, he peered harder.

This was no adjacent isle. He doubted that any land at all
existed past the clifftops, just as he doubted that Merlin's cape
housed limbs. They had travelled through time to be here, not
through any chartable sea. Whatever Merlin had meant by his
first answer, Peredur could imagine nothing ever beginning
here, but so much seemed to be screaming for an end.

The cargo of young menials in the hold looked petrified.
From the rank smell he guessed that some had already lost
control of their bowels. Why had they been brought? As
a gruesomely misplaced tribute levy, a senseless hecatomb

to bind the foundations of some spurious new-conjured kingdom?

Peredur's grip on his sword-hilt tightened.

'They will not leave this ship,' he declared to Merlin and, since the emperor was now coming up behind his former Regent, to once-great Arthur too.

Both looked back at him in unsurprised silence. 'Nor will you,' was all Merlin said, without a smirk this time. Then he turned to Arthur who immediately began to climb over the ship's side. When he was waist-deep in the water, he braced his back as somehow Merlin shuffled the mess of himself overboard and fastened on to him.

It took the emperor a long time and countless pauses to haul the Regent ashore, even though he looked no heavier than a bag full of air bubbles. Still Peredur would not drop his hand from his sword. He was the only armed man in this whole sorry company but that gave him precious little comfort.

Avalon, then. A beach-head to nowhere. Peredur could see through the grainy light a sizeable cauldron lying upturned, close to where Arthur and Merlin came to land. After setting Merlin down, Arthur tapped it, as if to see whether anything lurked underneath, then wedged it tighter into the shingle.

To either side, the small tribe of strays was busily foraging. Peredur could not imagine what they were stooped over looking for. Some appeared to be clearing aside the pebbles and wrenching up bigger rocks.

It crossed his mind that they were simply killing time as they waited to begin the business of raising up a new kingdom, or to make some kind of rendezvous. Arthur was certainly looking out to sea, way past *Prydwen*, maybe all the way back to a Logres to which he never intended to return.

But time here felt too lifeless to be killed. Already Peredur had guessed that no regular kind of day was going to break; there would be no stronger light than this dismal metallic wash. Its grittiness tired his eyes, making the emperor look like a wraith as he began to move among the strays.

He still walked athletically, but like an old man playing at someone younger. He had walked so differently around the camp fires in Outremer. Now he looked as if his greater spirit had deserted him, the way that the gods were said to have fled ancient Troy on the eve of its capture.

The strays were another matter. They seemed to be weaving in and out in some repetitive, pre-ordained pattern. Just as once they had shaped chaos with their stories, now they were doing it with the fluidity of their movements. Peredur began to suspect that this whole affair had been undertaken with their own interests, rather than Arthur's, primarily in mind.

But he was so mesmerized that maybe an hour passed before he realized that they were not foraging at all. The rocks and stones that they picked up were an end in themselves. As the apparently ever-greater number of strays milled about, they were piling handfuls of them, armfuls, around and then over the wedged cauldron.

In the poor light Peredur must for some while have been mistaking the growing cairn for the motionless Merlin. When he peered harder, he could see the dark soutane heaped on the shore beside the new structure, but no sign of the Regent himself. He shrank from thinking about what might be happening.

But he could not stop himself from seeing again that image of Merlin's great face fragmenting into a myriad lesser figures.

And now he was seeing it from inside the giant hill-figure's shoulder – along with everyone else – not from a position outside it. In his mind, Peredur had finally gone across that vital line. He could feel a massive protecting hand curling its fingers around him, around all those who very soon would be delivered.

At last all the activity was over, the story in moving flesh was finished, but clearly a new one was meant to be about to start in some other medium. The strays stood back stiffly in a semicircle. They looked like stones themselves: all that remained of one of the ancient giants' rings.

Arthur stood close to the cairn which they surrounded, surely now at the service of the strays rather than their master. Slowly he stepped up to it, appraised it, then plucked out one stone from near its summit. After a moment's pause he knocked out another, then one more. He stood back, looked at the result, only to step up and remove more still.

So it went on, as mesmeric in its way as the strays' earlier snaking. The emperor continued deftly to displace stones here and there, like a sculptor tidying the work of a set of apprentices. Occasionally he paced behind the pile to assess it from the back. Then Peredur was able to see how he was transforming it.

The boys in the hold too were watching. Peredur heard their soft gasps as the truth gradually revealed itself. *Replace the head . . .* their mingled exhalations might have been singing. The phrase came back to Peredur loud and clear. By scraping away at the cairn Arthur was fashioning a hideous leering face; as artless as an infant's incisions in a hollowed-out pumpkin.

Peredur looked on, remembering the way that Arthur had once ended a siege in Outremer by chopping down a tree and hurling it over the city wall. Here again they had entered the realm of symbols. Here was one final attempt to overcome what Merlin had called the highest spirit of reason. But now, even before the emperor moved on to the next stage of his labours, Peredur sensed the desperation behind this act of defiance, or atonement, or special pleading, or whatever else he had been made to believe it was.

When the assembled face was as fully realized as he could make it, Arthur stood directly in front of it. He looked as if he might be about to kneel, to do homage to his own crude construction. In fact, worse followed.

He flung back his cloak and, with the strays gazing on, he hunched his shoulders. At last he was asserting himself, declaring in his very posture that he knew this to be no more than an ill-advised parody, that his own loss of Logres was past any kind of cure. The spell, he accepted, had stretched and broken for good and all.

Peredur knew that he had taken out his penis. Moments later he saw the thick arc of urine splashing on to the heap of stones.

The emperor began to move again, still urinating, his outline blurred by its steam. He edged from one side of the head to the other, making sure no stone was left unwetted. Briefly a flap of his cloak fell forward from his shoulder to swamp the stream. Arthur hurled it back and continued.

Peredur felt his own bladder distend. Some of the boys in the hold were giggling in panic. Even they could see that this was no way to regain paradise. At last it was over. Arthur's hands dropped to his sides, his hunched shoulders sagged further, and then quite suddenly, side on to the ship and its gaping spectators, he collapsed.

His fall looked heavy, unbroken. Not one of the strays moved towards him. They had all long since given up on him. Merlin appeared to have vanished altogether. From inside the giant's outline, Peredur stared at the fallen Arthur with his failures piled up around him like the interest on a debt which, he now saw, was ultimately unrepayable.

The moment swelled then tapered. And Peredur felt the warm sea swilling around his thighs before he became aware that he had taken a decision and acted on it. Not a decision he had taken alone. His new instinct felt utterly unfamiliar yet entirely reliable. It was as if he had seen his own shadow beckoning to him, and then dutifully followed.

He strode closer to the bizarre coastal tableau, indifferent to whether he was about to change the necessary course of events or to trace a line long since laid down for him. *The place where all things begin and end* . . . But although Merlin might well have met some opaque end on the shingle there, Peredur knew in his blood that the emperor had to go on. He belonged in his own island. Dead, alive, or even somewhere in between the two, his place was always in that land.

He glanced around at the arc of strays as he stepped over the tideline.

Closer to, they were more like trees than stones, their ragged hair flailing in the gentle sea breeze. None of them looked back at him. The faces of some were twisted into thin smiles, the parts reduced to mimicry of their previous sum. These were the only true children of Logres: Merlin's spawn, inheritors of nothing.

Peredur smiled too. New certainties were rising inside him like mushrooms after rain. A far greater mind was now beating in his blood.

He understood that Merlin and Guenever, those two fragmenting cloud-faces of Logres, had been the father and mother of the Great Remaking, the twin supports not only of Arthur but of the kingdom remade for him. Now at least one of those supports had been knocked away.

Peredur chose to waste no time. The emperor was conscious, sodden with his own urine, his face cut and bleeding, his penis curled up spent on his lower thigh. The knight in the head-covered surcoat stooped down. He pulled the emperor to his feet, gripped him by one arm and with surprisingly little effort swung him up on to his back.

Turning again towards the sea, he felt Arthur's hands beginning to cling to his shoulders. The young men from the hold were scuttling about the ship, making it ready to sail again. They had understood. Maybe this was even the deeper reason why Arthur had brought them along.

When Peredur reached *Prydwen*'s hull, two of them jumped down into the water. They wanted to help him heave Arthur back up towards the waiting hands of half a dozen more.

But before Peredur let anyone else lay hands on him, he pulled the broken emperor around and loaded his penis back into his breeches. He himself then needed helping hands as he struggled back aboard.

The anchor was up, the oars engaged. Peredur lay on the deck with his head slumped against the almost imperceptibly twitching thigh of Arthur. He did not feel it. Already he was with the waiting masses.

As the ship surged back to the island he had left behind as Logres, the sky began to lighten.

TWENTY-NINE

Each day that week, Dyfric left his lodgings only after darkness fell.

Although he could not yet see them, he knew that thousands of pairs of eyes were trained on Camelot from below. Were he to walk the deserted streets by day he felt sure that he would be watched, as if the great city walls had been transparent. Even at night with no lamps or torches burning, he sensed that his own winding progress was being followed.

But the mausoleum had to be made ready, and only the former 'Archbishop' was now in a position to ensure that the ground was prepared.

He had not expected to feel so self-conscious after the last exodus. For years he had guessed that he would eventually be left here alone. Maybe he had been anticipating it ever since the Great Remaking. Neither as a court nor as a city had Camelot ever quite fully convinced him. It had always seemed like a place awaiting its final evacuation. No one who came into it had ever looked likely to stay. Least of all the emperor himself.

Dyfric was surprised that it had taken Arthur so long to

go. In his mind, he must have been going for so long – inside that poor, noble head of his which by the end had seemed so full of flapping, beating creatures. In a sense he had never returned from his travelling in Outremer, his first vain attempt at escape. In time it might even be said that he never truly made the transition from Albion. Either way, he had failed to prosper in Camelot.

But the manner of his going had been predictable enough. Abrupt, unheralded, unarmed; just seven days before his queen and captains were due to arrive for one more moribund Round Table.

Dyfric would never know whether the Lord of War had ordered the scullions and ostlers to accompany him, or if they had simply been afraid to stay on in his absence. In some ways they had felt love for him. They were the closest in the end that Arthur had come to sons of his own: wanted, acknowledged offspring. 'In sorrow,' Dyfric remembered a different god saying in another thwarted form of paradise, 'thou shalt bring forth children.'

The boys had hung back on their mares and ponies when Arthur rode up to the chapel before leaving. Dyfric had seen it all from his lodgings.

Without dismounting Arthur pushed back the door. For a moment Dyfric imagined he might be planning to duck and ride inside. Instead he only gazed at what he had never taken seriously, and which could now give him no last respite. He loosened the strap that bound his battered shield to his shoulder, swung it around and held it out in one hand.

He seemed to be making a plea with it, possibly even a protest. The painted device was clear to Dyfric behind his window. The mother and babe in arms which so faithfully echoed the image on the icon he had petulantly defiled all those years before. He wondered afterwards if the emperor had been presenting it specifically for him to see. But he was trying to impress someone far larger than himself when suddenly he wheeled his horse around and hurled the shield deep into the abyss from which his nemesis had arisen.

He had then ridden through the lower, postern gate at the head of his untried army. He rode straight-backed with his devil-black hair streaming, but his departure was still furtive. He could not leave his own city by its main gateway. Already – whatever measures he had in mind to shore up his eclipsed regime elsewhere – he had relinquished his right to high Camelot.

On the seventh day Dyfric left his lodgings a little earlier than usual. The sun was still setting, and a fine Spring rain freshened his face.

Although he was unsure why, he felt a greater urgency to be about his business that evening. The stillness on the surrounding plains seemed thinner. He could hear no sounds, no evidence of movement, but the air in Camelot was circulating faster, as if in anticipation of some change. 'Blows and wounds' he remembered with a smile, or would he see a wonder?

In Albion he would now have been preparing for the Rogation festival – a time for great, good-humoured outdoor crowds, when the litany of the saints was sung and the parish bounds were ritually beaten. During the past six days, Camelot's chaplain had been observing newly-invented traditions of his own that were not too dissimilar.

But as the week progressed, his confidence grew that his feet were being guided into far more ancient footprints. Just as once he had found the Glass Castle legendry as suggestively old as it was new, now he was finding his spontaneous circuits of the city fulfilling some much longer-held expectation.

In spite of the rain and the growing sense of an approach, he followed his chosen route slowly. Keeping to the centres of the streets, he proceeded in diminishing ellipses around the citadel. It was as if on the six previous days he had cut a spiral groove into the city, which led him on inexorably to the foot of the citadel's steps.

He seldom glanced about him. On the first days he had regularly darted looks from side to side, half to satisfy himself that the place was now quite empty even of the occasional roving peacock, half to fix in his mind a picture of the whole processional route.

Had he paused now, and turned his eyes on the cobwebbed seamstresses' parlours, the silent armourers' workshops and abbatoirs, or the tiltyards stretching away behind them, he would no longer have seen a dead city. Nor would he have seen it as it had been in its teeming times.

Already it would have appeared to him in the way it would be at the last: as a great, glassily-gleaming monument to a monarch who had ultimately failed to bring his people inside; a ruler whose essence was always seen most clearly in flight.

With every step, Dyfric walked further away from his chaplaincy. He was striding deeper into the priesthood of the cult of a Reborn Son, whose presence was reaffirmed across the kingdom each morning like a second layer of dew. No absent Lord of War, but a true Prince of Peace who possessed all his people equally – in death as much as in life – and who in turn was equally inhabited by them.

Replace the head . . . Replace the head . . . The words' insistence beat in Dyfric's bones as he reached the foot of the citadel steps and paused before ascending.

One name, one head, one hand. Now nothing was forgotten. This was the place where, almost twenty years before, Dyfric had stepped down from the wagon that had brought him through newly-made Logres into Camelot. Here beneath this splendid stairway, he had been hauled into position by some vast unseen hand to witness the passion of the Son and Mother.

With reopened eyes he saw the trail of blood as the blameless Mother had been made to heave her shrinking Son up to where the great stone Table was still in the making. But it was not the Son's blood, never his own. It was the blood of the Mighty, that Arthur had started to draw even as he had sired the Son on his own sinless sister. The Son whom the king had then tried to disown by drowning; the Mother whom he punished with exile and abomination.

But on that day of the Great Remaking both had returned only to suffer again: the Son forced to grow backwards into the Mother; she – raped one last time by the king inside the hill's cist from which, even more rashly, he had removed the protecting head of Blessed Bran.

Replace the head . . . And heal the stone . . .

Dyfric murmured the words aloud as he rose up the steps, carefully evading the spots and stains which still looked wet and fresh. At the top he was tempted to turn and look out across the plain. The rain had eased and there was still enough light left in the day for him to see. The air swarmed faster than ever.

A wonder was coming. There were no more blows and wounds.

He fastened his gaze on the mounted king, carved high into the arch to the hall. Hallowed Arthur on the back of a goat. His hubris had always been heading him toward tragedy, a king who decapitated his kingdom then imagined that he could hide by spreading himself across an empire.

Dyfric passed underneath feeling only pity. 'Emperor.' A word without weight. Arthur was no more an emperor than he himself was an archbishop. The Island of the Mighty recognized no emperors.

He deepened the hall's darkness on entering, briefly blocking the faint shaft of daylight that was its sole illumination. As ever, it seemed crowded at its shadowy edges; a motionless, wraithlike Company forced out from the centre by the sheer flat expanse of the Table.

Dyfric shuffled now, in deference to the absent: the final few still excluded from the new-yet-ancient Body Politic. He began his circuit of the stone, marvelling at the lack of even the tiniest crack. Of all the expectant inanimate elements of Camelot, this Table most eagerly awaited Arthur's return. Dyfric could almost hear the grain bracing itself. Had he rapped it with a knuckle, it would have answered: *Heal . . . Replace . . .*

But Dyfric did not rap the Table. Not that evening, nor on any of the previous six. All he was required to do was follow the groove which looped around it before taking him back out under the arch. And this time when he stood at the top of the steps – with his beating of the new bounds complete – he let himself look out over the walls into the steamy sunset.

He felt the imminence of the masses, but riding on a white horse from the east came a single figure. And while still too distant to be identified by any particular feature, this could have been only one person: the island's first lady and repository of its sovereignty.

Dyfric closed his eyes and remembered the morning more than a decade earlier when he had come, too late, to the top of these steps. That morning, he had been so mortified by her going. She had been back since then, of course. Once each year for the May Round Table. Once for each time she had found herself with Lanslod.

But year on year she had come as less of her old self than

before, less of the barren island queen who with Merlin had unmade Albion and replaced it with Logres. Dyfric had observed the steady transformation, at first concerned, later in wonder. It amazed him that Lanslod had not fully admitted to it too, and thus understood why Arthur had shrunk away in fear from continuing to serve her in those acts on which his kingship depended.

He opened his eyes and watched the pale white light go on ahead of her horse, the groove of her own which soon she would be following up the slope to the city's main gateway. This was Queen Guenever in nothing but her name and title. She raised her head, and although Dyfric could scarcely make out her shape, the light from her eyes told him that here, at last, was the Mother.

Shivering slightly, he retraced the steps back to his lodgings, pausing only at the lip of the abyss into which Arthur had flung his shield. It had not been enough. Arthur himself would not have been enough.

Heal the stone . . . Replace the head . . .

They had all travelled back in order to go forward. The new queen of this island's air, land and waters was coming into her city. Dyfric returned to his lodgings, knelt in front of the triptych and cleared his mind.

Later that night, as he lay in his bed before sleeping, he heard a stirring around the postern gateway below the gash in the hillside.

The new queen's people had come forward like the tide. A tide which would break the final circle by grinding away Camelot's walls in readiness for the second, even greater, coming.

THIRTY

Lanslod was in no rush to reach Camelot.

The horse he had been given at the anchorage went at its own pace. At times it seemed to be taking its own route too, staying on the broadest highways, carefully skirting the forest depths. Lanslod felt odd to be back in the saddle after so long. Odder still to be clean and cropped and dressed in the emperor's clothing; the very same doublet, breeches and thin-soled boots which Arthur had loaned him for his summonses to Guenever.

He was glad not to have been wanted on the voyage, whatever its nature or purpose. Unsurprisingly, no words had passed between himself and the emperor. But by having Lanslod refurbished, and then sending across to him his own horse, Arthur had made his preference plain enough. It had been a commission of sorts. And although Lanslod refused to see it as an act of succession, he knew now that during his time of wildness his old ambition had been only dormant, not dead.

He kept his mind as empty as he could. The occupied stretches of the land through which he passed looked empty too. Whole villages seemed to have been evacuated. Wayside inns stood open-doored, their fires all burned out.

Occasionally he saw movement on the higher ground. Children racing along crests. Once, when his own road took him above a shallow-sided valley, he saw a huge assembly. So huge that he looked away, as if from the sight of a naked relation.

No great carved or limed figure marked the grass here, but thousands upon thousands of people had arranged themselves in a perfectly still loop-and-knife formation. Hours later, he saw a second vast congregation darkening the larger part of a chalk horse.

Lanslod had little doubt that similar musters were taking place all over the waiting face of Logres. Scattered spots of humanity like dark raindrops on the lush green emptiness. He was resolved to find nothing surprising, nothing too strange to be engaged with. Simply seeing Arthur again had given him new steel. And at least while he was eating up the ground like this, he felt that he still had the necessary resources.

Coming closer to Camelot he tried to imagine that he was merely approaching another Round Table. The emperor and Peredur might have taken flight, but the Company was larger than them. It would have to be. Meanwhile the thought of the city on the hill drew him on, through night and day then night again.

As he entered the plain, shortly before dawn, his horse slowed almost to a standstill. At first Lanslod could see no reason for this. The creature seemed more wary than afraid. Its path forward became mazy, almost as if it were picking its way around obstacles that Lanslod could not see: the way that a horse might have skirted the night fires of a military encampment.

Lanslod did not try to urge it on. He too felt presences

around him in the dark, dewy mists. The same sense of multitudes as when he had been confronted by the young dream-knight on the last night of his wildness. Massed but benign. Nothing, yet, to give him pause.

As daylight filtered through, showing the city's mound with its turrets up ahead, Lanslod reined in the horse, dismounted and covered the rest of the distance on foot. He had never come to Camelot from the west. It had an unfamiliar look – even before he was close enough to see that the entire postern gateway had been removed, along with a surrounding section of wall.

There was no trace of debris or lighter-coloured stone dust on the slope. The gap in the wall was framed by smooth, continuous surfaces where blocks had been sheered off or taken out whole. It was as if a knife had been used from above to slice away the section like so much butter. But Lanslod paid little attention to that. The higher he went, the more fixedly he stared at the old cave-mouth which had thus been exposed.

He did not see the cairn at its lower lip until he passed through the gap.

Under the mists it was hard to tell where the sky ended and the dew-soaked grass began. The dark mass of stone was clear enough, but it seemed to have assembled itself in response to his looking, rising like the hump of some great sea serpent that now surrounded the whole of Camelot.

Lanslod went towards it, and when he was half-a-dozen steps away he saw the sword.

The cairn was squat and not especially high – just half Lanslod's own height. It was an unusual shape: fatter in the middle than at the top or bottom, with the sword lodged at an almost rakish angle in its flank.

He stared at it, blinking to make sure that it was no mirage.

But it was as real as the mist, lodged into stones that looked unusually blue in the early light. The sword was of no great beauty or size. *Take what is yours . . .* he remembered from the first Round Table.

Going forward again, it became clear that the cairn was in fact a single great knot of rippled stone, dark like petrified water, its colour and texture both similar to those of the Table. *I have no sword . . .* he remembered protesting before the rite of knighting in the forest.

His eyes began to moisten, and not from the mist.

He felt like a child in front of this. A child in an emperor's clothes. Beaten by a challenge that he had not yet even attempted. Tested and found wanting, purely for being himself.

He knew from the hilt's animal-head decoration – bull, bear, goat, ram – where this sword must once have belonged. In the scabbard that Arthur had for decades worn empty at his side. Lanslod glared at both stone and sword, as if he could wish them away through hard thinking. *Take what is yours . . .*

He ran a finger up the sword's flat shaft. The hilt's heads seemed to taunt him. He felt his tears' dampness at his mouth. He hated this. He felt more strongly than ever that he was being watched, from above, below, all around; even within.

He closed his hand on the hilt and braced himself. He did not step around to the side from which the weapon protruded. He grabbed it face on, as if he were about to draw it from a scabbard at the level of his own left breast. Already it was going to be hard to extract. This would make it many times harder. But he knew that he was making no more than a gesture.

He jerked his arm up and over to the right. The sword came free with a hiss.

Lanslod almost lost his balance. He staggered sideways for several steps, pointing the blade stiff-armed as if it were propelling him. Then abruptly he turned, expecting the mists to lift and the whole of Logres to reveal itself in loud, adoring applause.

But the mists stayed thick. No one was there. Lanslod gave a choked shout, not so much to draw attention as to express his own amazement – and, already, his profound confusion.

When he looked at the stone from this new angle, its contours were quite clearly those of a head. An aquiline nose, a firm chin, a hairless pate; its blank eye directed at the gap in the wall. Lanslod knew this young but old profile. And when he took just one step closer, he saw a red rivulet dribbling like ore from the slot where the sword's blade had been – from the head's temple, as it were.

He staggered again, this time up the slope. The sword was cumbersome, its blade proportionately short in relation to the hilt, but it was sharp enough to draw blood from the wind. Pausing, Lanslod laid it into the flat of his free hand, hefting it like a baby.

Tears coursed down his cheeks now. He looked through the blur at the sword as if it had betrayed the true him, dragged him way too far outside himself. He tried to laugh, but again he could make only the choking sound. The stigma of his success was too great. He had always been a man apart, but this was a newly intense form of isolation; as if he had been sworn to keep a secret so solemn that even he had been told no more than its first two words. He badly needed to be moving, pounding over ground again.

Launching himself up the slope past the chapel, he had no sense of achievement. He had to keep moving: run, fly – still holding the sword before him. He had to go on as if nothing had happened, on to the citadel, the hall.

An assembly, he was sure, would be waiting there for him.

He saw nothing to either side as he swept into the city's dawn streets. New light was rising ahead of him, not so much from the east as from the buildings up ahead. White, dazzling, making the citadel's high walls scintillate. He felt that he too was shimmering as he took the steps up to the hall, two then three at a time in his eagerness. *Take what is yours . . .*

He stormed through the archway and into the marble-pillared hall. There was no assembly. Nor any Table. Where once the great granite dais had dominated the chamber, now waters were lapping in a wide circular pool.

'You have come too soon,' said a low, female voice, which could have been the water speaking. 'This is not the place.'

Lanslod swung his head from side to side like a sandbag on a quintain struck by a sequence of lances. Then he saw her straight ahead – seated on a simple bench, shining in the shadows a short distance behind the spot where Arthur's throne normally stood. Dressed in a sleeveless white gown, her arms were crossed, and with her right hand she gripped her left shoulder. Lanslod at once became defensive.

'I've brought it,' he haltingly explained, brandishing the sword in one hand. 'From the head of stone. I took it.'

He tried to make it sound unexceptional but his quaking voice gave him away. He sounded as excited as a boy caught thieving. And he was more horribly conscious than ever that he was wearing the emperor's clothes.

'This is not the place for you.' She smiled at him, narrowing her eyes just a little, less in disbelief than in appraisal of the sword itself. 'You have come too soon.'

Lanslod looked back, knowing her but not knowing her. She was Guenever, but only in the sense that Guenever was the queen, the first lady of this island. She had the shape and features of Guenever, but was no more truly her than the stone head down below had been a thing of flesh and bone. What Lanslod saw was not the etiolated woman who had annually haunted this court and swarmed around him in bed. What he heard was not Arthur's childless consort. And what he felt, still, was not a single presence but a massed parade of them, just as he had seen inside the hill figure.

'I took the sword,' he protested, tears welling again.

'It belongs in the water.'

'But I took it! It was there, waiting to be taken, and I took it!'

'As you should have done. But it belongs in the water.'

'It was Arthur's. That has to matter!'

'Not any longer. Not after Arthur's misuse. Now it is superseded.'

'Superseded by what? And how?'

'Go back and you will see. The stone is still unhealed. The head unreplaced.'

Her eyes flashed at him. Eyes familiar from the Tower bedroom, but not Guenever's. The woman behind them was fleshing out this body just as Arthur once had filled out his cloak of hair and feathers.

Lanslod held the sword away from him – in one hand, tip upward – as if it were a torch that had now burned dangerously low.

The hall's vaulted roof seemed to be pressing down on him, pushing him closer to a land that he would never understand. He felt so crass stumbling around in this arena of an island, at the constant beck and call of its fickle higher powers, a fool called up from the crowd to be tricked and laughed at.

'Lady . . .' he called to her across the roofed-in spring, but he did not know how to continue. Her hair was loose, her face unpainted. There was such a different air about her now.

Raw; shorn of all that he had once found so forbidding. For the first time, Lanslod truly desired her.

Go back and you will see . . . She took her hand away from her left upper arm. There was an armlet beneath it; slim, golden. Lanslod knew it, and he knew whose it was. Apparently absently, she put a single finger to it and began to make it revolve against her flesh. As she continued to ease it around, it bulked larger and larger in Lanslod's vision.

Although she herself stayed distant, he could see that her narrow band of gold was shaped like a dragon, with a single red garnet eye. Round and round the beast went, swallowing itself once, twice, again, mesmerising Lanslod. He knew now where he had seen the bauble before – on Morgan's arm at her casting-down at the Great Remaking. *Go back* . . .

Morgan. The name came back smoothly, like a sword drawn up from a stone inside his head. Morgan, sister of Arthur and mother of Mordred.

On returning from Outremer, Lanslod had fancied that Logres had been subverted, occupied from within. Similarly, now, Guenever. The island's first lady retained her name, but her pullulating presence was Morgan's; a presence that arched over so many other women too. All were here: some, like Elayne, closely familiar to Lanslod. Others, like Anna of Orcadie, known but only by repute. Others still were simply names. They rang in Lanslod's head like a roll-call as the dragon went on circling: Moronoe, Mazoe, Gliten, Glitonea . . . All now gathered up in the goddess seated opposite.

But Lanslod was seeing the completion, where Arthur had sensed the slow conquest of his queen. For so long the emperor had been fighting his own rearguard action; first by attempting to put himself beyond Morgan's reach in Outremer, then by trying to use Lanslod to keep her at bay. All in vain.

Replace the head, replace the head . . . The old Guenever now was eclipsed; the emperor too was about to be usurped. But not, at the last, by Lanslod.

One name, he remembered. One name, one head, one hand.

He took two faltering steps closer to the spring which bubbled gently at the room's centre but somehow spilled no further. The sword in his hand had no meaning. Arthur had no meaning. The emperor had ceased years before to exist for his people. By hurling away his sword, Lanslod would erase him altogether. The emperor who was already far across the water.

But something held Lanslod back. Some residual loyalty perhaps. *One of you will betray me* . . . And Lanslod's dubbing of Mordred had surely been enough. There was a limit to the vengeance that a single man could keep on taking. His eyes stayed on the revolving dragon but in his mind he was making his own managed retreat. *Go back and you will see* . . . *The stone is still unhealed* . . .

Tearing his eyes from the armlet, he looked down. Although the roof was stone-built, he saw blue, gossamer-clouded skies reflected in the water's surface. Hours must have passed since he started to stare at the dragon.

He did not want to go back. Back down to where the Company's remnant would by now surely have gathered. His own momentum simply would not take him. And still he did not want to relinquish the sword, even if it had no meaning for him – or maybe because of that.

Without looking up, he sensed again that he was being surrounded. Not, this time, by the seated queen. He thought he heard footsteps behind him, muffled talk. A hand closed lightly on his left shoulder.

He swung around. As he did so, another two hands grabbed

his right arm, locked it, and a further pair wrenched the sword away from him. It was so simple. Three men had scarcely been necessary. One could have done it.

Caius. Lucan. Lanslod gaped from one to the other as they continued to hold him fast. Then he heard the dull slap made by the third knight's throw. He twisted around to find that it was Bediver. It happened to be Bediver; it could have been any one of the Company.

Half-supported now, Lanslod watched with the others as Arthur's sword bobbed flat on the water. If any of them had expected a prodigy he was disappointed, save by the fact that as soon as the weapon sank, the spring ceased to bubble. It was as if some gigantic submarine appetite had finally been satisfied.

Lanslod grinned wild-eyed at Bediver, who was wearing a discreet golden loop-and-knife pin on the breast of his tunic.

'You . . .' Lanslod breathed. 'You're the one. It was you who betrayed him.'

Bediver smiled with compassion. 'Do you not think he betrayed himself, long before he ever said that?'

Lucan and Caius tugged him around, gently, towards the arch. Bediver was already walking ahead of them into the daylight. Lanslod did not resist. *Go back and you will see . . .* Alone, he could not have done it. Alone he had been going in the wrong direction for such a very long time.

None of the three looked back at the new queen. Lanslod wondered if any of them had even seen her. Perhaps, unlike himself, they had not needed to.

THIRTY-ONE

Dyfric saw it all, from Lanslod's drawing of the sword to the Company's formation of a circle in front of the pit.

This was the last Round Table, with the stone head standing in Arthur's traditional position. By the time Dyfric stepped out of his lodgings, only a handful of places were still unfilled. The space that corresponded to the perilous seat was vacant. Lucan, Caius and Bediver were also absent – although, Dyfric imagined, not for much longer.

Naturally Lanslod was yet to appear; then there was Peredur. And Peredur would come. One man would have to return with the king. That honour seemed finally to have fallen to the knight with the severed-head blazon.

None of the knights turned to watch as Dyfric moved down the slope behind them towards the gap in the wall.

The men were like megaliths. Dyfric marvelled at their straight-backed stillness, their new expressions of serenity. Under Arthur's command, not one had ever looked so calm and sure. Each of them, even the closest, was focusing exclusively on the head. Dyfric wondered whether they had ceased to see anything else, if they had all now begun to scale the wall behind which paradise lay.

He paused and looked back through the space where Lanslod would soon stand. He saw what Lanslod would see; Lanslod, the John to the coming Son's Christ.

The unhealed head stared blankly out over the plain. Blood still dribbled down the left side of its face. And protruding now from its temple was a second weapon. Lanslod had delivered Arthur's sword, but only to clear a path for this far less impressive-looking knife, the truer key to the kingdom and to so much more besides.

It was a poor thing. Rusted, bone-handled, with two brass studs inserted for a firmer grip. None of these megalithic men would presume to close his hand over it. Even Lanslod, finally, would understand when he saw. Poor Lanslod, who for so long had looked as unbudgeably jammed into a lump of stone himself. He too, now, would have his deliverance.

Dyfric turned his eyes away towards the citadel.

Four figures were coming steadily down the slope like a single eight-legged creature. Only one was being supported, his legs moving loosely out of step with the others: Lanslod, defenceless now, having dispensed with Arthur's sword in the only way left to him.

As they came closer to the circle, Lanslod began to find his feet, and only Caius had to guide him to his place while Lucan and Bediver walked with purpose to theirs.

Lanslod's eyes met Dyfric's briefly before they fell to the triptych which he held, closed, in front of him. Caius allowed him to pause and look as Dyfric unfastened the icon's catch and opened out its leaves.

Lanslod showed no surprise to find each of the three panels as blank, now, as the eyes in the stone head above him. No king, no queen, no heir. His eyes narrowed, as if he might be about to smile, then gently he extricated himself from Caius, turned, and stepped up to his place in the assembly.

Dyfric watched the fingers of his right-hand curl when he saw the knife, but then they opened out again, and hung as loosely at his side as everybody else's. At last, after so many years of chasing his own tail, the king's first knight had come to rest.

As Caius too moved on, Dyfric closed the icon and continued down the slope.

He left the former city through the scooped-away section of wall. The gradient beyond it grew less steep. When he came to level ground, he was able to see the horse approaching slowly from the west. Just one horse, but its rider looked broader than a single man.

He watched transfixed as the creature came closer. Part of the rider's bulk was explained by a dark, billowing cloak. Dyfric recognized the hair and feathers before he identified the rider as Peredur, and only then did he notice that Arthur had been strapped to his back.

Peredur reined in the horse at the foot of Camelot's hill. He glanced over at Dyfric, who saw from his awkward posture and the tiredness in his eyes that he could not go on alone.

He went across, slipping the icon safely inside his vestments. Already Peredur was working at the buckles that held the slumped Arthur to him.

When he was finished, he shifted in the saddle and brought Arthur's torso around in his arms. The king's face, streaked with plastered-down hair, was striped with dried blood. The wound seemed to be high on his left temple, concealed by his swathe of hair. His eyes were closed, his lips apart. Dyfric reached up and took a share of the load, although Peredur still bore the brunt. He took Arthur under each arm and, staggering a little, eased him out of the knight's grip. Then, squatting, he laid him down on the grass.

Dyfric stayed on his haunches but at once took away his hands. He had never touched the king before. Even now, half-afraid of reprisal, he almost rubbed them together to remove any trace of what he had handled.

The figure on the ground was still a king, if only in the way that a carved wooden piece on a chessboard is a king. He still had to be relieved of his powers in their entirety; and when the game was over and the pieces packed away, he would continue to be a king. No one could ever change that. No one, even now, would want to.

While Peredur dismounted, Dyfric tried to study Arthur's face. He soon found it impossible. The slit of dark between his lips made him feel dizzy, as if he were being sucked down bodily into it, tight against his even rows of teeth, deep into the abyss that no man ever needed to know again.

Dyfric shut his eyes, gathered himself, then looked again, but this time only at the cloak. It rippled on the windless plain as the knight came up closer: each black feather fluttering as if in a fight to remember how to fly. Arthur's body seemed so shrunken inside it. Once he had seemed to be made of fire, but now his big bones had fallen in on themselves like sticks around a burned-out ball of grass.

The knight's boots came into Dyfric's line of vision, beside the laid-out king's head. They were pale-coloured, paler than Peredur's, almost white and quite unstained. Dyfric twisted his neck to look back to Camelot, not directly upwards.

Peredur had gone inside the wall and, without a backward glance, was taking his place in the ring. Now only one space remained.

Dyfric, still crouched, pressed his fingertips into the ground and pushed himself a short way back before rising to his feet.

If he had hoped to put more distance between himself and the new knight, he was foiled.

Wherever the newcomer's feet happened to be planted, the essence of him was everywhere. Dyfric felt as if a second circle now surrounded him, infinitely larger, deeper and more permanent than any that the Company could make.

He put both his hands over the icon which now lodged close to his heart, its edges softened by the fabric of his outer clothing. But he felt, rather, as if any number of hands were being laid upon him. Assuring him, encouraging him, enfolding him, preparing him for the moment of his own eventual assumption.

But that moment was not yet.

Dyfric felt the hands slide away to leave him agonizingly alone again on Camelot's plain. Alone, but for the king on the ground and the unarmed knight whose surcoat and mail were as pale as his hairless head.

A moment after Dyfric met his eye, this new knight stooped and effortlessly swept up Arthur in his arms. He could have been gathering in an armful of dry kindling. The king looked almost foetal, his legs hooked over his bearer's right arm, his head and shoulders pressed close to his knees.

Dyfric wondered only now whether or not Arthur was dead. It had not occurred to him before, even when he had been taking his weight, laying him out, searching his face. He seemed neither dead nor quite alive. He was warm still, and supple; there was breath in his body, but this was no longer the place where he could exhale it. The ether around him had ceased to be his own.

He was being cradled now in just one arm. With his free hand, the last knight was delicately smoothing back the hair from Arthur's face. When the bloodied temple was exposed, he leaned over and kissed it.

He raised his smooth head after a long pause, then looked at Dyfric as his tongue snaked out to clean first his upper lip, then the lower. One name, one head, one hand.

'It's not my blood,' he confirmed. His voice was so deep that Dyfric felt its rhythms first like a quaking of the ground. 'It was the blood he unleashed.'

In saying this he turned to face Camelot, and Dyfric's eyes were dutifully drawn to the great stone head, the source of all the bleeding. And then Mordred was striding towards it with his load, leaving him behind, bereft.

Dyfric took one step after him, hesitated, became confounded.

It was like watching an entire army withdraw – abandoning a siege, the outcome of which had suddenly ceased to matter to the war's strategy.

But this was not a war. After several steps Mordred put out his left arm and, with a gesture from his hand, he beckoned Dyfric forward.

'Come,' he called without turning his head, and the sound soared across the plain. 'Come inside.'

Dyfric set off up the slope, still clutching his nestling icon. The single figure up ahead was stretching away from him for as far as the eye could see. His flesh was this land, his bones its rivers, his breath the air around them all. And his place was in the time before time, the single moment that spread beneath the membrane of the Ages.

But whereas Dyfric expected him to go directly to the circle, to the stone, and to the knife that was waiting, he bypassed them all and headed on at once towards the citadel.

Dyfric glanced away to the knights, and saw that they had all taken several steps forward. The circle was now much smaller, and each man in it stood with his shoulders touching his neighbours'.

Through the one remaining gap, Dyfric saw the unhealed head of stone and he knew what he had to do. *Come . . . Come inside . . .*

Mordred was far away already. Each step forward that he took was also a step back towards the island's reviving heart, past Logres, past Albion; past the need for kings and queens and Regents. But this was no mere act of revenge against Arthur, nor Merlin, nor the previous Guenever. It was a restoration of the truest Body Politic; the kingdom made not for any king but for all its children indiscriminately.

Dyfric stepped up into the unfilled space in the circle, making it whole once more. As his shoulders came against those of the knights to either side, he felt the fusion; not only with the men on this sunlit slope, whose faces and names were already interchangeable, but with the crowds which now stood on hillsides from one end of this land to the other. Again, as equals, they were turning back into giants.

With the eyes of all, Dyfric saw the Son climb the steps of the towering citadel, pass into the hall, set down Arthur upon the water and leave him there, just as once he himself had been left on the waters by Arthur.

Dyfric in his circle saw it all through the walls, the light of the new Guenever having made the tower transparent. At the last, Camelot was reduced and raised to this single cautionary finger pointing up at the skies into which Mordred continued to climb. Here was the Glass Castle of legend, with Arthur embalmed inside it.

And the circle was shrinking again, converging on the old stone head.

The hand of every person present in the new Body closed, as one, on the hilt of that little knife. Then Mordred's hand reached down to surround them. As he lifted, they all came free with the blade from the bleeding rock. The healed head fell back into its niche inside the hill, and the opening closed over like a freshly-mended sky.

When Mordred set them down again as one, the Island of the Mighty was restored. The oldest spell of all had been recast: 'He who is head, let him be a bridge for his people.' Mordred would for ever be that presiding head, that bridge which would rise like a rainbow from past into present, from kingdom into firmament, and then arc back down again to this island at the heart of the earth.

Other best selling Warner titles available by mail;

The prices shown above are correct at time of going to press, however the publishers reserve the right to increase prices on covers from those previously advertised, without further notice.

W
WARNER BOOKS

WARNER BOOKS
Cash Sales Department, P.O. Box 11, Falmouth, Cronwall, TR10 9EN
Tel: +44 (0) 1326 372400, Fax: +44 (0) 1326 374888
Email: books@barni.avel.co.uk

POST AND PACKING
Payments can be made as follows: cheque, postal order (payable to Warner Books) or by credit cards. Do not send cash or currency.

All U.K Orders **FREE OF CHARGE**
E.E.C. & Overseas 20% of order value

Name (Block Letters) _____

Address _____

_____

Post/zip code: _____

☐ Please keep me in touch with future Warner publications
☐ I enclose my remittance £ _____
☐ I wish to pay by Visa/Access/Mastercard/Eurocard

Card Expiry Date

_____